THE GROWLER CHRONICLES
PHASE ONE

RUN

By
J.C. SAMPSON

Published by Bathgate Books

ISBN: 979-8-89048-009-5

Extra Content and News on J.C. Sampson at jcsampson.com

TABLE OF CONTENTS

BILLY HALLSON –
CALIFORNIA, OAKLAND CITY
CENTER – 1 P.M. DAY ZERO

Billy Hallson

Billy savored the sharp tang of his wine; its rich, complex flavors a reminder of his more affluent past, when money had been less of an issue. But times had changed, and so had he. He couldn't help but muse, toying with the wine glass in his hand, that life without the comforts of wealth felt like a song out of tune, harmony shattered.

The problem with me, he mused, *is timing. I married a woman just before she realized she was a lesbian. I bought a house just before the real estate crash, then had to sell it short and go bankrupt. Then I bought crypto just before people realized it was all bullshit.* He sighed and took a large sip of wine. He despondently looked down at his plain salad.

He chuckled and then reflected on a time when he had been happy, despite having nothing. He had been so happy in his tiny apartment, with his old, beater of a car, and his daily double max cheeseburger. *No more Maxi burgers for me,* he lamented, patting his stomach. *Not if I want to live to be fifty.*

Staring at the vibrant greens of his prescribed salad, he exhaled a world-weary sigh. Around him, the room buzzed with high-tech chatter and the undercurrents of office politics. It felt like a technicolor whirlpool, sucking him into its relentless vortex, day in and day out.

He set down his wine glass, its charm lost to him now. An image reflected at him in the glass—a middle-aged man, rounded with excess and pale from too many hours indoors. His doctor's stern warning echoed in his mind, a stinging reminder. *High cholesterol. Get active or...* He shut his eyes, shaking off the ominous words.

He was just in his forties, but it felt like his best years were draining away with each tick of the clock. *Change*, he mused, pressing his hand against his heart, pulsing under the weight of unspoken fear, *is a necessity*.

A wave of depression threatened to overwhelm him. *My marriage was a sham*, he thought. *The way she left me when I lost my job.* He remembered the day. Walking on to public transport with a cardboard box, he knew that everyone knew that he had been fired. The shame had cut him to his core. *She didn't marry me, she married an ATM machine, and when I stopped printing money, she ditched me and ran off with a woman.*

He remembered pretending to be working overtime that day. He remembered hiding the box in the garage so he could have one more night with his wife. They had sex and he'd gone to sleep.

In the morning, she had come in screaming. She had found the box. He sighed and closed his eyes at the memory.

From a couple of tables over, a jarring cough punctuated the ambient murmur. Billy glanced up to see a middle-aged woman, her back pressed against a wall, dressed in a garish shade of red. The wallpaper's pattern seemed to pulsate in rhythm with her coughing fit.

There was something ominous about the cough. It rumbled deep, resonating in a way that gnawed at his composure. A visceral reaction gripped Billy, his stomach twisting in unexpected discomfort. The sound seemed to slither under his skin, leaving a trail of unease that had him swallowing down a bout of nausea.

His gaze locked onto the woman, tracking the harsh rhythm of her chest as each cough seemed to tear from her very core. His fists clenched, his palms began to sweat, and his heart was drumming a quickening beat. The dull buzz of conversations faded, replaced by the grating sound of her escalating distress.

As her cough morphed into a choked gasp, Billy sprang from his chair. His mind flashed back to that first aid class; the dummy on the table, the instructor's calm voice teaching the Heimlich maneuver. His mind spun a quick fantasy—her grateful, teary eyes, a hefty reward...

Shaking the thought off, he darted across the space dividing them. With an adrenaline-fueled strength, he hoisted the woman to her feet. His arms encircled her, hands clasping in position as he delivered five abdominal thrusts. Panic threaded through him as he realized his error. *I'm supposed to do back thumps!*

4

In a hurried flurry, he administered five quick thumps between her shoulder blades. Her struggle continued; guttural, horrifying sounds clawing at the quiet. Her condition was worsening—a nightmare unfolding in slow motion.

Billy's eyes darted around the room, the weight of desperation pressing heavily upon him. A sea of faces stared back—wide-eyed, paralyzed by the spectacle before them. The silence was deafening, save for the ominous tick-tock of a wall clock.

"Is there a doctor? Anyone with medical training?" His plea echoed, swallowed by the thick fear choking the room. From the corner of his eye, he caught a young girl, phone held aloft, her fingers trembling as she recorded the scene. It hit him then, the stark reality of their apathy.

"Call an ambulance, now!" Billy bellowed, desperation raw in his voice.

Turning back to the woman, his heart dropped as her eyes rolled back, her body succumbing to a frightening stillness. An icy dread seeped into his veins, knotting his stomach. He looked up, his gaze sweeping across the room. All he met were expressions of shock, confusion, or morbid fascination.

Time seemed to stutter, the woman's skin morphing into an unnatural, sickly shade of gray. Billy was transfixed. A bitter thought flitted across his mind—urban apathy, a city full of eyes that watch but never act. No, he wouldn't be one of them. He would do something.

Sliding to his knees beside her lifeless form, he extended a shaking hand, pressing his fingers to her throat. The silent chorus of onlookers bore into his back, their collective fear a tangible weight on his shoulders. He forced himself to focus, his heart sinking as the grim reality dawned on him—she had no pulse.

The horror of the situation struck Billy like a sledgehammer. A tidal wave of nausea threatened to overtake him, his stomach churning with the stark reality of her lifeless form. He swallowed hard, trying to quell the bile rising in his throat, as his mouth filled with the metallic tang of panic-induced saliva.

Without a flicker of hope, Billy forced himself to start CPR. His hands rhythmically pushed down on her chest; each compression met with the unnerving crunch of her ribcage. Doubt clouded his mind, his thoughts churning like a whirlwind—was he doing this right?

His own internal berating roared in his ears. *Concentrate. Concentrate.* Amid the panic, an awful foam started to seep from her mouth. Then, like a lightning bolt, realization struck him—he hadn't checked for airway obstructions.

A tide of self-reproach surged within him. How could he have overlooked such a fundamental step? His earlier confidence crumbled, replaced by the cold, gnawing fear of his own inadequacy.

Billy, collect yourself, he commanded inwardly. He leaned in, his breath hitching as he gently pried her mouth open. The hushed murmur of the onlookers filled the air, a dissonant hum in the backdrop that served as a constant reminder—he was not alone in this ordeal.

His hands, slick with perspiration, trembled visibly. With a shaky determination, he forced the woman's mouth wider, peering into the unsettling darkness. A nebulous shape lurked at the back of her throat.

With a little trembling, his fingers plunged into the unfamiliar territory, reaching for the obstruction. It was frustratingly elusive, lodged deep in her throat. As he adjusted his grip, his fingertips brushed against it—not a solid object as he'd expected, but a viscous substance. It was slick, slimy, disturbing. What could produce such black ooze in someone's throat?

While his fingers were still lodged in her throat, a guttural growl erupted from her, an animalistic sound that froze his blood. Recoiling in shock, Billy stumbled back, his heart pounding against his ribs. The growl was not just menacing, it echoed with an otherworldly malice that filled him with dread.

His gaze met hers, and his breath stopped. Her eyes, once filled with fear, had turned a milky white, a chilling void of life. A primal instinct screamed within him—*this was wrong, all wrong.* This was not a mere case of choking. Something sinister was at play, something he couldn't begin to comprehend.

Billy's mind was a whirling tempest, desperately grappling with the incomprehensible. *Could this be a seizure? A psychotic episode?*

Without warning, the woman convulsed violently, her movements a whirlwind of raw, primal energy. Chairs and tables

7

scattered, crashing against the floor with thunderous echoes. The wait staff sprang into action, moving towards her in a futile attempt to control the situation.

She retaliated with savage ferocity, her teeth sinking into a waiter's arm, her face a grotesque mask of rage. A strangled curse escaped Billy's lips. This was madness.

A geyser of blood erupted from the waiter's arm as he tried to fend off her relentless attack. It was like a scene from the most gruesome of horror movies, the woman gnashing and snapping like a real-life zombie. The surrealism of it struck Billy— had he not felt her lifeless pulse himself, he would have dismissed her as simply deranged. Yet, her heart had been still, and that inky, sinister ooze in her throat...

His thoughts were abruptly interrupted as he realized his paralysis. Too much precious time had been squandered in stunned inaction. Instinct screamed at him to flee, to put as much distance as possible between himself and the monstrous woman. He backpedaled, almost tripping over a chair in his haste.

Suddenly, she pounced on a nearby waitress, who let out a bone-chilling scream, as if a demon from hell had descended upon her. The blood in his veins turned to ice. What was happening? His mind whirled, frantically trying and failing to make sense of the nightmare unfolding before his eyes.

A primal instinct seizjsed him, a desperate urge to survive. He knew he had to flee, but he was a heartbeat too late. She was already lunging towards him, her eyes vacant and predatory, her movements inhumanly swift.

Without thinking, his hands seized the edge of a nearby table, hoisting it up like a makeshift shield. She impacted against it, knocking the wind out of him. Desperately, he put all his strength behind it, striving to keep her gnashing teeth and clawing hands at bay. Around him, the restaurant had erupted into pandemonium. Patrons darted frantically for the exit; a stampede driven by sheer terror.

The woman's strength was a shocking contradiction to her small frame. Each snarling attack threatened to rip the table from his trembling grip. Despair curled around him like a vise.

Then, cutting through the chaos, the sound of sirens wailed in the distance. The doorway burst open to reveal a uniformed police officer, his weapon leveled at the monstrous woman. "Freeze!" he commanded, his voice a beacon of authority in the swirling storm of panic.

The woman abruptly shifted her attention to the new arrival, her milky eyes narrowing on him. He faltered, his confident facade giving way to raw shock. His eyes mirrored the horror that swept the room, his grip on the gun wavering.

"What the..." he stammered, stumbling back a step. "Freeze!" His voice, once a bastion of authority, now trembled with unease.

In response, she issued another guttural growl, deep and animalistic. A sound that mocked the concept of reason and civilization.

"Mother of..." His voice died in his throat; the last word swallowed by his rising panic.

With a savage snarl, she lunged at the officer. He squeezed off three rapid shots, each hitting her squarely in the chest, yet they barely seemed to phase her. Like an unholy creature, she was upon him, sinking her teeth into his throat. His horrified scream cut through the air, hanging there like a siren's wail.

"God damn!" another voice echoed as a second officer rushed into the chaos. His weapon was already trained on the bestial woman, the crack of gunfire almost instantaneous.

In a sickening display, the woman's head erupted in a burst of gore. The report was so deafening that Billy recoiled. The new officer was immediately by his fallen comrade's side, his gloved hands desperately trying to stanch the gushing wound on his neck.

Billy could only stand there, shock anchoring him in place. The sight of the growing pool of blood spreading beneath the wounded officer was a stark reminder of the grotesque reality. His mind spun. She wasn't just insane, she was...something else.

His heart hammered, a wild percussion echoing his fear. His hands trembled, a visible testament to the torrents of adrenaline running through his veins. It took a Herculean effort to tear his gaze from the lifeless form of the policeman, his mind whirling with the next step.

The reality sank in; the officer was beyond help. His untrained hands couldn't mend a torn throat, much less rewind the clock on death's swift advance. His gaze shifted, scanning the chaotic scene around him. Waitstaff, previously bustling with orders and dishes, now lay scattered, wounded amidst the debris.

His feet were moving before he had fully processed the thought. He maneuvered through the chaos towards them, his eyes assessing their injuries. Gnashed flesh marred arms and legs, teeth marks a grotesque testament to the savage attack. A cold dread coiled in his stomach. They needed help, and fast. Medical help, that was likely not coming anytime soon.

He grabbed a cloth napkin from the nearest table, the linen cool in his clammy hands. Moving quickly, he tried to stanch the bleeding on the waitress's bicep, his fingers staining with the warmth of her blood. He could see the terror in her eyes, mirroring his own.

The blare of sirens seemed to crescendo, the sound of salvation. Relief flooded through him as EMTs burst onto the scene, their uniforms a stark contrast to the nightmarish tableau. Now he could step back, let the professionals handle the carnage.

The first EMT kneeled next to the fallen officer, his gloved hands moving deftly to check for a pulse. Billy watched as the EMT slowly shook his head. "No pulse."

A cold shiver ran down Billy's spine. *I've never seen a dead person before today, and now...the officer bled out in mere moments.* The enormity of the bloodshed, the raw violence of it, bore down on him.

Billy looked on as the lifeless body of the policeman was respectfully placed onto a stretcher, a white blanket concealing the brutal reality underneath. The restaurant owner, a beacon of familiarity amidst the chaos, poured Billy a cup of tea, which seemed surreal but was very welcome. The rich aroma cut through the smell of blood and fear. He added a shot of whiskey, the amber liquid swirling into the hot tea. Billy found himself wishing it was just the whiskey. He kept the thought to himself, offering a wordless nod of thanks instead.

As the dust began to settle, time moving at a crawl in the wake of the horrific event, Billy found himself perched at a corner table nursing his fortified tea. The sound of approaching footsteps drew his attention, and he found himself facing a detective.

The man was clad in an unassuming black shirt and blue jeans, a stark contrast to the formality of the uniformed officers. A badge was clipped to his belt. There was an air of weary determination about him, his eyes reflecting the weight of countless crime scenes witnessed.

The detective extended his hand, his grip firm yet sympathetic. "Hello, Billy Halls, is it?"

Billy corrected him, "It's Hallson, Billy Hallson." His voice rasped out, strained from the adrenaline and horror of the night. Out of the corner of his eye, he noticed a glimpse of the white blanket on the stretcher. A policeman's lifeless hand peeked out from beneath it, a grim reminder of the events that had unfolded. He forcibly shifted his attention back to the detective.

"And your age, Billy?" The detective's pen was poised over his notepad, his eyes fixed on Billy, unblinking, searching.

Billy hesitated, an inexplicable wave of regret washing over him. *Why does he need to know my age?* "Forty-five...no, wait, forty-six," he corrected himself, the reality of his age suddenly seeming so much more significant. *I could have died here today,* he thought. *What would my life have meant? I have achieved nothing, just a failed marriage and a failing career. I am overweight, overworked and...and apparently, I am useless in a crisis. The biggest success I've had in life is getting the judge to lower my alimony payments.*

Questions from the detective droned on in the background of Billy's awareness, the nods and head shakes coming almost automatically. His focus, however, veered to a hand peeking out from the white shroud of the stretcher. It sent a shiver down his spine. *This morning, that policeman had woken up, had breakfast, took a dump and marched out his front door with no idea that his life was about to end.* The thought made Billy shake his head in wonder.

Okay, he thought, *I am definitely going to do more exercise starting today...well, tomorrow. Though, that policeman was probably in great shape, and it didn't save him. You never know what life will bring.*

He could not take his eyes off that hand. Suddenly, it twitched. Billy started, the motion sharp enough to snap him out of his semi-detached state. The detective, absorbed in his notetaking, missed the slight jerk of Billy's head.

A tiny spark of hope flared in the dark depths of Billy's heart—could the officer have survived? As swiftly as it appeared, he extinguished it. The memory of the gruesome wound was still fresh; survival was a far-fetched dream. "Just a post-mortem twitch," he muttered under his breath, attempting to dispel the cold dread slithering up his spine.

Why haven't they taken the body already, he thought. *I can smell it. It's like…rotten meat.* He fought the bile rising in his throat and swallowed hard.

His gaze remained fixated on the hand, his attention divided between the detective's monotone and the unsettling hand. Then, it happened again—the hand twitched. Billy's eyes widened and his mouth dropped open. The detective noticed his reaction and followed his gaze, but the body was motionless.

"The hand twitched," said Billy.

The detective looked doubtful. "I've seen a lot of dead bodies, Mr. Hallson, they are sometimes twitchy. I've even heard one groan."

Billy inhaled deeply, attempting to steady his racing heart. The hand tremored again, and this time, the body mirrored its movement. The detective's voice died in his throat; his attention riveted to the stirring corpse. With a sudden jerk, the body propped itself against the stretcher, the face concealed under the ghostly veil of the blanket.

The murmur of conversation in the restaurant abruptly stopped, replaced by an eerie silence that was quickly infected with the tension radiating from the dead policeman. Every police officer in the room froze, their attention magnetically drawn to the seemingly-resurrected figure. As the detective pivoted sharply at the sudden quiet, his widened eyes were a mirror, reflecting the unspeakable horror that was unfolding.

Amidst the terrified hush, a police officer's voice ripped through the silence, "What the hell is happening?!" The accusation in his voice was as clear as the shock etched on his face. "You declared him dead!"

Billy felt a cold dread snake its way through his veins, making his heart pound wildly against his ribs. His breath seemed to solidify in his lungs, and a sudden bout of nausea twisted his stomach in knots. The terrifying realization that the nightmare was far from over threatened to drown him in a sea of terror.

The EMT, visibly pale, was temporarily at a loss for words. He stuttered in disbelief, "B-but…he was…lifeless. Carotid… shredded. Maybe a… neurological spasm. I've heard…rare cases…" His voice trembled, barely audible above the mounting pandemonium. His eyes, wide with fear, remained fixed on the convulsing figure. Around him, the stunned silence had given way to chaos, the officers and restaurant staff whispering frantic prayers, cries of alarm and disbelief cutting through the air. The atmosphere was a volatile mix of fear and confusion, a potent reminder of their horrifying reality.

Suddenly, the dead officer convulsed with a jolt that sent tremors of fear coursing through the room. The EMT staggered back, his face draining of color, his eyes round with terror. Meanwhile, the police officers, initially confused and hopeful, sprang into action, rushing toward their reanimated colleague with a desperate bid to help.

One officer, braver or perhaps naiver than the rest, yanked off the covering shroud, revealing the ghastly sight. The corpse's skin was deathly pallid, eyes transformed into a milky abyss, and a disconcerting black ooze dribbled from his mouth like some monstrous infant's drool. The room drew in a collective, horrified gasp, the sound echoing sharply against the walls, amplifying the terror that had seized them all. The chilling sight punctured the bubble of denial they had cocooned themselves in, unleashing a pandemonium that ricocheted off the walls of the previously mundane restaurant.

Just as the truth dawned on the officers, the abomination that was once their colleague issued a growl so primitive, so alien, it sent an icy prickle of dread skittering across everyone's skin. *Holy hell,* Billy thought, his mind spinning in disbelief. This is real. *This is actually happening.*

With a speed that mocked the realm of the living, the creature sprang towards the officer who had unveiled its grotesque transformation. A sickening crunch echoed through the restaurant as its teeth sunk deep into the officer's hand. The man's scream, raw and full of excruciating agony, bounced off the walls, amplifying the heart-stopping terror that had ensnared them all.

Panic tore through the room like wildfire, sending officers scrambling back in disarray, their faces mirroring the unspeakable horror that had descended upon them. Hands shaking uncontrollably, they fumbled to draw their guns, training them on the monstrous parody of their former friend who was growling with unfathomable ferocity.

"What in God's name is happening?" The shout cut through the pandemonium, echoing ominously in the midst of the chaos, yet finding no answer. They were now grappling with a reality that far surpassed their worst nightmares, a reality that no amount of training could have prepared them for.

The creature's ferocity surpassed anything humanly conceivable. At first, the officers hesitated, caught in the throes of disbelief. Yet as reality crystallized, they responded the only way they knew how—guns blazing.

But it was as if the bullets were nothing more than stinging gnats to the monstrous entity. Unfazed by the barrage, it pressed on, its body a grotesque spectacle riddled with bullet holes, yet undeterred.

It was a nightmare made of flesh. The undead policeman, fueled by an unearthly strength, tore through the officers as if they were paper dolls. Its teeth sank deep, its claws tore through fabric and flesh alike. Two officers crumpled to the ground, their screams piercing the air as the creature mercilessly mauled them. Another officer recoiled, his arm marred by a vicious bite. He fell back, horror etched onto his face, clutching his blood-soaked sleeve.

The restaurant had been transformed into a war zone, a surreal theater of horror. Billy could only watch, paralyzed, as his everyday world morphed into an unending nightmare.

He could barely register the acrid smell of gunpowder in the air, or the coppery tang of blood that filled the room. His mind was racing, skittering around the edges of a terrifying reality he was reluctant to acknowledge.

Images from countless horror movies flickered through his mind. The inhuman strength, the gruesome transformation, the relentless hunger—it all pointed towards one horrifying yet ludicrous conclusion. A zombie. The word echoed in his mind, bouncing off the walls of his denial.

"But...they're just movie monsters...aren't they?" he muttered, his voice barely more than a whisper, lost amidst the pandemonium that had overtaken the restaurant. He tried to shake the thought off, but it clung to him like a sinister shadow, turning his blood to ice and his heart into a leaden weight in his chest.

Engaged in its macabre feast, the undead policeman gnawed at the officer's arm with an insatiable hunger. The officer's screams punctuated the air, a stark symphony of terror and agony. Suddenly, the gnashing of teeth and the screams were overtaken by the deafening roar of a gunshot.

Without warning, the undead officer's head erupted in a grotesque display. Bits of gore and brain matter splattered across the room, painting a horrifying tableau of violence. The source of the life-saving bullet, a grizzled, older officer, stood with his smoking gun extended, his grim face illuminated by the barrel's fading echo. The room fell into an uneasy silence, the only sound was the labored panting of the remaining officers and the sickening drip of the undead's remnants pooling on the floor.

Billy surveyed the chaotic scene that had unfolded in front of him. Half a dozen officers were writhing in pain, their uniforms stained with the grotesque reminder of their encounters. Their comrades, now makeshift medics, applied hurried bandages to the wounds, each one a potential death sentence in this new and horrifying reality.

His mind raced, pieces of the horrifying puzzle slotting into place. *Zombies... they had to be zombies. And if that were true, then each one of those bite wounds spelled a chilling future for the bitten officers.* Billy weighed the potential risks. He was unarmed, unprepared, and the night had already proven that anything could happen.

His gut screamed at him to run, to escape while he still could. And yet, his conscience nagged at him, guilt seeping into his thoughts for even considering leaving the wounded officers behind. He swallowed the lump in his throat and made his choice. Survival was paramount. He quietly rose from his seat, slipping unnoticed through the pandemonium, and made a beeline for the exit.

"Going somewhere, Hallson?" The detective's voice rang out, clear and commanding amidst the commotion.

Billy froze mid-step. *Damnit.* He knew he would be needed as a witness, but staying could mean the difference between life and a horrifying, gruesome death.

"I...need some fresh air," he stammered out, trying to keep his voice steady. "Feeling a bit queasy, you know?"

The detective's hawk-like gaze bore into him, scrutinizing his every move. Billy could almost hear the gears turning in his head. Seconds stretched into eternity before the detective finally nodded, albeit reluctantly.

"Alright. But don't go too far, Hallson. We'll need your statement," he warned, his gaze never leaving Billy until he'd stepped outside and into the comparatively safer night.

Breathing a silent prayer of gratitude, Billy made his way to the exit, every step carefully measured to mask his urgent desire to flee. Once outside, he made a show of staggering towards the side of the restaurant, hunched over as if battling a violent wave of nausea.

Out of the direct line of sight from the restaurant's windows, Billy quickened his pace. He spared a last glance over his shoulder at the scene of chaos he was leaving behind, before breaking into an all-out sprint. His heart pounded in his ears, mirroring the adrenaline-fueled beat of his desperate escape.

Billy sprinted away from the restaurant, the fear-fueled adrenaline providing him an energy he hadn't felt in years. He was unaware of his surroundings, his mind racing through the gruesome spectacle he had just witnessed.

As the frenzied chaos of the restaurant receded behind him, he began to slow his pace, his labored breaths echoing in the quiet streets. *God, I am so unfit.* A chilling realization began to take hold of him, and he skidded to a halt. The scene at the restaurant was not just a gruesome incident. It was just the beginning.

The woman, he surmised, must have been patient zero. A previously unknown infection had killed her and then brought her back from the dead, turned her into a monster that attacked anything living in sight. The bitten officers, Billy realized with a sickening jolt, were likely the next to turn. The beginnings of an apocalypse; something that until now, he'd only seen in the movies.

A wave of fear washed over him, but it was quickly replaced by an odd sense of grim determination. He was in a unique position, possibly the only one who understood what was coming. He had a head start, the chance to prepare, to survive.

He quickly formulated a plan. He would gather supplies, find a place he could fortify, and maybe try to warn people. It was terrifying, the thought of what was coming. But as the early afternoon sun beat down on him, he felt a surge of resolve. It was him against the impending horde. And he was not going down without a fight. The dread of the coming night loomed heavily in his mind as he rushed towards the uncertainty.

Amanda Willard – Oakland, Alta Bates Hospital – 2 p.m. Day Zero

Amanda Willard and Joshua Willard

Shirley's voice cut through the din of the busy hospital reception. "Amanda!" she called, her gaze darting from the ever-ringing phones to the expanse of the waiting room, scanning for the familiar figure of her colleague. "Are you leaving now?"

Tucked in a corner, Amanda Willard was standing, her back turned, as she filled out the last bit of paperwork from her grueling double shift. Her eyelids were heavy with exhaustion, her uniform a testament to the long hours she had put in. Hearing her name, she turned around, shooting Shirley a tired smile that didn't quite reach her eyes. "I'm trying to, Shirley. Just need to wrap up a few things here," she replied, her voice barely audible over the backdrop of hospital noise.

Shirley gave her a sympathetic look. "You look beat, honey. Joshua at the daycare?"

A nod from Amanda confirmed this. She ran a hand through her hair and sighed. "Yeah, and if I'm lucky, I can pass him off to his father for the evening and get some sleep."

Her words hung in the air as she turned back to her papers, her mind already wandering to the thought of a few precious hours of sleep. But the thought of Joshua's father filled her with misgivings. He was not a reliable or eager parent.

"There's been an incident downtown," Shirley announced abruptly, her tone shifting to one of gravity. Her eyes darted across the reception, her gaze resting momentarily on the TV screen showing breaking news.

Amanda looked up from her paperwork, her tired eyes squinting at Shirley. She swiped at her phone, checking for alerts. "Dead? Casualties? Why haven't I gotten a STAN alert?" She paused, scanning her phone again. She let out a sigh, shaking her head. "Nothing. Must not be so severe. I'm out of here, Shirl'."

Shirley hesitated, her mouth opening as if to say more, but then, perhaps sensing Amanda's exhaustion, she closed it again. She simply gave Amanda a sympathetic wave. "Go get some rest, hon, you've earned it."

Hauling her backpack onto her shoulder, Amanda trudged out of the ER, her steps heavy with exhaustion. The shrill wail of ambulance sirens pierced the air as she crossed the road, the relentless noise of the city compounding her fatigue.

She wrinkled her nose at the acrid scent of exhaust fumes mixing with the distinct smell of urban decay that clung to the city.

Signs of neglect and disarray were etched into the cityscape, a testament to a system struggling to keep up. The sirens seemed to echo her own sentiments, screaming out against the deteriorating state of affairs. "This damn city..." she muttered under her breath; her thoughts punctuated by the latest outbreak of violence. "Every day, it's one step forward and two steps back." Her hands clenched tightly around her backpack straps, channeling her frustration into the stiff fabric.

As she moved further from the chaos of the emergency room, her mind began to drift to a happier place, a sanctuary amid the city's madness—her little Joshua. The thought of his bright, innocent face brought a warmth that bubbled up within her, countering the chill of the city's harsh realities.

She could almost feel the sensation of his small arms wrapping around her in a welcoming embrace, the sincerity of his affection washing over her in a wave of pure, unadulterated love. She chuckled softly to herself, envisioning the familiar sight of his lips smeared with peanut butter, invariably sharing a bit of it with her during their enthusiastic welcome-home kisses. It was these moments, these precious, sticky, peanut butter-laden kisses that made all the trials of her day worth it.

She pushed open the door to the brightly lit daycare, the room filled with the infectious energy and laughter of children. She signed her name crisply on the checkout register, casting a quick glance at the clock on the wall before being buzzed into the pickup area.

Ludmilla, a care worker with a perpetually cheerful demeanor, walked in, guiding a small figure by the hand. Joshua. As soon as his bright eyes landed on Amanda, a grin spread across his chubby face. "Mommy!" he squealed, freeing himself from Ludmilla's grasp.

In a flurry of movement, he dashed towards her, his tiny sneakers squeaking against the tiled floor. With a leap of joy, he launched himself into her waiting arms, wrapping his arms around her neck in a joyful reunion.

Joshua took a deep breath, his eyes sparkling with the excitement of the day's tales. "I made a pasta necklace," he declared, holding his tiny fist up as if the said necklace was still in it.

Amanda couldn't help but laugh, planting a kiss on his forehead, "Wow, that sounds wonderful, honey."

"And we did a puppet!" Joshua continued, now animatedly moving his other hand as if operating a puppet. "And we had a new fire engine toy!"

Amanda's heart warmed at his innocent enthusiasm; her exhaustion momentarily forgotten. She listened attentively as Joshua continued his rambling narration of the day's events, punctuated by dramatic gasps and extravagant hand gestures. From Lilly throwing up in the sandpit, a particularly hot slide, a destroyed sand rabbit, an enforced nap, to a peanut butter and jelly snack without the coveted pea snacks and lemonade— he covered it all.

She kissed him on the forehead and carried him out.

"…I had to have strawberry juice, which is nice, but then I had to go pee but there was no one to take me pee because Miss Penny got sick, and Lilly was being sick so…"

Mid-sentence, Joshua's words brought Amanda's attention to a spreading dampness seeping into the side of her scrubs. She glanced down and spotted the culprit—Joshua's soaked pants. Her heart sank a little, another complication to an already exhausting day. Yet, as a seasoned trauma nurse, she'd encountered much worse than a little pee. She merely tightened her grip on him and adjusted him in her arms, protecting her remaining dry clothes.

"Well, buddy, sounds like we need to make a pit stop at home first," she said, masking her sigh with a forced smile. "Let's get you cleaned up before we think about dropping you off at your dad's."

As Amanda spotted their bus lumbering down the road, she tightened her hold on Joshua and broke into a light jog towards the stop. Each bump in the sidewalk sent them bobbing up and down, triggering peals of laughter from Joshua. Despite the exhaustion nipping at her heels, hearing his innocent, joyful giggles ignited a warm spark in her heart. The sound was like a soothing balm, momentarily easing the strains of her long, taxing day.

Three ambulances in quick succession screeched into the emergency room driveway, their red and blue lights flickering against the evening dusk. The squeal of sirens echoed in the air, a harsh reminder of the incident downtown. As she watched the frenzied scene, another shrill alarm rang out, drawing her attention to a convoy of police cars barreling down the road, their lights slashing through the shadows.

Ambulances Rushing to Ground Zero

The clamor of the city, its unceasing chaos, felt like a weight on her chest. The sense of desperation and danger was a far cry from the quiet, peaceful town where she had grown up. The city had promised opportunity and excitement, but all it offered her was exhaustion and a sense of dread.

The bus pulled up to the stop and Amanda moved to board, but paused as the driver stepped off the bus, his arm wrapped around a young man. The man was pale, sweating profusely, and staggering as if in a stupor. But what grabbed Amanda's attention was a trail of black ooze trickling from the corner of his mouth. The man rubbed his face and the black liquid smeared.

"Hold up, folks," the driver called out to the waiting passengers. "Just need to drop this young fella at the hospital." The crowd watched silently as the two men slowly shuffled towards the emergency room entrance.

Amanda frowned; her professional curiosity piqued. That black ooze...It was unlike anything she'd seen before. It could be dried blood mixed with mucus, but something about it seemed off, almost unnatural. She shook off her unease, reminding herself that she was off duty. But she couldn't help but glance back at the retreating figures, a prickling sense of apprehension creeping up her spine.

She stepped onto the bus; her attention immediately drawn to a commotion a little way down the street. A disheveled man was running wildly along the sidewalk, his shouts a discordant melody carried on the wind. He was frantic, arms flailing, as if the world behind him was on fire. A weary sigh escaped Amanda. It seemed Oakland had its fair share of distressed souls, their trials and tribulations worn like a second skin.

She found a seat near the middle of the bus, Joshua nestled securely in her arms. With the bus stationary, awaiting the return of the driver, they had a clear view of the disarray unfolding outside. She watched, her nurse's instinct alert and assessing, even as she kept her expression calm for Joshua's sake.

"Okay, buddy," she said quietly, her focus subtly shifting from the street's chaos to her son's innocent chatter. "Let's talk about your day some more while we wait, alright?" A casual normalcy to shield him from the unusual happenings just outside their temporary sanctuary.

"Phone!" Joshua chirped, his small hands reaching out with an enthusiasm that only a toddler could muster.

With a knowing smile, Amanda pulled her phone from her pocket. Her fingers moved deftly over the screen, unlocking it and navigating to Joshua's favorite game, 'BoBo the Bus'. As the cheerful music of the game filled the air, she handed the device to him. His eyes lit up, and he became fully engrossed in the colorful world on the screen.

A second man, a neatly dressed Caucasian, sprinted past the bus, his crisp business clothes incongruous with the panicked run. A young woman was hot on his heels, panting heavily. Amanda squinted, trying to discern what they were running from.

"What on earth...?" she muttered to herself. The unsettling scene unfolded like a ripple effect, with more terrified citizens sprinting away from some unseen danger to the west.

Sirens blared again, slicing through the air like the harsh cry of a mechanical bird. More police cars whizzed by, their lights flashing urgently as they converged to a point a few blocks away.

Well, there are enough emergency services headed to resolve whatever's going on, she thought and clutched Joshua closer, the usually comforting vibration of the idle bus now serving as a harsh reminder of their stationary position. An icy wave of dread washed over her. She needed to get her son away from here. Now.

"Mama, I got the blue squares," said Joshua, thrusting the phone into her face, his innocent joy strikingly contrasting the mounting fear in her gut.

"That's wonderful, Jo Jo," she responded absently, her gaze once again drawn westward to the now-significant crowd of people fleeing in terror.

The bus driver still hadn't returned. A pang of annoyance mingled with worry nagged at her. She eyed the open bus door, now seeming more like an unsecured gateway to danger. *Should I close it?* she pondered.

Before she could make a decision, her phone blared with an intrusive 'awooooga' sound. The blaring alert caught everyone's attention on the bus, all heads swiveling towards her. She winced, recognizing the sound instantly. A STAN alert. It was a critical incident call, beckoning her back to the emergency room.

I could just pretend I didn't get it, she thought. *I could spend the evening with Joshua instead of whatever nightmare Oakland has in store for me tonight.* She sighed deeply, for she knew she could not turn her back on those in need of her help.

Great, just great. She'd have to put Joshua back in daycare, which he certainly wouldn't appreciate. As if the situation wasn't fraught enough already.

Suddenly, the bus doors swung open to admit a hulking figure. The man, donning a mechanic's jumpsuit with the name tag 'Frank Ricci,' was a whirlwind of bushy hair, fear-etched lines, and dark skin. Without a word, he pulled the lever to shut the bus doors and took a seat in the driver's cabin.

"What are you doing?" Amanda demanded, her brows furrowing in confusion and concern.

"Getting us to safety," came Frank's terse reply, his gaze locked on the chaos unfolding outside.

"But you're not the driver and…well…you don't have the keys," Amanda pointed out, her voice laced with disbelief.

Frank merely flashed a silver object from his pocket—a lock pick set, Amanda realized. With an air of practiced ease, he began to work on the ignition. The hum of the bus engine firing up was his only response.

More frantic citizens were pounding on the bus door, their panic-ridden faces pressed against the glass. "Let us in! They're coming! Let us in!" Their pleas echoed ominously within the confines of the bus.

"I need to get off. I have to get to the emergency room," Amanda insisted, her voice straining with anxiety.

Frank's eyes met hers in the rearview mirror. "The emergency room would be the last place you'd want to be right now," he said, an underlying note of regret in his voice. "If you step off this bus, you might not last five minutes out there."

His gaze flickered back to the desperate crowd outside the bus. He hesitated for a moment, his hand gripping the steering wheel tightly. "I'm...I'm sorry," he muttered. Then, with a visible look of guilt, he pressed his foot onto the accelerator, leaving the screams behind.

"What's going on!" Amanda's voice cracked with desperation as she held Joshua tighter, sinking back into the seat.

"People...they're losing it. Biting, attacking...even killing. It's like something out of a horror movie." Frank's voice wavered, his knuckles white as he maneuvered the bus around a group of terrified pedestrians darting onto the road.

Glancing around, Amanda noticed the other passengers, a dozen or so people, all peering out the windows, their expressions mirroring her own alarm. Outside, the sidewalks were awash with panicked individuals trying to escape from something unseen.

'Awooga'! The harsh sound of the STAN alarm cut through the noise again. Hastily, she muted it, her mind racing.

Biting? Killing? It didn't make sense. She recalled a news article about a drug named flakka, which allegedly induced violent behavior. *Maybe*, she thought, *some reckless group threw a party, handed out tainted drugs, and this...this was the aftermath.* It was a horrifying thought, but it was the only explanation that seemed to fit the chaos unfolding outside.

"Were you an eyewitness to this...this biting?" Amanda's voice barely rose above a whisper.

Frank's affirmative nod was almost lost amidst the jolting of the bus. "Yeah, seen it with my own two eyes."

She pressed further, her voice filled with hope. "Could it just be kids, you know, teens, college students acting out?"

The bus lurched as Frank swerved to avoid a group of frantic pedestrians. He shook his head, his face taut. "No, it ain't just kids. It was all sorts of folks. Even saw a cop doing it. Then, an old lady. Hell, even a kid, couldn't have been older than...ten or so." He paused, swallowing hard. "And they all had this black goop around their mouths. It was downright sickening."

The other passengers exchanged wide-eyed glances, the color draining from their faces. Amanda felt a shudder run through her. She instinctively hugged Joshua closer, her mind racing. The image of the young man with black ooze around his mouth flashed across her memory. A chilling realization began to dawn on her. This was no drug-fueled party gone wrong.

Joshua laughed. She looked down at him; he was engrossed in his game.

She returned her gaze to Frank. "Black goop?" Amanda echoed, her brow furrowed in confusion.

"Exactly," Frank responded, his face hardened. "It's nasty and it'll chill you to the bone."

The thought of cops involved in this madness made Amanda's stomach churn. It didn't fit any patterns she knew.

A woman from the back piped up then, "Some guy on SnapChat said this chaos started near the Memorial Park."

An older man seated across from Amanda chipped in, "My wife just texted me. She said it's all quiet around Jack London."

Amanda found herself connecting the dots. "That aligns with what we're seeing. Most of the runners were coming from the west...but Memorial Park is quite a distance, ten, maybe fifteen blocks away."

As they passed the area of panicked pedestrians, Frank reduced the bus speed. The terror of the situation was gradually replaced by an eerie calm, the silence punctuated only by the distant wails of sirens.

"Could you drop me off at the Central Reservoir?" Amanda asked, attempting to assert some control over the situation.

Frank was silent for a moment as he navigated the streets. "I'm planning to get on MacArthur at Fourteenth. I can drop you there. It's just a block away from the reservoir."

Amanda nodded, appreciative of his decision. "Thank you."

An old man piped up suddenly, "Hey! Can you drop me at St. Vartan?"

"I'm not a damn bus driver!" Frank barked back; his eyes still locked on the road. "I ain't making no stops until Fourteenth."

Amanda felt a pang of anxiety at his harsh response. The situation was escalating, and it was becoming increasingly apparent that everyone was on their own in this chaos.

As the bus continued to rumble down the increasingly deserted streets, Amanda took a moment to process what was happening. She pulled her son closer to her, feeling the tremble in his little body as he clung to her, oblivious to the madness outside. She turned her gaze to the window, watching the eerily quiet city pass by.

Suddenly, the bus lurched to a halt, causing several passengers to stumble. She glanced towards Frank, and the color had drained from his face. Following his gaze, Amanda's heart seized in her chest. In the middle of the intersection, just a few blocks away, a crowd had gathered. But it wasn't the kind of crowd you'd expect to see, milling about in fear or confusion.

They were fighting, tearing at each other with a ferocity that Amanda found chilling. It was like watching a pack of wild animals. The distant sounds of their snarls, growls, and cries echoed down the street, making the hairs on the back of Amanda's neck stand on end. And then she saw it: the black ooze Frank had mentioned, smeared around the mouths of the combatants.

As the terror washed over her, Amanda found herself gripping Joshua tighter. Her mind was spinning with dread and confusion, but one thought was becoming increasingly clear: This wasn't some drug-fueled frenzy. This was something much, much worse.

"What's happening?" Joshua whispered; his little voice filled with fear.

"I don't know, baby," she murmured back, pressing a kiss to the top of his head. But in her heart, she knew they were on the brink of a nightmare beyond comprehension. And there was no telling how far they would have to go to survive it.

Thankfully, the bus moved forward, getting past the violence. After a few miles of driving, Amanda began to relax. *We are safe,* she thought with relief...*for now.*

SAMANTHA WINTERS – CLAPP SPRING, SANTA ROSA ISLAND

The Cult of the Phoenix had marched their new initiates up from the dock at a breakneck pace. They were late on a date where lateness mattered. The boat ferrying them from the mainland had been delayed by engine trouble. With aching bones and sweating brows, the initiates waited now to be granted entry to the cult's bunker.

A chill swept through Samantha Winters as she perched nervously on the rough-hewn log. Beside her, seven other cult initiates murmured prayers and whispered among themselves. They were a motley group, young and old, from different backgrounds, but united in their faith of the Prophet or, perhaps, in their desperation. Samantha knew she was different, however. She was here under the Federal government's watchful eye, acting as their reluctant spy within the Cult of the Phoenix.

She had been brought up to be a good Christian, going to church every Sunday, so pretending to be faithful to a false prophet was agony. The Phoenix group did not even claim to be Christian, their beliefs were…odd and secretive. There were whispers of mind control, but Samantha did not believe them. She had heard there was some genius behind it all, someone with an agenda, someone who even their prophet leader answered to.

In front of them, a man known as the Robe-bearer, an overweight figure clad in crimson and gold, engaged in a hushed, heated conversation with a door guard.

The discussion between Robe-bearer and the guard seemed to be intensifying, their voices taking on sharper edges. Samantha found herself holding her breath, hoping against hope that she wouldn't be discovered, that her mission wouldn't end before it began.

"Late today!" she heard someone shout.

Robe-bearer responded with a whisper and pointed back at Samantha.

More heated talk followed.

With a heavy sigh that seemed to deflate his ample form, Robe-bearer lumbered back towards them. His eyes were shrewd under a heavy brow, gleaming with an intelligence that made Samantha's stomach knot with unease.

"There's been a slight change in plans," he began, his voice grating like gravel under a boot. The initiates stirred restlessly, exchanging uneasy glances.

"They'll let us in," he continued, managing to sound both smug and soothing, "but not without a precaution." He paused, letting the tension build. "A small medical examination. Just a little thing, really." He waved his hand dismissively.

Samantha's mind began to race. A medical examination? That could pose a problem. She had no idea what they would be looking for, and what they might find. She was glad she had refused to wear a wire, instead she had her communications device hidden in a secret pocket in her pack.

"And why this sudden precaution?" Robe-bearer continued, his voice taking on a theatrical quality. "The Prophet himself is here, my children. We cannot risk bringing any...unpleasantness to his holy presence. I will proceed ahead of you, but the door guard will see to you."

With that, he turned and strode up toward a small shed which he disappeared inside.

A flicker of surprise lit Samantha's eyes. *The Prophet is here.* She found her hand sliding to the side of her bag, her fingers brushing over the concealed bulge of her communications equipment. It gave her comfort to have it as a lifeline, a tenuous connection to the world she had left behind but desperately wished to return to.

Images flashed through her mind, each one sharp with regret. Her family, huddled together in their detention room, their eyes filled with worry. The cold, impersonal office where they had threatened her with deportation. The bleak despair that had driven her to accept this dangerous mission.

A shiver ran down her spine. *What if the Cult found out?* The question loomed large in her mind, dwarfing everything else. *What would they do to me? They couldn't kill me, could they? They are not above the law.*

She remembered the long boat ride to this isolated island, Santa Rosa, they called it. She had never heard of it until the day of departure. She could still feel the icy sting of the wind as she was forced to sit on deck, the taste of salt on her lips, the sinking feeling of dread as the mainland disappeared from sight.

The feds better live up to their end of the deal…or…what could I really do if they just deport us anyway? She knew that she was powerless against the whole might of the U.S. government. *The government has rules*, she reminded herself, *unlike the Cult and their messianic leader, the Prophet.*

Back in San Diego, she had felt a semblance of safety, like help was just a phone call away. *I should have tried calling the ACLU.* But here, surrounded by water and fanaticism, she was truly alone. Would her tiny transceiver even work in this desolate place? She tried to push away the uncertainty gnawing at her. It was too late for doubts; she had made her choice, and now she had to see it through.

The door guard strode over to the log, an imposing figure in the dim light. His cold eyes swept over the group, settling on Samantha. A clipboard was gripped tightly in his right hand, a pen in his left, and a gun hung ominously in a holster, angled just left of his groin.

"Samantha Winters?" His voice was a low growl, turning her name into a threat.

She swallowed the lump forming in her throat and nodded.

A slow, predatory smile spread across his face, transforming into a disturbing leer. Her heart hammered against her ribcage, its frantic rhythm resonating in her ears. She felt a wave of cold fear washing over her, leaving her bloodless and pallid.

A sickening realization gripped her. She could be violated here, discarded, and forgotten. The FBI wouldn't bat an eye; to them, she was just a disposable pawn. A non-citizen with no rights. If she were to scream, who would even listen?

Would anyone believe me if I reported an attack from a member of the cult? How could I prove it? Would I even live to report it?

The feeling of fear and helplessness gnawed at her, making her shudder despite the warmth of the evening. She was a lamb among wolves.

She looked him in the eyes, but his gaze remained stubbornly fixated on her chest. His crude gaze lingered, taunting her, daring her to challenge him. She took a deep breath, her chest rising in silent defiance.

"So, 'Samantha Winters', huh?" His voice was deceptively soft, laced with venom. "We know that's not your birth name. Changed it to sound more American, didn't you?"

"There are many Samanthas in Mexico," she said. "And I didn't want to keep the last name of Xochitl because, frankly, I got tired of having to spell it." She held his gaze and nodded, refusing to back down.

A sneer curled his lips. "Of course, who wouldn't want to be an American?" He looked down at his clipboard, his tone taking on a mocking lilt. "Brought over the border when you were just a kid, twelve years old? Hmm?" He paused dramatically, as if savoring the next bit of information. "And you graduated as a valedictorian from your high school." He leaned in closer, the sour smell of his breath assaulting her senses. His voice dropped to a harsh whisper. "Benefited from a little affirmative action, did we?"

Her temper flared and she was barely able to prevent her hand from reaching out and slapping him, instead she snorted indignantly. "No," she said, her voice barely more than a growl. She had intended to remain silent, but his insinuation had pushed her over the edge.

His reaction was a dismissive chuckle. "No, huh?" He seemed to enjoy her growing discomfort. "Well, you guys are too late to be allowed in…"

Her eyes widened. What would the feds do if she was turned around? Would they honor their deal and not deport her family? *Mama, Papa, Sonia, Silvia, Carlos.*

He touched her hair, and even picked up a strand of it and wrapped it around his hand for a moment. "But I wouldn't want to risk the Prophet's wrath by refusing you entry, now, would I? Not after you caught his eye back in San Diego." With a sarcastic smile, he made a check mark on the clipboard. Shoving his pen back into his shirt pocket, he pulled out a paper tube and a small glass vial.

He ripped the tube open, revealing a bright red swab stick. "Open wide," he commanded, his dominance in the situation clear.

Such a gross man! An icy dread filled her as she realized the power this man held over her fate in this strange place.

She hesitated momentarily before finally acquiescing and opening her mouth wide. He took the opportunity to swipe the swab against her cheeks, across her tongue and then brusquely thrust it to the back of her throat. The sudden intrusion made her gag, causing her to choke and jerk her head back. The guard pulled out the swab just in time. Her eyes teared up.

"Ha! You're really going to need to get that gag reflex under control!" He guffawed loudly, clearly enjoying her discomfort. Still chuckling, he shook his head in amusement and placed the red swab into the vial. His expression abruptly morphed from mockery to concentration as he watched the swab. A few agonizing seconds later, the swab transformed to a startling green. "Well, you're clear. Go ahead and enter through that door. I still have to check the rest of these folks," he said, indicating the remaining initiates with a dismissive wave of his hand. A strange grin flitted over his face.

That was the most disgusting man I have ever met.

The door he pointed to was on the very small shed. "Here?" she asked, confused. "Where is the bunker?"

The door guard just waved her on.

She approached the flimsy looking, wooden door. The door handle would not turn. She furrowed her brow and tried harder. A harsh buzz filled the air, and the handle unlocked. The door was surprisingly hefty, and she realized it was made of metal and over a foot thick. The paint made it look very convincingly wooden. The inexplicable thickness made her hesitate as she entered.

Why on earth would they make such a thick door? Were they expecting to be raided all the way out here in the middle of this island…where no one knows they are located and with such an inconspicuous door?

As she pushed past the door, a flight of stairs loomed ahead, plunging down into an unseen abyss. She paused, casting a quick look over her shoulder. To an observer from the air, the location would appear as nothing more than an inconspicuous small shed or cabin, nestled amongst dense vegetation. She realized the bunker itself was entirely hidden underground. The realization sank in— she was cut off from the world. A sense of desolation washed over her. She would not be able to call for help after all. With a heavy sigh, she accepted her predicament—she was going to have to play along, for now.

She descended the seemingly endless staircase, one cautiously measured step after another. By her estimate, she must have descended nearly a hundred steps before the staircase took a sharp turn, leading her down another lengthy flight of a hundred more steps.

Just as she was catching her breath at the bottom, she was startled to see the door guard from earlier waiting for her. Confusion washed over her as she studied his familiar face. But how could he have reached here before her?

Reading the bewilderment in her expression, the man offered her a smug smile. "Don't worry, you're not seeing things. You just met my twin brother, John, up there." His light tone held a hint of amusement, suggesting he found her confusion rather amusing. Despite his words, Samantha found it difficult to shake off her initial shock. Two guards with the same unsettling smile.

"Oh, I see," she said, forcing a polite smile onto her face. Even though Nathan seemed more amiable than his brother, Samantha remained wary. She did not want to engage in a conversation, not wanting to give away any more information about herself than she had already. Instead of replying verbally, she merely nodded, her smile never reaching her eyes. She hoped Nathan would interpret it as a simple acknowledgment rather than an invitation to continue the conversation.

Robe-bearer was on his knees with his head on the ground, mumbling a prayer.

"Alright, Miss Winters," Nathan said, sounding somewhat apologetic. "I'm going to need you to undress for the medical examination."

Samantha's eyes widened and she involuntarily stepped back, the fear clawing at her from the inside. *It's happening! He's going to…*

Seeing her obvious discomfort, Nathan quickly raised his hand in a placating gesture. "Now, hold on. It's nothing personal. I won't lay a finger on you, I promise."

"We need to ensure that you have no wounds, no bites, or anything that could potentially pose a threat to the people inside," he explained, pointing to the huge metal sheets that formed an imposing set of sliding doors. "Only then can you go through the blast doors."

Bites? she questioned internally, feeling her brow furrow in confusion. *Why would bites be a threat to others?*

She took a hesitant step back, her fingers clutching the fabric of her shirt. "Shouldn't we wait for the others?" she asked, her voice wavering. There was a certain safety in numbers, and perhaps it would feel less intrusive if they all underwent this 'medical' examination together.

"Nah, they didn't make it in time. We're making an exception for you though," Nathan explained nonchalantly.

"In time?" Samantha echoed, her heart pounding against her ribs. "In time for what?"

A sudden burst of gunshots from above cut through the air, causing her to flinch. She instinctively glanced toward the stairs, her breath hitching. "What the hell?"

"Worry about that later," Nathan said, his tone professional despite the sudden chaos. "For now, let's get this medical examination done. Please undress."

Her eyes locked onto his, her mind churning. What choice did she truly have? The sound of gunshots still echoed in her ears, making the prospect of going back upstairs terrifying. "And you won't touch me," she stated, her voice hard.

Nathan raised three fingers, his expression grave. "Scout's honor. The Prophet would skin me alive if I even dared to cross that line with you." His words were serious, lacking any hint of jest, offering Samantha a shred of reassurance.

I have had worse inspections when ICE picked us up. She remembered their groping hands inspecting her for weapons and drugs. *Men!* she thought with such bile, but then she remembered her Papa, her little brother Carlos. There were good men in the world. Uncles and mentors flooded her memories. *Judge people as they come, one by one.* That was the mantra her father had taught her. *Never judge by the group. Never judge by the accident of birth.*

Fueled by a sense of resignation, she methodically stripped down, folding her clothes neatly and placing them in a pile. When she was bare, she stood tall and defiant, her arms spread in a here-I-am gesture.

Nathan's gaze ran over her body with clinical precision. "Raise your hands," he instructed. His eyes checked under her arms. "Turn around."

As she turned, she faced the staircase where John, the guard from above, was making his descent towards her. His gaze was lewd, hungry, and a thin trail of drool glistened on his lower lip. He came to a halt, his eyes raking over her with unabashed interest.

Any decent man would avert their gaze.

Nathan, seemingly oblivious to his twin's lecherous stare, concluded his inspection. "Well, I see no bites," he said matter-of-factly. "You're perfect."

"She sure is," John added, his voice thick with innuendo.

Samantha felt her skin crawl, her previous fears threatening to surface again. But she swallowed them down, holding on to her defiant stance. She was a survivor, she reminded herself, and she would get through this too.

"Your willingness to serve the Prophet and his most sacred order...It has pleased him greatly," Nathan remarked, his voice taking on an ominous undertone. "Devotion like yours, it's always rewarded...If not in this life, then assuredly in the next."

His words hung in the air, a veiled promise and threat all at once.

Finally, after what felt like an eternity, Nathan said, "Alright, you can get dressed now."

She spun around, her hands shaking slightly as she hastily grabbed her clothes. Her movements were rushed and erratic, a stark contrast to the methodical undressing she'd performed moments ago. The chill of the bunker's air had never felt so biting. She could feel the twins' eyes still on her, their unwelcome scrutiny like physical weights. She had to get out of this place. She had to survive.

"Is the surface door sealed?" Nathan asked John.

John looked up the stairs momentarily, turned back to his brother. "It is," John replied.

"There you have it," Nathan said, his gaze still fixed on John. "The end of days has begun."

John simply smiled and nodded in agreement, the words hanging heavy in the air. "Fucking A," he replied after a moment, breaking the quiet tension. "Even if Robe-bearer couldn't marshal his initiates here on time. Moron."

Robe-bearer stood, gave John a withering stare, then turned to face the doors. "The Lord runs by his own time, and the time is…death," he said.

A pause filled the air, only to be interrupted by a massive, thunderous noise that shook the very ground they stood upon. Clunk, clunk, clunk. Samantha flinched, the ominous clanking noise echoing in her ears. The blast doors were opening. Slowly but surely, the massive sheets of metal began to slide apart, the spectacle eerily punctuating the men's disturbing exchange. The finality of it all settled in Samantha's gut, a cold dread threatening to consume her. The world was changing around her, and she was far from sure it was for the better.

With the heavy doors fully opened, a blast of stale, cold air hit Samantha. The space beyond was dimly lit, the vastness of it barely discernible in the weak light. Nathan motioned her forward, and she felt herself automatically take a step towards the daunting unknown.

The guards remained behind her as she moved into the cavernous space, the sound of the blast doors grinding closed behind her echoing ominously. The only source of light came from a dim bulb hanging from the ceiling, casting long, monstrous shadows around the room.

At the far end of the room, a door cracked open, spilling a sliver of warm light onto the cold concrete floor. A silhouette appeared in the doorway, too distant to make out any features. Samantha squinted, trying to discern the figure in the darkness, a sense of unease crawling up her spine.

"Welcome, child," a voice called out from the figure, echoing through the vast chamber. It was a deep, soothing voice, carrying an edge of authority and command.

With that, the door closed, plunging the room back into shadowy silence. Samantha was left alone in the darkness, the cryptic welcome resounding in her ears. The silence was deafening; the mystery of the figure and the voice leaving a chilling question in her mind: What had she gotten herself into? A sense of dread filled her as she realized the extent of her isolation. Alone, in an underground bunker with a mysterious figure, far away from anyone who might help her. The last thought that filled her mind before the chapter closed was a desperate plea: She had to find a way out of here, and fast.

BILLY HALLSON – CALIFORNIA, OAKLAND CITY CENTER – 1:30 P.M. DAY ZERO

Billy Hallson – The Getaway

Billy's pulse pounded in his ears as he darted his eyes around, his mind racing with the adrenaline of survival. He felt the primal urge to sprint the three blocks back to his apartment, but a more rational thought pushed through his panic. *No,* he decided, his gaze falling on the chaos that had unfolded. *An officer infected six others before they managed a head shot. What happens when all the police are infected?* He gulped, his palms slick with sweat. *There is going to be a major outbreak of growling zombies spreading out from that ground zero restaurant. The average Californian doesn't carry a gun. Anyone unarmed doesn't stand a chance against one of those rabid creatures.* He needed a car.

His apartment, located in a bustling, downtown area where parking was a luxury, didn't come with a parking spot, prompting him to sell his car long ago. Since then, the reliable Oakland public transport had been his mode of transit. He cringed at his ill luck, his heart hammering against his chest. Then, as if struck by a bolt of inspiration, he thought about renting a U-Haul truck. They were sturdy and spacious and could easily serve as temporary refuge. At nineteen bucks a day for in-town use, they were also affordable. Billy nodded to himself, a grim sense of resolve settling in. *Yes*, he thought, *that could work.*

Is it wrong that I just want to save my own ass? If I stay here, I might be able to help people. The feeling of guilt made him grunt. *But…seriously, what can I do? If I tell people I think there is a zombie apocalypse about to happen they will think I am another damn crazy in a city full of crazies.* The pace of running began to slow as his limbs began to hurt.

I have no gun; I have no weapons at all. He remembered the ferocity of the woman once transformed. *If I stay, I just die. I can't do any good.*

A sudden, piercing pain sliced through his side, halting him in his tracks. Dammit, he thought, doubling over, clutching his side. He was pathetically unfit, a stark reality driven home by the painful stitch after a mere two blocks. Panting, he glanced around before crossing the street to his bank. The threat of the infected officers turning rabid loomed ominously over him, but he felt he still had a small window of time. A plan began to form in his mind—withdraw all his cash, then head north.

After the bank, the storage center was his next intended destination. In his recollection, they always had U-Haul trucks for rent. A good cover, and a feasible escape vehicle. Plus, with his money on hand, he wouldn't have to rely on the unpredictability of electronic transactions during a city-wide panic. A thin, grim smile crept onto his face. It would have to work.

As Billy stepped into the bank, a faint, musty scent of old money and the cold sting of disinfectant greeted him. He noted, with some relief, the absence of a crowd. The hushed whispers and soft humming of computers were the only sounds disturbing the otherwise tranquil space. Without hesitation, he moved towards the closest teller.

"I'd like to withdraw all my money," he stated, tapping his card on the reader.

The teller looked up at him, a hint of fatigue veiled behind her glossy eyes. Her smile was plastic, a rehearsed reaction that never reached her eyes. "Uh-huh," she responded, her voice holding a disinterested monotone as she started tapping away at her keyboard.

Tap, tap, tap. Each passing second increased Billy's impatience, the silence of the bank punctuated only by her rhythmic typing. He swallowed, his throat dry, and took a deep breath, trying to quell the nervous energy radiating off him. His gaze kept darting back towards the entrance, half-expecting the chaos to follow him in any second.

How many keystrokes does it need to do this simple transaction, he wondered. Surely there should be one button to withdraw, and then enter the amount.

Tap, tap, tap, tap, tap, went the teller, pressing a hundred keys in rapid succession.

He looked at her nails; they were long, and he wondered how she could do her work with ungainly looking claws

The teller exhaled heavily and started counting out his money. The droning sound of sirens suddenly filled the air outside, jarring in the otherwise quiet bank.

Could it be happening already? Had those cops turned sooner than he'd thought? The idea was unsettling. He imagined the infected running rampant through the streets, spreading the horrifying condition with frightening speed.

Just how fast will this thing spread? He remembered in college learning about the frightening speed of exponential growth. *If one zombie infects four people before being killed, and it takes fifteen minutes for the next generation of zombies to turn, and each one of those infects four people…then how long before all four hundred thousand people in Oakland are infected? Fifteen minutes means four people infected. Thirty minutes means sixteen…then its two hundred fifty-six…* He had always been good at math. He closed his eyes as he continued the progression. *In two hours and fifteen minutes, a quarter of a million zombies will be wandering Oakland. Fifteen minutes later, there'll be no living people left. And I cannot warn anyone.*

"No," he muttered under his breath, attempting to rid his mind of such terrifying thoughts. He forced himself to focus on the teller, who was still counting his money with an air of aloofness, completely unaware of the chaos brewing outside.

The math is missing some variables. People will fight back once they understand the risk. Zombies might not be able to infect humans so easily once humans know what's happening. However, it'll be harder to defend when there are hordes of them.

The teller began to carefully recount the bills, but the noise of the machine seemed to echo in the tense silence of the bank. Billy felt a bead of sweat trickle down his temple and his heart thudded painfully in his chest.

"Please, I trust the counting machine," he urged, his voice edging on desperate. "I really need to leave."

Just as he said this, the bank's doors swung open, causing a wave of city noise to pour in, sirens shrieking in the distance. He turned sharply at the sound, his breath hitching as he half expected to see one of those...things...lumbering through the entrance. But it was just another customer, blissfully unaware of the pending horror outside.

Turning back to the teller, he hastily grabbed his cash, stuffed it into his wallet, and without a word, bolted towards the exit, leaving the dumbfounded teller behind.

The moment he stepped outside, he felt a cold chill run down his spine. The usual hum of city life was tainted with an undercurrent of panic. People hurried in all directions, their faces painted with confusion and fear, mimicking his own feelings.

Is it happening already, or is it the usual rush of the city?

He launched himself into a sprint toward the storage center. His mind raced. *God, I hope they have a truck...I hope they can do the paperwork fast.* The ominous wail of the sirens grew louder in the distance, a grim reminder of the looming threat.

Calm down, Billy boy, he told himself. *There are always sirens in the city.*

Every person he passed, every car horn that blared, every siren that wailed made his skin crawl. The city was on the brink of chaos, and he needed to get out. His legs moved faster, adrenaline fueling his run. He knew he must not be caught on foot when all hell broke loose.

With each step, a dull ache resonated in his thighs, begging him to stop. He had only managed to run a block before exhaustion forced him into a walk. Gasping for breath, he wiped the sweat off his forehead, his heart pounding like a drum against his ribs.

A solitary, ten-foot truck sat idle in the courtyard of the storage center. Billy rushed into the office, barely noticing the cool blast of the air conditioner as he approached the receptionist. "I need to rent that truck. It's just for the day, local travel," he said, practically throwing his license and credit card onto the counter.

The receptionist, a young woman more engrossed in her phone than her job, glanced up at him. She lazily nudged a form towards him. "Fill this out, please," she said with a disinterested drawl.

Suddenly, the piercing wail of sirens from two more cop cars shattered the dull hum of the office. She looked up, her boredom briefly replaced by curiosity. "What's going on out there?"

Billy, eyes fixed on the form, replied quickly, "Some sort of fight at a restaurant, I think."

His hand shook slightly as he hurriedly filled out the paperwork. Each siren in the distance was a ticking clock, urging him to move faster.

Outside, the sirens were joined by the sound of distant screams and the faint aroma of burning rubber wafted through the open door. "Must have been one hell of a fight," the receptionist mused, standing up and beginning to saunter towards the door, her curiosity piqued.

"Excuse me," Billy interjected, sliding the form towards her with a sense of urgency creeping into his voice. "Can we please speed this up?"

Caught off guard, she turned back, eyebrows raised, and reluctantly sat back down. As she did, a man in a disheveled suit sprinted past the front door, his face a mask of sheer terror.

The receptionist squinted at the form, crinkling her nose. "You should really work on your handwriting, you know. Is that Billy or Gilly?"

Billy couldn't help but shoot her a 'are you serious?' look, which she cheerfully ignored. "It's Billy," he clarified, the edges of his patience beginning to fray.

With an exaggerated "Okaaaay," she started tapping away on her keyboard, the monotonous clicking threatening to send Billy over the edge. Just then, a woman and a child dashed by the office, the woman's frantic cries barely audible over the incessant tapping.

If a zombie comes charging into this store, then this was the worst mistake of my life, but if I can just get the truck and get out of town then…

She finally stood up, keys in hand, and moved towards the door. "Let's do a walk around the vehicle."

Without a moment's hesitation, Billy grabbed the keys. "I accept the condition of the vehicle. I need to go. Now." His words hung in the air as he raced towards the truck.

"Return it with a full tank or you'll be charged," she hollered after him, her voice fading into the clamor outside.

"I will!" he shouted back without turning around.

A cacophony of gunfire erupted from the direction of the restaurant, the shots pounding in his ears like an ominous drumbeat. The noise ricocheted off the buildings around. People were darting in every direction, their faces etched with stark terror, their movements mirroring the desperation in their eyes.

The receptionist was now caught in the human torrent, her once bored expression replaced with one of bewilderment and fear as she squinted towards the chaos.

But Billy had no time to consider her—every instinct was screaming at him to get moving, to escape. Barely noting the grit underfoot, he sprinted towards the truck, the keys jangling in his trembling hands. The engine roared to life under his touch, an orchestra of mechanical sounds cutting through the gunfire.

With a jolt, he jammed his foot on the accelerator, and collided with a small post. The scrape of metal against concrete filled the air, but Billy ignored it, and it did not slow the truck down.

"Hey!" he heard the receptionist yell, her voice a fading echo in his rearview mirror. But he had already dismissed her from his mind. He was laser focused on one thing only: escape.

The violent shattering of the truck's wing mirror startled Billy, snapping him out of his survival-induced tunnel vision. His heart pounded wildly as he processed the reality—a stray bullet had found its way to his vehicle. His knuckles whitened on the wheel as he hastily veered the truck to the right.

The unexpected turn catapulted him into a narrow alley, a labyrinthine refuge from the main street chaos. Flooring the accelerator, he urged the vehicle forward, desperate to escape the gunfire-laden air. But his rapid advance was abruptly halted when an adolescent boy wandered directly into his path.

"Jesus! Get the f…" he began and then noticed the boy looked weird. The pallor of his face was deathlike, and an inexplicable black ooze seeped from his mouth, staining his lips and chin. No visible wounds marred the boy's body, fueling Billy's growing unease. An unnerving realization crept in; *infection wasn't solely spread through bites. It could be a virus. It could be airborne. That lady, who was the first to turn, had no wounds on her.*

The boy's head jerked upwards, his lips peeling back to reveal a monstrous snarl. With an abrupt, jerky motion, he launched himself at the truck like a wild animal. Billy's eyes widened in horror, his foot slamming down on the accelerator in instinctive response. The boy clawed his way onto the sloped hood, bashing his skull against the windshield with enough force to spiderweb the glass.

Billy's hands were white knuckled on the steering wheel. He held his breath, foot bearing down on the gas pedal as the truck picked up speed. After a tense, heart-stopping fifty yards, he hit the brakes with all his might. The sudden stop sent the boy tumbling off the hood, skidding along the grimy asphalt of the alley.

Without a second's hesitation, Billy slammed his foot back down onto the accelerator. The truck lurched forward, rolling over the boy with a gruesome crunch that resonated in the enclosed space of the alley.

I just ran over a human being.

He closed his eyes for a moment as bile rose in his throat. He swallowed and grimaced. He then glanced in his wing mirror in time to see the boy leap back up. The boy's body was mangled, bones were showing, but nevertheless, he started shambling after the truck.

For a moment, Billy hesitated as he watched the impossible sight of the boy dragging mutilated limbs with sinews and torn muscles.

"For the love of God!" he shouted, gripped the steering wheel, and slammed his foot on the accelerator.

He glanced at the spider-webbed windshield and let out a shuddering breath, the gravity of what he'd done—and what he might have to do again—settling in his stomach like a block of ice. The boy's snarling face was etched into his mind, a haunting image he knew would stay with him long after this day was over.

As he drove on, the sounds of chaos receded behind him. His mind raced, thoughts whirling like a cyclone. The world he knew was falling apart. He had no idea what lay ahead, what horrors awaited him. But there was no going back. Not now.

Just that morning, Billy had awoken under the weight of his mundane existence, clouded by a haze of disappointment. His failing career was a glaring mirror reflecting his unfulfilled dreams back at him. Every attempt to get a better job led to rejection emails, each of which felt like a slap, each unpaid invoice a testament to his perceived worthlessness.

Then there was the haunting specter of his failed marriage, a phantom that hung over him like a pall. The facade of love that once brought warmth and companionship was extinguished, supplanted by indifference, enmity, and eventual separation. The void his ex-wife left was more than just the absence of a person—it was a gaping chasm in his soul, an emptiness that no amount of TV dinners or late-night beers could fill. What about her? Should I try to save her? She doesn't even live in this city anymore. Thank God I have no kids to worry about. Imagine that. A sadness settled on him. I lost my marriage before we got that far.

His physical health was yet another battle he was losing, his burgeoning weight a stark, visible testament to his profound unhappiness. Every day, the mirror presented him with a reflection he hardly recognized. The man staring back at him was a stranger, a sad shadow of the person he once aspired to be.

Yet now, in the face of a world collapsing around him, a surprising revelation hit him like a sledgehammer: he yearned for the very life he had been so dissatisfied with. The drudgery of his job, the lingering sting of his failed marriage, even the cruel taunts of the unforgiving scale—they were all facets of a life that, despite its imperfections, was irreplaceably his.

This newfound realization struck a chord within him. His fight was no longer against his personal failures, but against an unfathomable, existential horror. His life, mired as it was in failures and disappointments, had become a precious commodity to be defended with every fiber of his being. What seemed a constant struggle earlier had morphed into a desperate battle for survival. And he was ready, with every ounce of his strength, every bit of his will, to wage that war. The fight had just begun, and Billy had never felt more alive.

Just then, a chilling howl echoed through the streets, making Billy's skin crawl. It wasn't a sound that any human should be able to make. Instinctively, he knew the sound was coming from these undead creatures, these zombies, these…growlers. It was a grim reminder of the new reality, the terrifying unknown he was hurtling toward. He knew that his life had changed forever.

Amanda Willard –
Oakland, 14th and
MacArthur – 3 p.m. Day Zero

Bert

It was a short walk home from where the bus driver had dropped Amanda and Joshua off. She was trying to make sense of what she had seen downtown. She was sure that the police would have it under control. She brought up the local news report on her phone.

Male News Announcer: We are getting reports of a riot near West Oakland. Police say that the cause of the violence is as of yet, unknown.

Female News Announcer: That's right, Gary. The police never understand the true root cause of violence in this city. But I can tell you what it is. It is three hundred years of institutionalized racism. That's what is behind this…and let's not call it violence… let's call it what it is, resistance. It is resistance to injustice.

Amanda put the phone away and chewed her lip thoughtfully. *I am sure more details will become evident tomorrow when I get to work.* She knew she would have to explain not responding to the STAN alert. *I had a toddler in my arms and my bus had been basically hijacked.*

A feeling of guilt overtook her. She felt she had let people down. Whatever the crisis was, she was supposed to respond to STAN alerts. *People may have needed me, but I could not leave Jo Jo at daycare with all that violence going on. Besides, it can't have been that bad of a crisis, I have not received any new STAN alerts.*

Little Joshua sat high on her shoulders, his small hands clutching her hair for balance as they made their way down the last stretch of pavement. Their home awaited them around the corner—a tall, sprinter van, a humble dwelling by society's standards, but one that served all their needs. As she walked, her eyes skimmed over the rows of luxury townhouses, an ironic contrast to their own living situation. Amanda was a nurse, a professional respected in society. Her wages weren't meager—on the contrary, she earned a healthy income that was nearing six figures. Yet, with the skyrocketing prices of housing in the city, even she had been priced out of a traditional home. The city had a lenient approach to what they called 'stealth camping', and so, she and Joshua made do with their mobile haven.

As Amanda reached the van, a familiar figure emerged from the vehicle parked beside hers. Meredith, her neighbor and a fellow dweller in the city's ad-hoc community, was wrangling her son, Daryl, Joshua's frequent playmate.

"Hey, Amanda," Meredith called out, a note of worry tinging her usually jovial voice. She gave Daryl a little push, ushering him forward. "Do you think you could spare a moment? Daryl's not been feeling well."

Amanda balanced Joshua on her hip as she fumbled to unlock the van. "Of course, Mer," she replied, pushing the van door open. "Let me just get Jo Jo settled."

Meredith nodded, her shoulders drooping slightly as she let out a sigh. "This phase of theirs, right after getting out of diapers...it's trickier than I thought." She looked down at Daryl, who was pulling at the hem of her dress. "Can't wait for this little one to be done with it."

Amanda eased Joshua onto the pull-out ironing board affixed to the van's side wall, a makeshift changing table in their compact living space. Methodically, she stripped him of his boots, slipping off his soiled trousers and underwear, and tossed them into a laundry basket tucked conveniently below. With practiced ease, she wiped him clean using a pack of wet wipes from the adjacent drawer.

Upon rummaging through Joshua's clothes drawer, she was met with an unfortunate realization—only one pair of trousers remained. A wave of frustration washed over her. *Great, another laundry run,* she thought, mentally adding it to her growing list of chores.

With Joshua cleaned and changed, she helped him down to the van's floor, setting him up with his iPad to keep him occupied. As the digital lullaby of children's programming began to play, Amanda turned her attention back to washing her hands. The familiar smell of the antibacterial soap momentarily calmed her rising stress. With a final rinse and shake of her hands, she turned back to Meredith, ready to lend her assistance.

"Don't worry, little man. Let's see what's up," Amanda cooed, attempting to keep her voice light and cheerful. She reached for Daryl, expecting to be met with the familiar heat radiating from a feverish child. Instead, her hand was met with an unsettling coldness. Odd, she thought, her brows knitting together in concern. She noted the absence of shivering, which was unusual for a cold body.

"Alright, champ. Can you show me your tongue?" she asked, maintaining a comforting smile. Daryl complied, revealing a disturbing sight—his tongue was speckled with an unfamiliar pattern of black spots.

Meredith, who had been nervously watching the entire examination, wrung her hands. "It's those spots that worry me, Amanda. They just appeared suddenly. Do you know what they could be?" The anxiety was clear in her voice, and Amanda knew she needed to tread carefully with her response.

A chill ran down Amanda's spine as she recalled the man with black ooze on his face and the disarray and fear she'd witnessed at the hospital earlier. Could Daryl's condition be related to whatever was causing the citywide distress? The thought was terrifying.

Slowly, she traced the black spots with her gaze, trying to understand their nature. A disease that has traveled so far from the

71

initial outbreak in such a short period could have catastrophic implications. Could they be on the precipice of a citywide epidemic?

She looked at Meredith's anxious face and bit her lower lip. She knew she had to tread lightly. The last thing she wanted was to trigger a panic. Balancing her own fear and maintaining an aura of calm was going to be a monumental task.

Amanda's fingers trembled slightly as she pulled out a tongue depressor and a pen flashlight from her chest pocket. "Open wide," she instructed, her voice both firm and soft.

Daryl obediently widened his mouth, revealing the ominous black substance lurking at the back of his throat. With careful precision, she pressed the depressor on his tongue and shone the light, illuminating the stark contrast of the black lining against the pinkish hue of his oral cavity.

She withdrew the depressor. Smears of the strange black substance coated the depressor, stark against the wooden surface. A wave of dread washed over her. That wasn't blood. Whatever it was, it was something entirely unknown.

"Excuse me for a moment, Meredith," she said, her tone shrouded in professional calmness, belying the rising apprehension within her.

She moved back inside her van, leaving Joshua engrossed in his iPad world. From a corner, she retrieved a compact box and delicately extracted a microscope—a high-end piece of equipment that she had luckily snagged for a mere twenty dollars at a garage sale.

She put the black substance from the tongue depressor onto a glass slide, and the slide into the microscope. The device buzzed to life, its screen radiating a soft glow in the cramped interior of the van. With a quick setting adjustment, the image amplified to a forty times magnification. Amanda squinted at the screen. The unknown substance appeared like a stretch of black sand, speckled and grainy.

Adjusting the microscope to a massive six hundred times magnification, the sand grains morphed into black specks sprouting long tendrils. It was bacteria, she realized, but of a kind she couldn't identify. The tendrils reminded her of the infamous cystic fibrosis bacteria, acting more like legs than anything else. A sinking realization dawned on her—she was dealing with crawling bacteria, a facet she was not prepared for. *A black pseudomonas?*

"Tell me, Meredith," Amanda ventured, "you don't happen to have a personal physician, do you?"

The response was a bitter laugh, laden with the reality of their shared economic struggles. "Sure, let me just check my overflowing bank vault," Meredith retorted, her sarcasm echoing in the confined space of the van.

Suddenly, the piercing wail of sirens sliced through the conversation, its persistent cry growing louder from the west and the north. Both women exchanged a glance of shared unease, their attention drawn to the urgent clamor echoing down the streets.

Amanda took a deep breath, returning her focus to Meredith. "Listen, Meredith, I can't pinpoint what it is, but it's certainly bacterial. You need to get Daryl to the emergency room as soon as possible. But not here in Oakland, it's too chaotic. Drive him south. Inform them it's bacterial—they'll most likely prescribe antibiotics. And Meredith...be quick." The urgency in Amanda's voice underscored the gravity of the situation, and the urgency of the sirens outside mirrored it.

Meredith hoisted Daryl onto her hip, her face creased with bewilderment. "Why not Oakland?" she questioned, the furrow in her brow deepening.

Amanda's gaze strayed towards the ominous sounds of chaos from the city. "Something's happening out there, Meredith. I can't be certain, but I heard talk of...biting incidents."

"Biting?" Meredith echoed, her voice trembling with rising apprehension and confusion. Amanda noticed how she unconsciously pulled Daryl closer, her eyes reflecting the flicker of fear that Amanda herself was trying hard to suppress.

Amanda shrugged, weariness seeping into her voice. "I wish I could accompany you, Meredith. But I've just finished a double shift, need to refuel the van, need to get some food and..." she wanted to say she was getting very concerned about what was happening in the city and was considering making an escape to somewhere more rural, but she did not want to alarm her friend. "...I need to do some laundry."

As Meredith's face fell slightly, Amanda felt a pang of guilt. She was interrupted by the thudding roar of a helicopter, its spotlight piercing the twilight sky. The sight seemed to solidify the escalating situation, making it all too real.

"God, things really are falling apart tonight," Meredith muttered, her voice a whisper against the drone of the helicopter. "Do you reckon it could wait till morning?"

Amanda met her gaze, the gravity in her own eyes mirroring Meredith's growing concern. "I wouldn't risk it, Meredith."

Meredith looked around furtively. "Don't you…have anything, from your little clinic?"

Amanda froze, her eyes darting around instinctively as Meredith's question hung in the air. Only the closest in her circle knew about her clandestine sideline; a pop-up clinic for the homeless, running on medications supplied by a contact who worked an incinerator at the hospital, and handed over expiring medicines for free. Usually there was nothing wrong with the expired medicines, and they were very expensive, so saving them for the uninsured seemed like just common sense. But those treatments were dispersed anonymously, a necessary safeguard against the threat of prosecution.

A simple mishap, an allergic reaction, or worse, a fatal incident, could lead to a criminal investigation. One wrong step could mean more than losing her nursing license. It could land her in prison.

She remembered she did have something in her box of salvaged medicines, which was a very powerful antibiotic, but it had lots of potentially fatal side effects, and she simply did not have the equipment to handle a serious reaction.

"Sorry, it's really dangerous to just treat something when you don't really know what it is. I am sure the hospitals will have some

75

expert who can figure it out and know how to treat it…I simply have no clue."

Seeing the hope in Meredith's eyes dim, Amanda shook her head regretfully. "I wish I could help, but whatever this is...I don't think I have the right medication for it. It's best if you get him to a hospital as soon as possible."

A flicker of suspicion crossed Meredith's face, but she only nodded. "Okay, Amanda. Thanks for your help." Her voice wavered slightly, and she shifted Daryl in her arms, as if the extra weight suddenly became too much.

Amanda watched her, a pang of sympathy twisting in her chest. "And, hey, where's Phil? Can't he take you?" she asked, hoping to ease some of Meredith's burden.

A bitter smile tugged at Meredith's lips. "Phil? I sent him packing."

Amanda blinked, momentarily taken aback. The news of their breakup hit harder than she expected. "Meredith..." she trailed off, lost for words, her eyes reflecting a mixture of concern and regret.

Amanda's sympathetic words hung in the air. "I'm sorry to hear about that."

As she began to retreat into her van, a sudden movement down the street caught her eye. A figure was sprinting full tilt, panic etched clearly on their face. Amanda's brow furrowed. West Oakland, the epicenter of the chaos, was seven miles away.

No, this couldn't just be an extension of the same issue. Perhaps the problem had a broader origin than just one location.

With a newfound sense of urgency, she gently pushed the camper door shut, her mind already buzzing with questions and worry. The clunk of the door echoed ominously around her. But there was no time to dwell on it. Fueling up her van was now a priority she could not afford to delay.

The gas station was just shy of a mile from where Amanda's van was parked, a distance that under normal circumstances, would be covered swiftly. But these were far from normal circumstances. Every few feet, the piercing wail of sirens ripped through the night air, each one a harbinger of the crisis unfolding to the west. Her eyes flicked from one speeding emergency vehicle to the next, their flashing lights casting an eerie, disquieting glow on the deserted city streets. A chill ran down her spine, the once familiar surroundings now seeming ominous and fraught with peril. As the reality of the situation sank in, a sobering thought wormed its way into her consciousness. The city, with its congested streets and densely packed population, was perhaps the last place she wanted to be.

Pulling into the Quick-E Gas, Amanda hoisted Joshua onto her hip and set about filling the gas tank along with two five-gallon cans she had stashed for emergencies. With her son's curious gaze following her every move, she stepped inside the all-night mini convenience store, the artificial light stinging her tired eyes. She hadn't planned for an impromptu road trip, but she realized she needed to be prepared.

Searching the shelves, she quickly amassed an assortment of sustenance—two large bags of nuts for protein, several liters of soda for caffeine, a horde of chocolate bars for sugar highs, and a box of thirty energy bars, a practical choice for long, uncertain hours ahead. She piled it all onto the counter, the shopkeeper's eyebrows inching higher with each addition. Ignoring his inquisitive stare, she paid for her haul and made a hasty exit, the urgency of the situation looming larger with every passing second.

As she returned to the van, a man was waiting nearby. His dark skin was worn by time and weather, and his clothes hung loose on his frame. She vaguely remembered his name was Bert, a familiar face amongst the homeless community. The reek of decay clung to him, but Amanda was unfazed. Years of nursing had introduced her to far worse odors.

"I'm hungry," Bert rasped, his voice sounding like it had been strained through gravel.

Amanda hesitated. Every item in her grocery haul felt crucial now, a lifeline she might need in the near future. And yet, the reality of her own precarious situation gnawed at her, she had narrowly avoided living on the streets. She knew how easily someone could slip through the cracks. Contrary to popular belief, the number one cause of homelessness in Oakland wasn't drug use, or alcohol use or even mental illness, it was the loss of a spouse. She knew anybody can fall on hard times. With a sigh, she handed Bert a chocolate bar.

"Thank you, good lady," Bert said, his teeth glinting as he unwrapped the bar. "I'm Bert. God bless you."

"I remember you, Bert. Just stay safe, okay?" she replied, her eyes meeting his briefly before he shuffled away, his gratitude echoing in the cool evening air.

"Bless you too, lovely lady and lovely boy," Bert called back, already disappearing down the street.

Securing Joshua safely inside the van, Amanda proceeded to fasten the two five-gallon gas cans onto the rear. As she adjusted the straps of the last can, a soft, rhythmic sound broke the silence. Turning, she saw a small figure standing barefoot in the middle of the cross-section—a young girl. She looked to be in her teens, her black hair was wet and hung over her eyes.

For a moment, Amanda could only stare. Motherly instinct surged within her, a visceral urge to comfort and protect. "Hey there," she called out gently. "Are you okay?"

As the girl turned, Amanda's words caught in her throat. The sight was horrific, almost monstrous. Black ooze dripped from the girl's mouth, her eyes had a milky sheen, and her expression was contorted into an eerie snarl. The symptoms matched the ones she'd seen earlier.

The *'biter thing'*.

Suddenly, the girl let out a bestial growl and launched herself towards Amanda. Panic gripped her, and for a moment, she was frozen in place, just watching this monster approach in a whirl of gnashing and flailing limbs.

"Fuck!" whispered Amanda, as she stumbled backward, throwing her arms up instinctively in defense. The girl was mid-air, lunging towards her, when a loud thwack! echoed through the air. Out of nowhere, Bert, the homeless man, swung a baseball bat with all his might, striking the girl's head mid-flight.

The force of the hit sent the girl sprawling backward. She convulsed violently on the asphalt for a chilling moment, then lay eerily still. Amanda's mouth dropped open as a mix of horror, shock, and gratitude washed over her.

"See, you gotta aim for the head," Bert's voice cut through the eerie silence, his tone gruff yet strangely calm. He paused, squinting down the dimly lit street. "You'd best be on your way, missy. More are coming, you see." He pointed, his hand shaking slightly, towards a horde of silhouettes, their slow, relentless advance sending a chill down Amanda's spine. The distant groans carried by the wind echoed a grim warning, adding an urgent, haunting note to Bert's words.

Amanda's pulse raced as her gaze darted from the encroaching horde to Bert. "Thank you," she managed, her voice strained with adrenaline. She fumbled with the keys, the roar of the van's engine shattering the silence. The chilling sound attracted the crowd's attention and their slow amble turned into a horrifying sprint; their faces distorted with savage intent.

With horror, she realized she had made her and Bert the center of the horde's focus. She looked at Bert and she looked at the ravenous crowd of monsters crashing towards her.

She made a decision she knew was rash. "Bert!" She flung the passenger door open, her voice barely audible over the roar of the engine and the growling of the crowd. "Get in, now!"

He nodded, his eyes never leaving the oncoming threat as he jumped into the van. With a swift stomp on the pedal, she peeled out of the gas station, the tires squealing against the asphalt.

But she had left it too late. Some of the infected had jumped on the van as she accelerated eastward, towards the MacArthur freeway. She heard them dragging behind, holding on to the bumper, and she heard one on the roof. She swerved the wheel side to side and all but one fell off the bumper. The one on the roof fell down to the side, where it clung for a moment.

She stamped on the break and then immediately on the accelerator. The jerking motion knocked the remaining two off. As she accelerated away, she noticed a small group of people on the side of the road had emerged from a restaurant to see what the noise was. In her wing mirror she saw the two infected run towards them, but she refocused her eyes on the road ahead, so she never knew for sure what happened, but she heard the faint sounds of screaming.

Amanda murmured, her eyes glued to the road while her thoughts spiraled, "All these people...biting."

Bert, his gaze fixated on the scene unfurling in the side mirror, grunted in response, "Zombies, that's what they are. Not the old fashion, shambling kind either. These are sprinters and jumpers and gnashers and...growlers."

She glanced at him, a mixture of disbelief and fear etched on her face. "Zombies don't exist. They're...biters, that's for sure...and they sure do growl a lot. Growlers."

Bert shrugged, his gaze never leaving the mirror. "Whatever you call them, there's a whole damn army of them."

She shook her head in disbelief. "I just don't understand how something can spread so quickly."

"That's what I thought when the homeless community burned down," Bert said with a little moan. "One campfire and then one tent, a few cardboard boxes. It seemed to happen in slow motion at first, then suddenly, everyone was running for their lives."

Amanda remembered the fire he talked of. There had been many deaths. She had treated horribly wounded people. It seemed so unfair. People who had no luck in their lives. People who had no loved ones to help them. Then adding to their burdens, after months of agonizing rehabilitation, they were left with horrific disfiguring burns. *Life can be brutal.*

She risked another look in her own wing mirror. Her breath hitched at the sight of the throng of bodies, a relentless tide surging towards them, though she was putting distance between the van and them. They were becoming just shadows under the faint city lights. The growlers filled the expanse, turning the once familiar streets into a haunting spectacle. She looked down a side street and saw more of them surging forward. "God...they're...everywhere," she managed, the sheer scale of the situation sinking in.

The ravenous horde continued sprinting after the van, their relentless pursuit mirrored in the rear-view mirror. In the distance behind, she saw a divergent group peel away, the Quick-E shop their new target, the glinting allure of prey within the well-lit interior too enticing to ignore.

Opposite them, a car skidded to a halt, its screeching tires punctuating the ominous silence. As she passed the car, she saw the surprised and fearful expression on the driver's face as he saw the growlers charging towards him. There was no way for her to communicate with the driver. In her mind she screamed for him to turn around, but it was too late. Seconds after she passed the car, she watched in her rear-view mirror as the horde descended upon it, a wave of growling destruction smashing the car's windows in mere seconds.

A cold dread seeped into her bones, the echo of her close escape resonating within her. Her foot pressed down harder on the accelerator even though the pedal was already on the floor, the van lunging forward, eager to widen the gap between them and the chasing nightmare. As buildings and familiar landmarks blurred in her peripheral vision, a chilling realization settled within her. She needed to avoid populated areas...and freeways, potential chokepoints.

The freeway was a bad idea, she realized. Everyone with a car and an ounce of sense would be trying to get away from the city and the freeway was the obvious choice. She needed to be smart. She needed to calm herself and actually think.

How to get out of the city, and where to go?

She knew there was a lesser-used road through the canyon that would get her to less populated areas. She brought the van to a safer speed and adopted her new course.

As the city lights faded into obscurity in the rear-view mirror, Amanda's pulse began to decelerate from its frenetic rhythm, aligning more closely with the steady thrum of the van's engine. The terror and chaos of the city's unravelling seemed to diminish with each passing mile, morphing into the hum of tires against asphalt and the symphony of nocturnal creatures that serenaded the darkening landscape.

Beside her, Bert sat in silence, his eyes fixated on the unfolding expanse of the road ahead. The flickering dashboard lights illuminated his weathered face, each wrinkle etching a story of struggle and survival, punctuated by a life that had forgotten to be kind.

There was a profound sadness in his gaze, a silent testament to his years on the unforgiving streets. Yet, there was a strength in his quiet resolve, an enduring spirit that had withstood the trials of life and emerged, unbowed. In the crisis that had just unfurled, he had displayed a fearlessness, a readiness to act, that belied his humble exterior.

"Zombies, huh?" Amanda broke the silence, her voice barely above a whisper. The thought was preposterous, laughable under normal circumstances. But tonight, it didn't seem all that far-fetched.

Bert chuckled dryly, a gravelly sound that seemed to startle the silence. "Believe it or not, ma'am, the streets teach you to expect the unexpected. Zombies, biters, the end of the world—ain't nothing that surprises me no more."

His words lingered in the air, cloaked in an eerie prescience, their echoes whispering tales of an impending reality they were racing towards.

SAMANTHA WINTERS – CLAPP SPRING, SANTA ROSA ISLAND

The Prophet

Samantha studied the bunker doors, towering monoliths of cold steel, as they reluctantly parted, revealing an expansive, dimly-lit cavern that stretched farther than her eyes could discern. The labyrinth of wires, machinery, and technology seemed to pulsate with an eerie life of its own, the hum and whirr of its systems filling the air with an undercurrent of electrical energy. It was both intimidating and mystifying, a testament to the fanatical commitment of the cult to their elusive cause.

This was no rudimentary construction, hastily cobbled together in the dead of night. This was a fortress, meticulously crafted, intended to withstand whatever catastrophic event they were so desperately preparing for. Samantha felt a shiver of apprehension crawl up her spine. Whatever the cult had been planning, it was much larger and far more sophisticated than anyone on the outside had imagined.

The realization was a bitter pill to swallow. She'd been sent here under the pretense of infiltrating a fringe group, extracting information on their beliefs and intentions. She was supposed to be spying on a bunch of religious crazies. But the sight of the monolithic blast doors told a different story. The enormity of their construction suggested government involvement, something clandestine and complex. Samantha chewed on her lip as the implications sank in.

Now, standing on the precipice of the cult's world, Samantha was no longer just an observer. She was a pawn in a game of subterfuge and manipulation, caught between a ruthless cult and a government that seemed to be playing a dangerous game of its own.

The weight of the situation settled around her like a shroud. But she squared her shoulders, pushing aside her fear. She was here now. The only way out was through, to unravel the secrets buried within this clandestine fortress and expose them to the light of truth.

The blast doors gave way to an expansive hall. At the far end, a stage loomed ominously, flanked by corridors snaking deeper into the unknown. Gathered in a near-perfect semicircle were about twenty individuals swathed in pristine white frocks, their faces an unreadable blend of anticipation and reverence. A young woman scurried, her white frock flapping against her legs, to join the formation, her face flushed with embarrassment.

At the heart of this congregation stood a figure of authority, a middle-aged, black man garbed in a crisp, white jacket and matching trousers. He extended his arms in a grandiose gesture of welcome, the warmth in his smile at odds with the cold sterility of his attire. "Ah, John, Nathan, and our final initiate." His deep voice resonated through the hall, infusing the air with a sense of anticipation that Samantha could taste on the tip of her tongue. "Welcome. The day of days has already begun, and indeed, it is glorious."

"Indeed," echoed John, the measured tempo of his words echoing in the cavernous hall. "The boat was late. But we've done our due diligence."

The man in the white jacket advanced with purpose, his confident strides in contrast to the unease coiling in Samantha's stomach. "I am the Doctor here," he announced, his hand reaching out to Samantha in a greeting as warm as his wide, beaming smile. "I am Doctor Evers."

A wave of uncertainty washed over Samantha as she regarded his outstretched hand. Doubt clung to her like a second skin, a byproduct of her situation. Yet, she couldn't afford to arouse any suspicion here. After a moment's hesitation, she extended her hand and accepted his firm handshake.

While she grappled with her confusion and fear, she couldn't help but notice the near-reverential tone in Evers's voice.

Her eyes scanned the room, the white frocks and the strange, unbroken unity of the people around her sent shivers of unease crawling down her spine.

"It's all part of His divine plan," Evers said, his eyes alight with fervor. "The reports are already flooding in. The world is changing,

Samantha, and we are privileged to witness it. To participate in it." His words held a fanatical zeal that made her stomach churn. "Soon, we will gather in the auditorium with His Holiness. His divine retribution cleanses the earth of sin."

His words echoed eerily through the room, bouncing off the sterile walls and sending a wave of apprehension through Samantha. The sheer magnitude of his claim was unsettling, her mind raced to make sense of what was happening. *Cleanse the world?*

Evers turned to her with a wide smile on his face, his eyes sparkling with an unsettling kind of excitement. "Now, shall we prepare for God's divine wrath?" His words rang in her ears.

What is he talking about?

A screeching sound split the air, pulling Samantha's gaze over her shoulder. The colossal blast doors were grinding shut, a monolithic barrier rising between her and the world outside. Her pulse quickened, her breath hitched in her chest, the cold realization seeping in like icy water: she was trapped.

"Novice Bethany!" Evers' voice boomed, echoing ominously off the stone walls. "Fetch me the Prophet's gift."

The young woman in the semicircle dipped in a low bow. "Immediately, Doctor," she replied, her voice echoing faintly as she disappeared down the right corridor.

Suddenly, Samantha's attention was yanked to the wall by the flicker of electronic light. Several large screens hung there, casting a ghostly pallor over the room. A news report flickered to life, silent images of terrified people fleeing down a city street. The images, devoid of sound, seemed to scream all the louder in the echoing silence.

"What is going on?" asked Samantha.

"Such madness," Evers commented casually, his gaze focused on the screens. "The world outside descends into chaos, while we here are safe, preparing for salvation."

Despite his words, Samantha felt no comfort. Instead, fear continued to slither through her veins. She glanced around the room, at the impassive faces of the cult members, all engrossed in the chaotic scenes unfolding on the screens.

A knot formed in Samantha's stomach as the images on the screen depicted a scene straight out of a dystopian nightmare. People sprinting, terror etched into their faces, their panicked screams eerily silent in the lack of audio. Buildings, once towering monuments of human achievement, were now ablaze, great plumes of smoke billowing skyward.

But why? What had triggered such chaos? Samantha's mind raced, her gaze darting back and forth between Evers and the screen. Dread coiled within her, her skin prickling with unease as the magnitude of her situation settled upon her. She was trapped here, in this place, with no idea what horror was unfolding beyond these walls.

Meanwhile, Bethany returned, holding a gleaming silver box in her hands. She handed it to Evers with reverence, her eyes downcast. Evers opened the box to reveal a gleaming syringe filled with a bright-green liquid. Samantha's heart dropped.

"Initiate Samantha," Evers addressed her, his voice cold and clear. "This is the divine elixir that will protect you from the world's ongoing purification. It will keep you safe from harm. It's time for your vaccination." The cult members turned their eyes towards her, and Samantha felt a chill creep up her spine.

She mustered a meager voice, the words teetering out as if on a tightrope. "I...I don't understand what's going on," Samantha admitted, her eyes wide and frantically seeking solace in the chaotic scene unfolding.

"God's vengeance," Nathan chimed in, an eerie calm in his voice as he casually strolled past her. As if cued by his statement, the group arranged in the semicircle began to mobilize, busying themselves with arranging furniture around the room. A hefty sofa, looking strangely out of place, was pushed directly in front of the large screens, and the harsh clattering of numerous stiff, utilitarian chairs being hauled into rows behind it filled the room. The stage was being set, and Samantha couldn't shake the feeling that she was about to be thrust into the starring role of a horrifying spectacle.

Her gaze flitted back to the injection, a foreboding suspicion gnawing at the pit of her stomach. *It looks like poison.* The thought gripped her as she instinctively recoiled a step backward.

Evers was quick to assuage her fears. "Don't worry, child," he soothed, his voice holding an unsettling edge of tranquility. "We've all taken it. Come on, roll up your sleeve. Non-dominant hand."

His words did little to quell her apprehension, but Samantha knew she was cornered. *It's not like I have a choice. I must find a safe place to contact someone.* With a resigned sigh, she surrendered to her predicament and obediently rolled up the sleeve of her left arm.

Evers smiled and pushed the needle into the flesh of her arm. The sting was not as bad as she expected but, as he applied pressure to the plunger, a fiery sensation spread out from her arm down her body. It felt like her body was hollow and was slowly being filled with lava.

"Ugh!" She grunted.

"Ha! Yeah, it has a little burn to it, doesn't it?" Evers said.

For a moment, she felt the pain would overwhelm her, she felt panic beginning to take over but then the burning sensation started to fade.

"Hoooo, that was…intense," she said.

"Right," Evers announced with an air of finality, pulling back the needle with a flourish. "You are officially purified."

She rubbed her shoulder and breathed a sigh of relief that the pain was over. A sudden sound startled her. The screens on the wall erupted with a mixture of screams and shouting with an announcer saying something over the top.

"That's right Melinda, authorities say the violence in Oakland has now spread to other towns in California. We have actually lost contact with the crew we sent to Jack London Square and the images you see are from the roof of our satellite building. Our small crew there have requested authorities to help them evacuate."

Samantha stared at the screens, trying to make sense of the chaos unfolding. This didn't resemble normal civil unrest; the pattern was all wrong. Instead of a united front clashing with law enforcement, people were savagely turning on each other. A knot of dread formed in her stomach. Something was terribly off.

On the adjacent screens, different news channels flickered to life, each broadcasting scenes of identical turmoil. From the aerial view of a helicopter, hordes of people sprinted down the streets, fires raging in the background. The clamor from the screens was almost unbearable until, abruptly, the volume was muted.

"Rapture!" echoed a voice from the far end of the room, silencing the muffled chaos from the screens. All heads swiveled towards the source—a towering, obese man swathed in a silk suit and sporting a striking red tie. The scars of past acne battles speckled his clean-shaven face. "This is the rapture, and we are the saved." At this proclamation, every individual in the room, including Evers, Nathan, and John, knelt in unison. Taking a deep breath, Samantha reluctantly followed suit. She had never encountered the Prophet in person, but she instantly recognized him from the portraits festooning the cult's San Diego headquarters. Except, in those portraits he had been a thin man, with no acne, in a cavern, wearing a business suit and surrounded by adoring worshipers. He had manufactured his own reality.

The Prophet lofted a bible high in his right hand. "Since you have kept my command to endure patiently, I will also keep you from the hour of trial that is going to come on the whole world to test the inhabitants of the earth."

"Amen!" said the crowd.

The Prophet continued. "For the trumpet will sound, the dead will be raised imperishable, and we will be changed."

"Amen!" responded the crowd.

"But not my flock. Oh no, not my flock. For I have gathered you to me. Did not our Lord say, 'Because you have kept my word about patient endurance, I will keep you from the hour of trial that is coming on the whole world, to try those who dwell on the earth.'"

"Amen!" shouted the crowd, louder than before.

"Amen!" shouted the Prophet.

"Amen!" screamed the crowd.

The Prophet ambled towards the sofa with an air of quiet authority, his movements deliberate and commanding. He lowered himself onto the plush fabric, the screens casting flickering shadows on his aged face. Two youthful devotees, their faces marked by both reverence and anxiety, scuttled towards him. With a magnanimous gesture, he beckoned one to nestle at his left side, the girl's face blooming with relief. However, his hand morphed into a dismissive wave towards the other girl, whose crestfallen expression was swiftly concealed.

His gaze then swiveled towards Samantha, his eyes like onyx in the stark room light. With a barely noticeable crook of his finger, he summoned her. A cold shiver cascaded down Samantha's spine, her heart churning in her chest. Steeling herself, she padded towards the Prophet and gingerly lowered herself onto the seat on his right side. His grip was firm around her left hand, a sign of control she found unsettling, yet she dared not pull away.

With an eerily calm yet authoritative voice, the Prophet commanded, "Bear witness with me, as the antiquated world crumbles to dust, and behold the dawn of a new era that will be under my reign." In a seemingly orchestrated maneuver, he gestured an elegant twirl with his left hand, a specially designed remote control reflecting in the dim light. Instantaneously, the room was once again filled with the chaotic sounds from the screens, the harsh reality of the outside world invading the sanctuary they were in.

A reporter could be seen on a rooftop, his voice sounded panicked and desperate. Samantha recognized the reporter as Jack Princeton, a seasoned professional.

"Never in my decades as a journalist have I witnessed such a scene of total mayhem. Chaos reigns supreme from every corner of the city as I speak to you live from the rooftop of the Oakland Museum," came the harried voice of the reporter, the backdrop of a city consumed by violence framing his desperate countenance.

"Authorities are struggling, powerless against this unanticipated and brutal wave of civil unrest. We've received reports that some of these rioters have breached the building we're in." His eyes darted nervously around, betraying a sense of underlying fear. "Our only hope now is to barricade ourselves in and hold out until help arrives."

The Prophet's fingers tightened around Samantha's hand, his lips curling up into a perverse smile. "Oh, this will indeed be a spectacle," he remarked with disturbing calm.

The screen flickered and captured the terror-stricken eyes of the reporter as he glanced behind the camera. With a shaky pivot, the lens was directed towards the throng of bodies bursting through barricaded doors and surging onto the roof. They were not just humans in the throes of panic, but grotesque parodies of their former selves—grotesquely injured, their eyes blazing with a rabid, unnatural hunger. They stormed towards the camera, their ghastly screams slicing through the air. The feed froze, leaving behind the petrifying image of a man, a young policeman from before the madness, transformed into a gnarled, demonic apparition.

"That...that was a police officer!" Samantha exclaimed; her voice choked with disbelief.

The Prophet chuckled, his eyes gleaming with perverse delight. "Oh, he used to be," he corrected, an eerie calmness lacing his voice.

Samantha trembled, her mind a whirlwind of terror and confusion. She whispered, as if afraid to voice her question aloud. "What's happening?"

His hand found its way to her thigh. She ignored the unwanted intimacy, there were more pressing matters. Leaning in, his lips brushing against her ear, he murmured with an ominous undertone, "What you're witnessing, my dear, is only the commencement. Phase one, if you will."

As she sat beside the Prophet, the nightmare unfolding on the screens seemed to seep into the room, permeating the air with a sense of chilling dread.

Her eyes were drawn, magnet-like, to the frozen image of the erstwhile policeman turned savage. His once uniform-clad form now epitomized the very antithesis of the order and safety he'd been charged to uphold. His milky eyes, the maw twisted into a macabre grin, the seething malice emanating from his very being— it was an image that branded itself onto the canvas of her mind, promising to haunt her dreams for an eternity.

She became aware that the Prophet's hand on her thigh was now squeezing and rubbing. His unwelcome touch felt like a surreal intrusion on her spiraling thoughts. He seemed to revel in the horrifying spectacle, his face lit by the spectral glow of the screens, his eyes gleaming with an unholy light. His calm acceptance of the chaos, his perverse delight in the downfall of civilization, it was a stark contrast to the terror welling up inside Samantha.

He is enjoying this. He is excited. What kind of monster rules this freakish cult?

Just what had she gotten herself into? What was this 'phase one' the Prophet had spoken of with such excitement? Her mission had been to infiltrate, observe, and report. But she'd plunged headfirst into an abyss, the depths of which she was only beginning to fathom. And as she looked at the gleeful Prophet and the carnage displayed on the screens, she knew the abyss was gazing back at her. She had come here to betray. To be a traitor in their midst.

The orders from the FBI were clear. They had blackmailed her, exploiting her precarious immigration status. It was an impossible choice, either deportation for her and her family or to venture into the heart of the unknown, infiltrating the enigmatic doomsday Cult of the Phoenix. The former would mean ripping away the life they had built from scratch, returning to a country ravaged by poverty and political unrest. The latter held its own share of dangers, the extent of which she was now beginning to grasp.

Samantha's heart clenched at the thought of her little brother, his wide-eyed innocence, his dreams of attending college and building a life here. And her parents, who had worked tirelessly, braving exploitation and bias, just to give their children a better life. Their hopeful faces swam before her eyes, superimposed on the gruesome images flickering on the screens. She was doing this for them, she had to remember that. Every moment of terror, every iota of confusion and revulsion that she was feeling now, was a price she was paying for their safety, for their future. Samantha felt her resolve harden. No matter how deep this abyss was, she was not going to let it swallow her. She had too much at stake.

She closed her eyes to reflect for a moment. *The accident of birth, the perverse malfunction of evil men, the whims of...the gods playing dice with humanity. How do I even try to be master of my fate?* She could feel the Prophet's hand on her thigh. *How far is this all going to go? Do I have the strength to survive?* She gritted her teeth and snorted. *Yes, I do.*

Billy Hallson –
California, Rockridge –
3:00 p.m. Day Zero

The Tunnel

Despite the chaos unfurling a mere two miles south, Rockridge's supermarket seemed untouched by the madness, a bubble of normalcy.

Billy was there, stockpiling emergency supplies with a fervor that left his credit card gasping for mercy. He'd already swept through the sporting goods store, acquiring an arsenal of knives, camping gear, dried food, and bows and arrows. Now, the ten-foot truck was parked outside the supermarket, waiting to be loaded with an assortment of survival goods. Billy's shopping cart was a testament to his priorities, a balance of practical and comforting items. Gallons of water, canned food, protein bars, and boxes of cereals were topped with an unlikely survival item—beer and chocolate.

As the candy bars jostled against the cans in his cart, Billy couldn't help but feel a knot of worry tightening in his stomach.

The usual hum of the supermarket felt unnaturally loud against the backdrop of his thoughts.

The critical item glaringly absent from his collection was a gun. His fingers itched for the cold, solid weight of a firearm, a tangible assurance of protection. But California, with its laws and mandatory waiting periods, proved an obstacle to his immediate need. The irony of the situation was not lost on Billy; when he needed a gun the most, he couldn't have one. His palms sweated around the handle of the shopping cart as he felt the magnitude of his vulnerability creep in.

His uncle Joe had trained him to use guns, from handguns, rifles to machine guns. He had kept a small handgun in his apartment, but it was stolen in a burglary, so now he was unarmed, prone, and he did not like the feeling.

He couldn't help but marvel at the glaring silence of the emergency broadcast system. Despite the chaos unfolding, there was not a single blaring siren or solemn announcement to alert the populace. It was typical, he mused bitterly, his jaw clenching in a familiar rhythm of frustration. He'd always had his doubts about the system's efficiency, its red tape and bureaucracy, and the tendency to keep citizens in the dark when they most needed to know. The system was designed for emergencies, and now, in the heart of one, it was stunningly mute. His scorn for the government deepened, rooted in a foundation of past disappointments and the bitter taste of betrayal.

There had been news reports, but they had given the impression of civil unrest. *I guess no news reporter wants to end their career by declaring a zombie apocalypse.*

He couldn't help but notice another individual among the scarce crowd in the supermarket, a middle-aged man standing out in his camo trousers, a stark black shirt, and a conspicuous red baseball cap. His cart was piled high with what Billy recognized as emergency supplies, mirroring his own stash.

Others are starting to understand.

Their paths crossed again in the desolate parking lot; two strangers bound by the same unspoken concern. The man in camo caught his eye and offered a single nod, his gaze steady and unflinching. There was a tacit understanding in that gesture, a mutual acknowledgment of the unfolding catastrophe. Billy returned the nod, feeling an uncanny solidarity with this stranger. He climbed into his truck, his mind whirring with the implications of their silent exchange.

Some people are figuring it out… but still I can't warn anyone. No one would listen. They might alert the authorities and try to get me put in the looney bin. Although maybe the authorities are beginning to figure out there is a real problem.

A sense of unease tightened in Billy's gut as he mulled over his limited options. Oakland was steadily descending into chaos, and staying put wasn't an option. But running aimlessly towards the east held no promise either. It was then, amid the whirl of thoughts, a realization surfaced.

Uncle Joe! A touch eccentric and largely reclusive, the man had chosen to seclude himself in the outlying area of Lamorinda, a mere ten miles eastward. Apart from his quirks, Uncle Joe had an impressive collection of firearms. He also lived in an isolated house nestled within an expansive canyon. Billy could almost visualize the sanctuary Uncle Joe's residence could offer in these tumultuous times. With this thought, a plan began to coalesce in his mind. Uncle Joe's—it wasn't just an option; it had suddenly become his only hope. *Yes,* he decided, *that's the plan.*

Didn't Uncle Joe build a bunker in his basement…

Retrieving his phone from his pocket, he swiftly dialed Uncle Joe's number. As the ringing tone resonated in the quiet of the truck, he kickstarted the engine and set his course towards Highway 24, aiming for the Caldecott Tunnel. A four-lane passageway boring through the hills. The tunnel served as a geographical threshold dividing the bustling urban sprawl of Oakland, Berkeley, notorious for crime and smothered in fog, from the sun-soaked, bucolic suburbs of Lamorinda to the east.

An involuntary grimace formed on Billy's face at the thought of Lamorinda. He'd always found it tedious—devoid of job opportunities, devoid of any semblance of a nightlife. It was a place where even the most run-down homes bore price tags that were utterly nonsensical to him. *Millions for a shack!* But now, despite his distaste for the area, it was his target destination—the place where hope was waiting.

The phone kept ringing. *Damn, he's not going to answer.*

"Mailbox full...goodbye," Joe's automated message echoed in Billy's ear before the line cut off abruptly. Sighing, Billy hung up the phone, his knuckles white against the steering wheel.

The on-ramp to Highway 24 sprawled out before him, choked with cars. Could people already be aware of the chaos brewing at the city center? Or was it just the typical logjam that kicked off the rush hour in these parts? He heaved another heavy sigh, his gaze sweeping across the sea of stationary vehicles.

Just then, a flicker of motion caught his attention in the rear-view mirror. A lone figure darted through the maze of stalled cars, their hurried movements lending an unsettling edge to the otherwise mundane traffic scene.

Through the tight frame of his rear-view mirror, Billy saw more figures emerge, weaving their way between the cars, their movements frantic and disjointed. A shiver of dread crept up his spine. Surely the nightmare from the city center couldn't have spread this far already. *Even someone sprinting from the restaurant, adrenaline fueling their speed, wouldn't have made it this far so quickly...* unless...A chilling thought began to take form in his mind. *What if these creatures never tire? They just sprint and sprint and kill and spread their infection.*

They were getting closer, and he was trapped on the ramp. *Fuck! Why'd I get myself stuck in traffic.*

The first wave of runners stormed the ramp, a stampede of panic and confusion. Among them, one man caught Billy's eye. His eyes were wide, saucers of raw terror, and foam bubbled at the

105

corners of his mouth. He was a picture of pure fear, not infection...yet. The infected couldn't be far behind, Billy realized, his pulse quickening. Behind the terrified man, hundreds of frantic people surged up the ramp, an unstoppable human tide.

A young man with Asian features scrambled onto a nearby car, desperately seeking a refuge. But his hope was short-lived. He was swiftly tackled by a hulking figure, a man with an eerie, milky-white gaze and grotesque black stains smeared around his mouth.

Billy's heart hammered in his chest, echoing his thoughts. *Shit, shit, shit!* He couldn't stay paralyzed in the middle of this unfolding horror. His grip tightened on the steering wheel, knuckles blanching. With a grim determination, he slammed his foot onto the accelerator, ramming into the car ahead, before reversing into the one behind. The jarring impacts jostled him in his seat but opened a narrow escape path. Swerving hard to the right, he propelled his truck through the boundary fence, off the ramp, and down the grassy embankment onto a less congested side road.

His mind raced, drawing a mental map of the convoluted roads surrounding him. Each of the typical routes leading to the tunnel were going to be choked with traffic or overwhelming chaos. *I need a path no one else will be taking.* A bitter taste of bile tickled the back of his throat as his hands tightened on the steering wheel. But then, an epiphany cut through his growing despair. In this uncharted nightmare, legality was a luxury he could no longer afford.

His foot slammed down on the accelerator, driving the truck faster down the side road. He knew it ended with a fence enclosing a utility yard, but that was no longer a deterrent. When the wire mesh fence came into view, he didn't relent. With a cacophonous crash, the truck bulldozed through the barrier and jolted over a curb, sending the rear axle bucking into the air. He winced, mentally urging his vehicle, *Don't give up on me now, truck, you're my only ticket out of this mess.*

The roar of a motorcycle erupted behind the truck, a reminder that he was not the only one desperate to escape the growing madness. Pushing his own fears aside, he focused on the path unfolding before him. Navigating around towering transformers, he knew the highway lurked just beyond.

The screech of tires, a symphony of rubber and grit, echoed through the air, confirming his two-wheeled shadow was still on his tail. *Whoever is on that bike believes I have a plan to escape this bedlam,* he reasoned, forcing down a flicker of uncertainty. *I just hope his faith isn't misplaced.*

With a final surge of energy, his truck rammed through the final barrier, a fence shielding the highway, and he navigated up the steep embankment. But the sight that met him was one of utter chaos. The highway, once a vein of steady traffic, had transformed into an unmoving wall of metal and panic, all heading in the same direction—east.

That's what I expected but I am thinking outside the box. He drove the truck down the embankment and through the fence again. The motorcycle was right behind him. He knew his idea was dangerous and would have him jailed in normal times. *Oh shit, this is going to suck.*

Burying his foot on the accelerator, he veered off onto a side road, streaking eastward until the path ahead turned into a congested maze of halted vehicles. He swiftly banked left onto an overpass that crossed the jammed freeway, his motorcycle pursuer abandoning him.

The biker must assume I am heading in the wrong direction…he might be right, but it's a gamble I have to take.

The decision was logical—the roads branching off this bridge pointed west, a direction far fewer people wanted to venture in the midst of this madness. His eyes lingered on the motorcycle, its rider skillfully darting between the stalled traffic, a beacon of agility and speed heading for the tunnel. A fleeting sense of envy struck him. *Should I have chosen a bike instead?* But the thought quickly dissipated. A bike, after all, offered no shelter against the horde or the capacity for the precious cargo he carried. His trusty truck, it seemed, was still the better choice.

Following the bridge, his only choice led him onto a ramp headed west. Unaware of the pandemonium engulfing the city center, a sizable flow of traffic was still heading west. He took the ramp heading the wrong way against the flow of surprised and angry vehicles. He headed east on the westbound Highway 24.

"Billy Hallson, you're an absolute madman," he said, grinning. A symphony of angry horns echoed around him, their blaring disapproval punctuating the throbbing beat of his adrenaline-fueled heart.

He pressed on eastward; the looming specter of the tunnel instilled a growing dread within him. He was acutely aware that the narrow shoulders, his lifelines, ceased to exist at the tunnel. *Alright, you've got yourself this far, genius,* he chided himself, the grip on his steering wheel tightening. *But what's the play once you hit the tunnel? What's the next move?*

Billy's gaze swept over the eastbound lanes, separated from him by a formidable barrier of trees and a gaping ditch. The horde had surged onto these lanes, their violent frenzy stark against the ordinary backdrop. An infected girl, in a grotesque display of savagery, smashed her head through the window of a Prius. The scene was so appalling that even the westbound traffic slowed, drivers' attention ensnared by the unfolding horror.

As the tunnel ominously approached, panic began to grip him. A deadly countdown was ticking in his mind: once the horde reached the westbound lanes, there would be no escaping them. The grim finality of his situation was now as inescapable as the concrete walls of the looming tunnel.

With no time left to plan, he swerved into the onslaught of westbound traffic. Car horns filled the air, a deafening symphony of panic and confusion. Drivers were swerving desperately to avoid the lunatic who dared to defy the direction of traffic. A sleek white Audi missed him by a hair's breadth, its silver bumper leaving a telling scratch on the side of the truck.

He pushed the pedal to the floor, his eyes fixed on the dance of the vehicles ahead of him. Every movement required the utmost precision, a ballet of speed and control. Every gap in the flow was an opportunity, and he seized each one, accelerating just in time to slip through. The frenzied pace of his drive, the blaring of horns, and the streaking of the tunnel lights all faded into the background as he focused solely on his path. He'd almost made it through the labyrinthine chaos of the tunnel when he spotted a pair of compact cars side by side, matching each other's speed with uncanny precision.

Both the obstructive vehicles screeched to a halt right in front of him. He slammed on the brakes, the truck lurching to a stop, inches from disaster. *So close,* he thought, the tunnel's end mere yards away. *I almost made it through the tunnel.* He noticed the driver in the car ahead, his face twisted in fury, but he couldn't afford to worry about that now.

With determination, he pressed the accelerator, slowly edging the truck forward. The driver in front of him opened his mouth in shock and mouthed an obscenity. The smaller car creaked and protested, inching backward under the truck's relentless pressure. Hope flickered as he realized he only needed to push a few more yards. However, his heart sank as another car pulled up behind the one he was shoving, leaving only a few yards of space. Undeterred, Billy kept pressing forward.

The driver of the car being pushed backward continued to stare at Billy, his eyes wide with disbelief and tinged with apprehension. The truck's progress was slow, just a few inches per second. The truck was contending with the resistance of two cars. Despite its compact size, the truck boasted a surprisingly sturdy engine and lower gears. Added to that, the weight of the emergency supplies lent it extra traction, enabling it to gradually, relentlessly push both cars back.

Billy could see more cars pulling up, but he also spotted to his relief—the end of the tunnel meant the side shoulder would be open. As soon as he cleared the tunnel, he maneuvered his truck onto the shoulder and clear of the cars. He noticed the bewildered drivers clamber out, hastily pulling out their phones to capture his unorthodox escape.

He put his window down and screamed at them. "Get out of here! They're coming!" All he got back were looks of disbelief or amusement.

Casting a quick glance towards the eastbound and westbound lanes, he took in the sight of the now immobilized traffic, a sea of metal stagnation. Desperate figures darted amongst the cars; their hopes of escape now limited to their own two feet.

Shifting his gaze back to his own path, he pinpointed the exit ramp and, sticking faithfully to the shoulder, directed his truck downward. A raw urgency surged within him, fueling his determination to reach his uncle's place. Despite the promise of its isolated location, he knew that such refuge could merely postpone the inevitable onslaught. He hoped his uncle had built a strong refuge, because the horde would eventually reach it. The glimmer of hope was now a lifeline he had to clutch onto with every ounce of his resolve.

As the wheels of his truck kicked up dust, his mind raced. The view through his windshield seemed unreal, a nightmare playing out in the harsh light of day. The once familiar landscape was tainted now, a scene from a dystopian world that felt alien, hostile. There was an odd duality in his state of mind, a mix of terror and exhilaration. For so long he had lived an ordinary life and now, everything was reduced to survival, every choice consequential. His mundane comfortable life was at an end, and he had never felt so alive.

In the rearview mirror, he caught glimpses of chaos unfolding behind him. Unruly mobs were swarming the highway, discarding the shell of civilization they once wore. The very rules that governed society were crumbling in the face of fear. The sight only intensified his resolve.

His fingers clenched tighter on the steering wheel. Sweat trickled down the side of his face, a stark contrast to the chill that ran down his spine. He turned on the radio, seeking a distraction, perhaps even some news of salvation. The stations were broadcasting mundane news items or cheery pop songs. The lack of news about the violence and chaos was eerie. There should be an announcement from the emergency broadcast system or frantic pleas for help. A pop song blared as if mocking the crisis. He immediately switched it off, the chilling song amplifying his growing anxiety.

The afternoon was fading, and the encroaching darkness mirrored the dread creeping into his stomach. As the familiar signpost for Lamorinda drew nearer, he could not help but cast one last look at the city he once called home, now a burgeoning epicenter of pandemonium. Would he find safety in his uncle's home, or would he be merely delaying the inevitable? Time, he knew, was no longer a benign force but a ticking bomb. It was a fight for survival now, and Billy was going to give it everything he had.

PROFESSOR MARK PRESTON –
THE SKY LOUNGE –
WASHINGTON D.C. – 8 P.M. EST

Professor Mark Preston of the CDC

Nestled in the heart of Washington D.C., the Sky Lounge was a beacon of grandeur, replete with an L-shaped bar that swept across the room like a beckoning finger. It boasted panoramic views that encompassed the iconic White House, the sprawling National Mall, and the rest of the vibrant downtown area. This was where Professor Mark Preston, the esteemed Director of the CDC, found himself that evening. He was caught in the whirlwind of a fundraising event whose cause was lost on him, a testament to the myriad of obligations tethered to his high-ranking position. Despite the seeming disconnect, he recognized such events as necessary networking opportunities, a platform to drum up support for his own significant endeavors.

Gritting his teeth, Mark picked at his plate of grilled chicken, the blandness mirroring his sentiments towards the evening. The crowd of politicians swarming around him was as flavorless as his meal, their empty promises and superficial charm leaving a sour taste in his mouth. He loathed the undercurrent of deceit that ran through their laughter and jovial banter, the two-faced pretense that was all too common in these political gatherings.

These fundraisers used to be so much better with Margie, he thought, remembering his wife. *We would have made fun of these people. She would have broken the ice for me.* He sighed deeply. The wound of her absence was so fresh. *All my expertise couldn't save her from lung cancer.* His career seemed to lose its purpose after her death. Now all he thought about was retiring and moving to an isolated island. *Peace and quiet and absolutely no politics.*

"Ah, Professor Preston!" Senator Reynolds boomed across the room, his voice commanding attention. His expansive grin failed to reach his calculating eyes as he beckoned Mark over, gesturing to the man beside him. "I've been enlightening our chief whip here about your request for...ah yes, CDC reserve emergency equipment." His tone was jovial, but the barb was clear. "Douglas here finds the concept rather interesting. He's under the impression that our government should be focusing on tightening the belt, not loosening it on extravagant purchases that may never be put to use."

Mark suppressed a sigh. "Well, it may seem like wasting money to buy a fire extinguisher for your home, but when it is on fire, it doesn't seem like a waste at all."

Douglas, a rotund man whose flushed complexion spoke of his Texan roots, responded with a hearty slap on Mark's shoulder. "Well, Preston, in my neck of the woods, we don't go buying boots until we're sure it's gonna rain!" His booming laughter echoed through the hall, but his eyes held an unmistakable challenge.

Sheeze, is it not obvious what a stupid statement that is?

"Actually, sir," Mark interjected, holding Douglas's gaze, "the bulk of the emergency equipment we're discussing is primarily manufactured in your home state of Texas. Investing in these supplies could directly boost your economy."

Douglas opened his mouth to respond but was cut short as a figure edged into their conversation circle. A young man, the strain of significance etched on his face, appeared with a vivid, red bow tie bobbing at his throat. Mark recognized him as a low-rung intern—hardly the person he wanted interrupting this pivotal conversation.

"Not now," Mark said, attempting to dismiss the intern while not diverting his attention from Douglas. "Now, if the esteemed gentleman from Texas would—"

"Professor Preston, it's of utmost urgency," the intern persisted, an edge of panic creeping into his voice.

With a thin veneer of patience, Mark turned his attention to the intern. "Alright, what is it?" He bit back his exasperation, hoping it didn't seep into his tone.

The intern shifted uneasily, his gaze darting around the room. "We have a major situation brewing on the west coast...It's an emergency."

Mark's brow furrowed. "What kind of emergency?" he demanded, feeling the first prickle of real concern.

Douglas, meanwhile, lifted his champagne flute, downing half of it with gusto.

The intern's response was so preposterous it momentarily stunned Mark. "Reports are coming in of...zombie-like attacks in Oakland, California," the intern stammered.

Douglas spluttered on his champagne, the liquid spraying from his mouth. A moment of choking was followed by a burst of raucous laughter that echoed through the hall.

Douglas managed to get a grip on his laughter, wiping his eyes. "Boy, whoever put you up to this...they're a genius! That's the best laugh I've had in months. Zombies, of all things!"

The intern's face grew paler, his voice shaky yet insistent. "No, sir, it's...it's not a joke. It's real."

Mark could barely contain his irritation. This wasn't just unprofessional; it was downright absurd. The intern had just torpedoed any future he might have had in this field.

Douglas gave the intern a hearty slap on the shoulder, pushing him slightly off balance. "Zombies in Oakland? Son, the only zombies I know there are called liberals!" He barked a loud laugh, clearly enjoying his own joke.

The intern did not take his eyes off Mark. "Sir, the CDC..." the intern tried to interject. He hesitated. "There are zombies in

Oakland, California," he finally said, rushing the words out in one blast.

Suddenly, the crowd parted to make way for two men in crisply tailored black suits. Their stern faces and imposing presence were unmistakable. They were secret service.

"Sir, we need you to come with us," one of the agents said, grabbing Mark by the shoulder in a manner that made it clear this was no request.

Mark, despite his esteemed position, couldn't help but bristle at the thought of being escorted in this manner. His experiences as a black man had instilled an innate wariness towards law enforcement, one that not even his lofty status could fully erase. He felt that being marched out of a building made him look like he had just been caught pick pocketing.

"I'll accompany you," he acquiesced, his voice tinged with resentment. "But know this, I find this highly absurd."

As he watched the agents' stern faces, a pang of anxiety flared within him. They were not here for a casual visit, something serious was at hand. He shook off the ludicrous thought that sprung into his mind... *zombies, of all things! When I find out what's really going on, heads will roll for this. But…what could be mistaken for zombies. Some kind of narcotic? Some new synthetic party drug?*

As the suited men escorted Mark away from the buzzing conversations and the warm light of the Sky Lounge, the air seemed to thicken with an ominous sense of uncertainty. The clinking of champagne glasses and the murmur of diplomatic conversations began to dull into a dissonant hum, slowly fading into the distant background.

The city's usual shimmer, visible through the tall glass windows of the Sky Lounge, looked colder now. He knew something serious was going on on the west coast, but what could it be? Oakland was a long way from Washington, but the gleaming light from the National Mall appeared eerie, as if the city itself understood something was not right.

Even as he found himself dwelling on the absurdity of the situation, the intern's words echoed in his head, "There are zombies in Oakland, California". Despite his scientific rationale resisting, the thought began to germinate. The laughter of Senator Douglas, the apprehension in the young intern's eyes, the cold silence of the secret service agents; everything painted a bizarre picture, a reality far removed from what he had known.

I need data. I can't do my job without data. He fumbled in his pocket for his phone and looked up news for Oakland.

"Violence hits downtown Oakland," one headline read.

"Famed reporter dies in Oakland riot," read another headline.

"Police join with rioters," read another article's headline.

Mark looked at the agents who walked with an urgent yet contained pace, their eyes locked straight ahead, faces devoid of any emotion. They were men trained for crises, but he couldn't help but notice a rare flicker of concern in their gaze. It was all becoming too surreal. What awaited him at the White House? Would he be walking into a situation so absurd that it threatened to shatter his perception of reality?

As he was led out of the Sky Lounge, the heavy doors closing behind him, Mark felt a chill run down his spine. The world outside was about to change, or maybe, it already had. The question was, was he ready for it? The unknown had a peculiar way of stoking the human imagination. As he walked away from the muffled laughter and the clinking glasses, he felt a strange knot in his stomach. He was stepping out of the familiar and walking straight into the jaws of the unimaginable. The world was holding its breath, waiting, watching, as a new, terrifying chapter seemed ready to unfold.

Okay, he thought, *let's just imagine it is zombies…how does that work? Obviously, it must be something that only looks like zombies. There are drugs that make people violent. I've seen footage of people riddled with bullet holes but still fighting…the amazing effects of adrenaline.*

As he tried to form rational explanations for what he saw in the headlines, he found himself thinking of a Shakespeare quote: "There are more things in heaven and Earth, Horatio, than are dreamt of in your philosophy."

AMANDA WILLARD –
SHEPHERD CANYON PARK –
6 P.M. DAY ZERO

The Van Gets Surrounded

Guiding the van eastward towards the serene Shepherd Canyon Park—a modest slice of verdant land on the periphery of Oakland's suburbs—she found solace in the untroubled roads, devoid of both traffic and the ominous presence of the infected.

A sideways glance at Bert revealed him propped against the passenger door, his eyes sealed shut. A gnawing worry tugged at her conscience. Had she been imprudent to let him hitch a ride? A chilling prospect flickered in her mind: what if he was carrying the infection?

Bert was the physical embodiment of neglect: unwashed for days, teeth stained and unbrushed, hair matted with remnants of countless nights spent on the dirt. He seemed like a potential host to a thriving colony of lice.

An unexpected sight caught her eye. A glimpse of flesh above his right ankle revealed an ominous mark—a bite. The sight struck her like a chilling breeze, its cold fingers of fear creeping up her spine. Had Bert been bitten? She hastily pulled the van to the side of the road. Bert remained unmoved, locked in a deep slumber, oblivious to her rising panic.

Casting a glance towards the back of the van, she found Joshua nestled comfortably in his bed, lost in dreams. Turning her gaze back to Bert, the beads of sweat dotting his forehead told an alarming tale. He's ill. The realization dawned on her with a sickening thud.

Never once peeling her eyes from the potential threat, she cautiously slid out of her seat, her fear clenching her stomach in a vice. She extended a trembling hand to the upper storage compartment, fumbling slightly as she pulled out a small lockbox. Her fingers danced over the buttons, punching in her code. The box clicked open, revealing her trusted Sig firearm, and its corresponding magazine. Her breath hitched as she gently inserted the magazine into the firearm.

With a resolute grip on the gun, she directed it at the slumbering Bert. "Bert," her voice trembled, breaking the silence. The single word hung in the air, heavy with dread.

"Huh?" Bert mumbled; his eyes still firmly shut.

"Is there...Do you have a bite mark on your leg?" Her voice was barely a whisper, her eyes filled with fear and uncertainty.

He looked at her with a weary expression. "Sure do," he replied, as he nestled his head back against the cool window.

"When did that happen? Who gave you that?" The urgency in her voice heightened.

"Ah, happened last night. Had a bit of a tiff with a mutt over a sandwich. Darn critter claimed the victory."

A line of perspiration trailed down his temple. "I'm not feelin' so hot actually."

Infection! The word screamed in her mind. She spared a brief glance at Joshua, still peacefully slumbering, before her gaze snapped back to Bert.

"Bert, you have to leave. Now," she declared, her voice low yet assertive. No response. "Bert. Out. Now."

His gaze met hers in an extended, uneasy silence. His eyes moved to the gun she clutched, his brow furrowing. The silence seemed to fill the space between them.

"I'm not infected, Amanda." His voice was soft but filled with unyielding certainty, his gaze steady. "A dog bit me, not a person."

Amanda's breath caught in her throat, her palm damp with sweat against the cool metal of the gun.

"I...I need you to get out," she stammered, straining to keep her voice low enough not to wake Joshua. Each word was a battle against the panic threatening to overtake her.

Bert locked eyes with her, his gaze holding a heaviness that briefly morphed his rugged exterior into a soft vulnerability. His eyelids then drooped, his gaze breaking away as he acknowledged her command. "I'll get out if you really want me to," he began, his voice a gravelly whisper. "But, Amanda, you know me. You've patched me up in that free clinic of yours more times than I can count. Antibiotics, lotion, bandages..."

Bert, with his tangled hair and weather-worn features, was a familiar face from the clinic. But that prior connection seemed trivial now, extinguished by the looming threat he could pose to Joshua. Her resolve hardened, and she clutched the gun tighter.

She took a deep breath, her fingers tightening around the cold grip of the gun. She swallowed, trying to force the words out, "I want you to—"

"Wait," Bert interrupted, rolling up his pant leg with a swift, frustrated motion. He pointed at the bite wound, his eyes fixed on hers. "You've seen enough wounds to know the difference between a human bite and a dog bite, haven't you?"

Amanda's eyes fell on the wound. The pattern, the ragged edges—they did resemble a dog's bite. But in this panic-fueled moment, her normally steadfast knowledge seemed shaky. She'd seen enough human bites in her medical career, seen the stark difference. But doubt crept in now, clouding her judgement. Could she really trust her experience, her gut, amidst the chaos?

"Wait, Bert," Amanda stuttered, her voice choked with emotion. A sudden brainwave hit her, causing her to pause midsentence. "Don't move, just...wait right there."

With measured steps, she swiveled her chair and made her way to a cabinet at the back of the van. Her hand trembled as she reached for the top shelf, extracting a small, cardboard box with a label that had faded over time. She rummaged through it and resurfaced, holding a pair of handcuffs lined with pink fur.

She turned back to Bert. Tossing the handcuffs in his direction, she tried to steady her breathing. The handcuffs landed in Bert's lap, their pink fluff a stark contrast against his grimy clothes.

Bert stared at the cuffs and then back at Amanda, confusion etching lines into his dirt-streaked face. "What the hell is this?"

"Loop those through the bar under your seat and then cuff your wrists," Amanda instructed, her voice firmer now.

Bert hoisted the handcuffs high, eyebrows wiggling suggestively as a roguish smile twisted his lips. "Got a bit of a wild side, do ya, doc?" His chuckle was low and gravelly, causing her cheeks to heat with embarrassment.

"Just put them on, Bert," she said, blushing.

Complying with a roll of his eyes, Bert maneuvered awkwardly to affix the cuffs, grunting as the constrained position drew a sharp curve in his back. "So, how long do I gotta stay tied up like some pink fluffy criminal?"

Amanda mulled over his question, a pang of uncertainty churning in her stomach. The timeline for the infection was unknown, especially given the chaos unfolding. "I...I don't know," she admitted, her gaze fixated on the gaudy handcuffs now shackling Bert.

I know nothing about this infection.

"And where exactly are we headed?" Bert asked.

Amanda blinked, momentarily stunned by his question. A plan, she realized, was something she severely lacked. "I'm not sure," she confessed, "but anywhere... anywhere that's not here seems like the right idea. Somewhere away from people."

As she spoke, her hands worked of their own accord, retrieving her phone from her pocket. A desperate need for information gnawed at her. Tentatively, her fingers typed into the search bar the unthinkable words, 'zombie outbreak'.

Incredibly, reports of a zombie outbreak in Oakland California, turn out not to be a hoax. Confirmed reports of a transmissible disease turning people into mindlessly violent automatons. Outbreak has also been reported in Sacramento, and possibly in San Jose.

She searched for how long it takes after zombie bite before they turn.

Some reports are saying that people turned less than fifteen minutes after a bite, other reports say it took thirty minutes. There are many reports that people have become infected without even being bitten. The source of the infection has yet to be discovered.

"For how long should I...?" Bert's words trailed off as a sudden noise outside the van jarred them from their conversation.

An eerily guttural sound echoed in the near silence, setting both their nerves on edge. Amanda peered out the window, just in time to witness a macabre scene. An infected adolescent girl had just sprinted past their vehicle. She skidded to a halt less than fifty feet away, her movements resembling an unhinged puppet. She was barefoot, with blood stains on her jeans and shirt. There was a rip in the flesh of her calf and her right foot was torn almost in half. Her nostrils flared, savagely sniffing the air as though she were a beast hunting prey. Her eyes, devoid of human warmth and filled with a hauntingly milky-white hue, darted about manically before freezing on Amanda. The intensity of the stare sent a cold shiver down Amanda's spine, leaving her, and a now silent Bert, in an uncomfortable limbo of fear and anticipation.

"It's one of those growlers," said Bert.

"Shit!" said Amanda as she started the van. *They reached here so quickly! I must stop underestimating this.*

The infected girl emitted a primal snarl, her mouth a dark cavern of tar-like sludge that slithered down her chin in grotesque rivulets. With an unholy shriek that pierced the air like a death knell, she lunged towards the van in a horrifying display of inhuman speed.

In one fluid movement, Amanda jammed the gear into drive and mashed her foot down on the accelerator, sending the van roaring into motion towards the growler. The collision was imminent and inevitable, a sickening crunch echoed in the confines of the van as it hit the girl and rode over her with a jolt that reverberated through Amanda's body. She winced, her knuckles white against the steering wheel, the bitter taste of dread lingering at the back of her throat.

Bert winced in tandem, a slight groan escaping his lips. Amanda stole a glance at him, trying to discern if the grimace was a result of his awkwardly contorted posture or the ghastly event they had just witnessed, or perhaps his first growl as an infected.

Satisfying herself that he was not turned yet she concentrated again on the road. She found herself drawn to the wing mirror to see the damage she had done to the growler.

A chilling sight met her eyes—the infected girl, her legs mangled in an unnerving ballet of twisted flesh and bone, was dragging herself along the asphalt. Behind her, a sickening trail of black, coagulated blood snaked its way along the road, an unforgiving testament to the horror they had just escaped.

That blood...it's as black as dried ink, Amanda mused, her professorial instincts stirring within her despite the terror of the situation. *But how is it fueling the muscles? How is respiration functioning, if at all?"* A chilling thought crossed her mind, the academic curiosity a stark contrast to the gruesome reality. *Could it be the bacteria? Perhaps they're crawling, consuming the host...or deriving energy from whatever the host ingests?"* Her voice trailed off into the grim silence of the van.

""Where are we headed?" Bert's voice wavered, betraying his nervousness.

"East," Amanda's voice was ironclad, resonating with unyielding determination in the confined space of the van.

Bert winced, his head slamming into the door as Amanda swerved around a tight turn. "Avoid the freeways or highways," he gasped out, the words escaping in labored breaths. "Everyone and their mother will have the same idea."

"I already had that thought," she responded, her eyes flicking momentarily to the rearview mirror. "That's why I have been heading to the canyon route." The van rumbled as if in agreement, tires gripping the road as they plunged into the welcoming shadows of the canyon.

The van's engine growled like a tamed beast beneath her control, a lone, resounding echo against the silent, ominous scene of the approaching canyon. As she pressed deeper into the enclosing darkness, her gaze flitted back and forth between the road and Bert, tension knotting in her stomach with each glance.

Bert, squished uncomfortably against the door, was unusually silent. He watched the passing darkness of the canyon with a calm resignation that felt heavier than the oppressive silence. The handcuffs gleamed in the scant light. Sweat beaded on his forehead, his shallow breaths noticeable in the confined space. Each hitch in his breath strummed the chords of tension that were wound tight within Amanda.

He's sick, he is definitely sick...Though it is understandable to get sick from a dog bite...but can I take the risk? What if it is airborne? What if...the right thing to do, to protect Jo Jo, is to throw Bert out the back of the van and speed away. A measure of callousness might be necessary to survive this apocalypse. She took a few breaths as her uncomfortable thoughts threatened to overwhelm her. *Perhaps human kindness is a more powerful weapon for survival.*

She shook her head and stared out the window. The moonlight painted an eerie landscape outside the van, casting elongated shadows that danced like ghostly specters in the night. The canyon was an amphitheater of echoing silence. The only sound in the vast, empty canyon was the rumbling of the van, a mechanical heartbeat pulsing against the stillness.

An abrupt flash of movement in her peripheral vision had her foot slamming on the brakes, the van skidding to an abrupt halt that made Bert grunt in discomfort. Her adrenaline surged through her veins as her eyes scanned the looming darkness outside, alert for the slightest hint of movement. It was a rabbit, or maybe a fox. Or perhaps, it was something far more menacing.

Something is out there.

Behind them, the infected girl had disappeared into the distance, but Amanda knew that danger still lurked unseen, ready to strike when they least expected it. The tension in the van was a tightly drawn bowstring waiting to snap. With each passing moment, the uncertainty of what lay ahead amplified, leaving an unsettling question hanging in the air—what's next?

MARK PRESTON – THE WHITE HOUSE – WASHINGTON D.C. – 10 P.M. EST

Whitehouse Meeting

"Excuse me?" President Mitchel scoffed, his eyebrows arching in disbelief. "If this is a jest, it's ill-timed. You've just derailed a crucial negotiation."

The President occupied the plush, worn leather of the oval office couch, his cowboy boots audaciously kicked up onto a chair of French antiquity, indicating the casual nonchalance with which he often approached his high office.

"Damnation, Dern!" President Mitchel barked at his chief of staff, his brawny fist colliding with the mahogany coffee table beside him.

Dern was an Obama look alike, but if anyone mentioned it, he'd have punched them in the face. He was unperturbed by the President's outburst. He straightened his tie and maintained eye contact. "I find it hard to believe this is a hoax, Mr. President," he intoned, his voice betraying a rare note of concern. "The reports are streaming in from all over—Oakland, San Jose, Sacramento...The scope alone suggests this isn't some elaborate prank."

President Mitchel held Dern in a stone-hard stare, the silence stretching between them before he finally shifted his ice-blue eyes towards Mark. "Fine," he drawled, leaning back into the plush upholstery of the couch and steepling his fingers before him. "If it comes to light that this is all some monumental prank, there'll be a reckoning. Now, Professor Preston," he paused, casting a sidelong glance at Mark. "How about you enlighten me on what exactly can cause the dead to rise and attack?"

"Nothing does," said Mark. "Well, nothing we know of." He shook his head, the weight of uncertainty evident in his voice. "It's unlike anything we've seen before. I have just had one phone call with my staff, so I do not know much. I can only assume that the infected aren't technically dead, but they just seem impervious to severe injuries—similar to reactions observed in individuals high on PCP. The way they behave mirrors symptoms of rabies in animals, but we've done no testing yet," he said, raking a hand through his hair. "One of my staff believes it might be bacterial, but it's nothing identifiable. The sudden simultaneous spread in three separate cities is another puzzle altogether. It's all...inexplicable."

President Mitchel swiveled towards Dern; his eyes narrowed. "Could this be a biological attack?" he asked. Dern met the President's gaze, his shoulders lifting in an uncertain shrug. "It's difficult to conceive of it as anything else but man-made," he admitted, the gravity of his words settling heavily in the room.

135

It took a moment for those present to absorb the consequences of it being a biological weapon.

President Mitchel's voice cut through the silence, tension edging his words. "As briefings go, this sucks. When can I expect a comprehensive briefing?" He jabbed a finger at an unseen map, his brow furrowing. "Could it be the Russians? I need to know our response capabilities, now!" His demands echoed through the room, underscoring the urgency of the situation.

Dern's face contorted into a grimace as he divulged the unexpected. "Believe it or not, there exists a contingency plan for a zombie apocalypse." His words hung in the air.

"Are you joking?" President Mitchel challenged, his voice a mix of incredulity and amusement.

Mark too, was taken aback. "Really?" he echoed, his eyebrows arching in surprise.

Dern nodded, his tone steady despite the bizarre conversation. "Not the CDC, mind you," he clarified. "General Bugmount, the Commandant of the Marine Corps, led a wargame once. Codenamed 'BAZ for Biochemical Attack – Z', they theorized it would prepare us for an array of bio attacks."

President Mitchel responded with a nod; his eyebrows arched in a bemused expression of disbelief. "So, what's the course of action? How do we salvage these cities?" he queried, leaning forward slightly.

In a tone weighed heavy by the words he was about to speak, Dern delivered the chilling verdict, "Sometimes, in the defense of a city, one must entertain the necessity of its destruction."

President Mitchel's jaw slackened, his eyes widening in surprise.

"Destroy...what?" questioned Mark, the last word emerging as more of a bewildered whisper than a coherent question.

The room fell eerily silent. The grim truth hung in the air like a ghastly specter. Mark shifted his gaze between Dern and President Mitchel, seeking clarity. "Sometimes in the defense of a city, it becomes necessary to destroy...what?" He echoed his previous question, desperate for a different answer.

President Mitchel, breaking the silence, replied in a low, heavy voice, "The city itself. To defend a city, it may be required to destroy the city."

"Are you out of your minds?" Mark's incredulity morphed into a shout, the words echoing harshly in the tense confines of the room.

Dern's expression hardened. "Time is of the essence," he declared, the stern tone indicating the gravity of the situation. "We're unsure about the genesis of this situation, but the infection is proliferating at an alarming rate. We need to annihilate those cities."

A shadow of concern crossed President Mitchel's face. He rubbed his chin thoughtfully. "Such a decision could significantly impact my reelection campaign."

Dern's voice was soft yet resolute when he replied, "Mr. President, these are Democratic strongholds, cities in a state that wasn't going to back you. In a paradoxical twist, initiating a nuclear strike on a few Californian cities might resonate with your supporters. You could portray it as divine retribution on the sinners. It transforms you into a wartime leader, unflinching in making tough calls. It could even result in your statues gracing town squares."

President Mitchel nodded and smiled. "They never build statues to peace time Presidents." He turned to Dern. "So how do we blow up some Californian cities?"

"Wait, hold on!" Mark's voice echoed in the room, strained with disbelief and desperation. "What about armored forces? We could just deploy tanks. They're practically impenetrable. They can engage without fear of retaliation."

The President considered this, his countenance reflecting his inner thoughts as it shifted from anticipation to disappointment. "Well, that does sound plausible. I require a detailed military briefing."

Exhaustion etched on his face, Mark ran a hand over his features. *Jesus! Why do we always elect idiots!*

As the room's conversation drifted towards the logistics of war, Mark found himself drowning in a sea of unrealities. He glanced at Dern and the President, the two of them engulfed in their gruesome brainstorming session. The buzz of their planning, an unbearable hum that intensified Mark's throbbing headache. He found himself, a microbiologist, ensnared in the midst of a discussion where collateral damage was the theme, a truly ludicrous situation.

Dern's hand animatedly skimmed over an aerial map on a screen, pointing out likely targets. The President leaned in, his hardened gaze fixed on the unfolding war strategy. For a second, Mark allowed himself to examine the President: the creased forehead showing a facsimile of concern, the cold determination in his eyes, and a hint of glee hidden deep within that unnerved him. *It's almost as if he has been waiting for this moment.*

The metallic taste of fear, anger, and disbelief coalesced in Mark's mouth. *This is all wrong. There should be another way, a humane way, a scientific way.* He clenched his fists tightly, his nails digging into his palms as he held onto his sanity in a world that had seemingly lost its own. *Science will save the day, not the military.*

An eerie silence fell on the room as Dern ended his monologue on battle tactics, looking to President Mitchel for approval. Mark caught his breath, looking at the two men before him. The fate of entire cities and millions of lives hung in the balance, a tightrope strung over a chasm of chaos.

Mark had no idea what would happen next, but he feared the answer might forever change the world.

BILLY HALLSON –
CALIFORNIA, LAMORINDA –
7:00 P.M. DAY ZERO

Canyon Critter Roadblock

Billy felt a shudder of contempt ripple through him as he surveyed the place. *God, I hate this dump*, he thought. He had made it through Orinda and was almost to the end of Moraga the next town. The town was built with only a single road leading in and out. During a zombie apocalypse, which Billy now found himself in the middle of, this seemed like a tactical blunder of the highest order.

Uncle Joe's quaint abode perched on the fringes of the town, only accessible via a decrepit bridge that groaned and shivered over a sometimes-tempestuous creek. The house sat ensconced within the enigmatic realm known as 'The Canyon.' This secluded corner of the world was populated by a motley assortment of characters who were collectively dismissed as 'canyon critters' by the town's more conventional residents. These 'critters' were viewed with a mix of condescension and wariness, their unconventional lifestyles clashing with the town's more traditional sensibilities.

Billy remembered walking in the Canyon as a child and meeting a canyon critter that lived in a tree. The disheveled woman had scared him, but ultimately had proven harmless.

The Canyon was an enigmatic web of serpentine roads that slithered aimlessly through the undulating landscape. Each road was a mirror image of the last, burrowing mazelike through the hills and often culminating in exasperating dead-ends.

Billy often mused that The Canyon was a place where trouble found trouble, a place that seemed unwelcome to outsiders, although in Billy's experience the inhabitants were the friendliest of neighbors. Any outsider brazen enough to incite trouble within its confines would swiftly find themselves cornered not by conventional law and order, but by an indomitable assembly of well-armed 'critters.'

These canyon dwellers, fiercely independent and distrustful of outsiders, prided themselves on settling their disputes without resorting to involving law enforcement. In Billy's eyes, the Canyon critters were akin to the stereotype of hillbillies. He had heard enough stories to know to avoid getting on their bad side, so he made it a rule to avoid crossing them.

As dusk began to slink over the Canyon, bathing the landscape in hues of melancholic orange and bruised purples, Billy switched on his radio which sputtered into life. News bulletins started pouring in, carrying ominous updates on the escalating situation in Oakland and, alarmingly, now Sacramento which was far to the east. He realized he was rapidly becoming surrounded by the infected. He better get to Uncle Joe's fast.

Billy's grip tightened on the steering wheel as he listened to the reports, his eyes darting warily from the road that coiled in front of him to the rear-view mirror.

The radio announcer's voice crackled through the speaker, filling the cab of the truck with an uneasy tension. "Well, folks," he began, the forced cheeriness in his voice belying the gravity of his words. "It appears that the epidemic has clawed its way into two more cities. Both Dublin and Fremont are now in the grips of the infected hordes."

Billy swallowed hard, his gaze flicking briefly to the radio. The idea of the infection spreading so quickly was a hard pill to swallow. The panic and confusion of the past few hours had been bad enough when it was just Oakland.

How did it jump to a different city… even at full run, a zombie would not reach Fremont so quickly. Something else is happening here.

"The origin of this infection still eludes us," the announcer continued, his tone sobering. "Our medical experts are grappling with the mystery, desperately working around the clock to uncover some answers."

Billy could imagine the chaos in the labs, the scramble to understand an enemy that didn't discriminate, didn't hesitate. An enemy that seemed hell-bent on reducing humanity to mere prey.

"And in response to the escalating crisis, the state government has activated the National Guard," the announcer relayed. Billy's stomach sank further. The National Guard's involvement confirmed the severity of the situation.

"San Francisco remains untouched for the moment," the announcer added, a note of wonder creeping into his voice.

Wait, I thought there was a report saying San Francisco had succumbed too. I expect things are confused and hectic in the newsrooms.

The announcer continued. "An entire regiment of Marines is stationed on the Bay Bridge, a bulwark against the tide of infection attempting to spill over from Oakland. They are taking extreme measures, shooting anyone attempting to cross into the city."

Billy shivered at the announcer's words, the reality of their new world settling heavily on his shoulders. The Marines, America's finest, reduced to shooting their own to prevent the spread of the infection. It was a grim thought, and a grim indicator of what lay ahead.

A regiment, that's like, three thousand marines.

"Sadly, it seems that the eastern front of Oakland hasn't been as successful in holding back the tide," the announcer added, a note of dread lacing his words. "The infected have managed to breach the Caldecott Tunnel. They're spilling out the other side like a swarm of locusts, laying siege to the towns that lie helpless in their path."

Billy gripped the steering wheel tighter, knuckles whitening as the realization dawned on him. *The infected must be less than a mile away.* Each passing second, each word from the announcer's mouth, drove home the stark reality: the world as he knew it was collapsing.

Damn! I could encounter the infected at any moment. I must find Uncle Joe's.

He brought out his phone again and tried to dial him.

"Mailbox full…goodbye," said Joe's voice. Billy hung up and growled.

Even the GPS was lost in the canyon.

"And now for more grim news, I'm afraid," the announcer's voice resonated through the vehicle. "The infected have overrun downtown Orinda, leaving chaos and destruction in their wake."

Billy's eyes widened at the update. *Orinda. So close.* He shook his head and turned off the radio. *Silence is probably wiser right now so I can concentrate on my immediate surroundings.*

Just as the drone of the announcer's voice dwindled into silence, Billy's headlights unveiled an unanticipated obstacle. Nestled in the heart of this isolated stretch of road was an impromptu roadblock. An anarchic jumble of forsaken vehicles and crudely assembled barricades sprawled across the asphalt, an unwelcome interruption to his unhindered journey.

Emerging from the tenebrous backdrop, figures, heavily laden with weaponry, stepped into the eerie glow of the headlights, their faces hidden beneath the grotesque masks of shifting shadows. For a heart-stopping moment, the world held its breath, then the silence was shattered by a stinging command. As they gestured authoritatively for Billy to halt, he obediently responded, his fingers clutching the steering wheel with an intensity that made his knuckles white and his hands quake.

145

As they advanced toward his truck, their weapons poised menacingly, a shiver of dread skated down Billy's spine. The chilling question gnawed at him: would they discern his uninfected status? Or would their fear and paranoia overshadow any semblance of reason?

His truck grumbled to a stop, the rhythmic drone of the engine slicing through the still night air, mirroring the palpitations of his heart pounding like a wild drum against his rib cage. Shrouded in the glaring blaze of the truck's headlights, the figures converged. With a motion of their hands, they gestured for him to lower his window.

Grudgingly, Billy obeyed. It dawned on him, as sharp and as cold as the night air, that the days of law and order had faded into oblivion. Now, in its stead, emerged a jungle law, one enforced not by gavels but by firearms. He had always had the conviction that civilization was a fragile veneer, barely restraining the feral beast lurking within every human. And now, that primal creature was ravenous, waiting for the flimsiest pretext to pounce. The chilling knowledge pierced him—if they decided he was an undesirable, there would be nothing standing between him and a swift, brutal end.

An uneasy silence stretched between them as they stared at Billy, their eyes assessing, calculating. Then, the one who seemed to be the leader, a broad-shouldered man with a gruff voice, broke the silence.

"State your business," he demanded, his voice cutting through the tense silence like a knife.

"I'm...I'm headed to the Canyon," Billy stammered out, his throat suddenly dry. "My Uncle Joe's place."

"You mean Joe Hillson?" said the man.

Billy nodded.

"Well, that conspiracy nut job is going to be full of I-told-you-sos."

I don't think he ever thought there would be a zombie apocalypse. He just thought the illuminati would come for his guns one day.

"And where are you coming from?" another man, taller and leaner, questioned from beside the leader.

Billy swallowed. "Oakland," he managed to say. The men exchanged glances, their expressions unreadable.

"Any contact with the infected?" the leader asked, his gaze boring into Billy.

Billy shook his head emphatically. "No, no contact. I've been careful."

The men nodded, seemingly placated by his answers. The leader signaled to the others, and they began to inspect his vehicle. Their movements were precise and efficient. They rifled through his belongings, their hands methodically searching through the contents of his truck. Every so often, they would pause to examine an item more closely, but each time they would replace it and move on.

Billy watched as they conducted their search, a gnawing anxiety twisting in his stomach. They were thorough, their professionalism a stark reminder of the grim reality they were all facing.

Finally, after a seemingly endless stretch of time, they finished their search. The leader returned to Billy's window, his face a mask of stern authority.

"Step out," he ordered, gripping a gun on his hip.

Billy was acutely aware of his lack of options. All he craved was to escape from these people, from everyone except his Uncle Joe. But, reluctantly, he opened the truck door and stepped out into the pool of stark light. He felt the weight of their gazes on him, loaded with silent threats. They could snuff out his life, loot his supplies, and his disappearance would dissolve into the fabric of this unfolding nightmare, unnoticed and unmourned.

"Turn around slowly," the man ordered.

Billy did as he was asked.

"You're clear," he announced, his voice gruff. "As you know Joe, we'll let you go. Keep out of trouble and head straight to your destination. It's not safe to be out here."

With a final nod, they stepped aside, allowing Billy to continue his journey. As he drove away, the imposing figures of the roadblock grew distant, their silhouettes blurring into the dark, and the canyon road stretched out before him, a path filled with uncertainty and fear.

It's no surprise to me that the canyon critters got roadblocks organized so quickly. I swear half of them have been planning a showdown with the government my whole life. Years of growing weed and living like hippies.

He had just begun to relax, his hand reaching out to turn the radio back on, when the air was pierced by a chilling sound, drowning the crackling static. The rapid-fire burst of automatic weapons rang out, their echoes shattering the canyon's stillness. A cold shiver ran down his spine. He whipped his gaze to the rear-view mirror, eyes straining to decipher the horrifying scene unfolding behind him. The roadblock was lit by the harsh, intermittent flashes from the gunfire, casting an eerie, flickering shadow-play of armed figures in combat.

The men at the roadblock were now fighting for their lives against the very threat they had just questioned him about.

Reality sank in; the infected were almost upon him, and the infection was spreading faster than he had imagined. He swallowed the lump in his throat and pressed harder on the accelerator, the desperate fight at the roadblock receding into the darkness behind him.

SAM BUTCHEART -
YERBA BUENA ISLAND

Every day since he and his tank had been stationed on Yerba Buena, Lieutenant Sam Butcheart, had asked himself one question—*why?* Russians are not going to invade San Francisco. There's no place to do tank training exercises. The only answer he could come up with was that it was going to be some kind of recruitment campaign, but so far, no civilians had been invited to take a tour of the three tanks that had been offloaded.

Even with its inherent question, the posting was far from undesirable. San Francisco, despite its profound and striking decay, was a city of delights. The cityscape offered its multifaceted charm to its residents and visitors alike. By day, it boasted the bustling Fisherman's Wharf, bougie restaurants, its sights and smells a constant adventure. As night fell, the city transformed, with the Tenderloin and SoMa districts awakening to a life of their own. This was a city that knew how to cater to the wants of a young man, even as it masterfully drained his hard-earned salary.

Sam Butcheart found himself roused from his hangover-induced slumber by none other than a major, an occurrence as disorienting as it was rare. The unwelcome shake of reality jolted through him, causing his hazy world to come into abrupt focus. It was an unsettling way to start the day, a rank breach in military norms that left him blinking against the daylight, struggling to process the unfolding reality.

He stared for a moment and was about to jump out of bed and salute when the major put a hand on his chest. "Stay there! I need to give you an order that is going to be the weirdest damn order you ever heard of."

"Sir?"

Sam was handed a slip of paper.

OPERATION ORDER 323/B - Operation "Cleansing Thunder"

1. Situation: Our forces are tasked with the elimination of the undead threat in the city of Oakland, which has resulted in severe civilian casualties and disruption of governmental operations. The city is overrun by infected and has been declared a quarantine zone.

2. Mission: Viper One, Viper Two, and Viper Three Tanks of 1st Armored Division are to mobilize immediately, enter the city of Oakland, and neutralize all undead hostiles. Civilian casualties are to be disregarded due to the extreme threat level and the risk of further infection.

3. Execution:

Intent: Our primary goal is the swift and thorough eradication of the undead to halt further infection and to pave the way for the re-establishment of secure, controlled zones.

Concept of Operations: The tanks will enter Oakland from the 3 main ingress routes [refer to map]. Eliminate the infected.

Tasks: Units are to neutralize all undead threats, maintain communication with HQ, and provide status reports every 2 hours.

Coordinating Instructions: All units will maintain radio silence unless reporting. Should any unit come under threat from uninfected hostile elements, rules of engagement are under Appendix A.

4. Service Support: All tanks have been stocked with enough fuel, ammunition, and provisions to last 72 hours. Extraction will be available at predetermined extraction points on an as-needed basis.

5. Command and Signal: Command: Operation "Cleansing Thunder" is under the direct command of General Hind.

Military discipline stopped him from throwing the order away with a "Are you serious!" comment. *It must be some kind of test. An order is an order and I'll obey it... for now.* He saluted and acknowledged his acceptance.

As Sam approached his tank thirty minutes later, he noticed Jones, his driver, propped unsteadily against the hull. "Feeling alright, Jones?" he asked, not needing a response to confirm the man's hangover.

Jones offered a weak smile, squinting against the daylight. "Yeah, yeah...If I'd known I'd be wrestling fifteen hundred horses today, I wouldn't have been matching you shot for shot last night," he grumbled, his voice gravelly with regret. He shook his head slowly before hacking a rough cough and spitting on the ground. "I'll manage," he added, attempting to reassure his Lieutenant.

Yeah, if I'd known I'd be leading a column of three tanks over the bay bridge towards Oakland, I might have traded the tequila for bud. I still don't think it's real. I mean… it can't be. At some point they'll call us back and give us a pat on the back for following orders without question. Although… maybe we are supposed to question. We're taught to think for ourselves… So far, no order has been illegal. But if I come face to face with an innocent civilian, I am not just going to roll over them.

There were marines on the bridge, they had set up a roadblock and defenses. There were a lot of machine guns pointing down the road toward Oakland.

The marines allowed the tanks through the barricade and then sealed it behind them. It was a surreal experience for Sam. He was riding atop the turret along with gunner Barry and loader Liam.

Barry kept shaking his head. "What do they actually mean by undead? I mean… they can't actually mean zombie, right?"

"Fucked if I know, G," said Sam. "They didn't cover this in Master Gunner Course?"

Liam shook his head gravely. "This has got to be an exercise of some kind. This isn't real. Although, you know zombies are based on a real thing."

Sam gave him a scornful look.

"It's true," insisted Liam. ""Y'know, when we talk about zombies, the whole concept goes way back, all the way to Haitian Vodou. It's a complex tapestry of African, indigenous Taino, and French Catholic traditions. In Vodou, a bokor, kind of a sorcerer, would use his magic to revive the dead...."

Sam sighed deeply. *Working with Liam is like working with a Goddamn professor. He seems to know everything about everything.*

"But here's the kicker," continued Liam excitedly. "These dead folks, these 'zombies', they'd come back without their souls. The bokor would control them, make 'em work, pretty much as his personal labor force. It's a real thing, swear to God. I saw a documentary on it once."

Sam shook his head. "You saw a mockumentary more like. There has never been such a thing as real zombies like in the movies."

Liam waved a finger in the air. "Now, they weren't the flesh-hungry monsters we see on the silver screen today," he said shaking his head. "No, they were more like pitiful figures, trapped under the bokor's spell. The whole brain-eating, rotting-corpse thing is a pretty recent, and I'd say, Hollywoodized, interpretation."

"So, it's Voodoo magic?" Sam said with a derisive snort.

"No magic," Liam said defensively. "It's chemicals. The documentary said that these bokor were using some form of neurotoxin, maybe something like the poison found in pufferfish, to induce a death-like state in their victims. Then, they'd use a hallucinogen, to keep 'em docile and compliant."

Sam spat. "But, as for us actually seeing real zombies walking around? That's still the stuff of movies and nightmares, right?"

Liam shrugged. Sam nodded.

"I am not so sure," said Liam. "Scientists keep sciencing you know. Coming up with all kinds of weird new shit."

"Nah! This is just a training exercise of some kind. We will get called back before we fire a shot."

"Straight after our semi-annual? I don't think so," responded Sam.

Sam looked at the traffic jam that had piled up at the toll booth. No cars had been allowed through for the last three hours. "They would not cause this mayhem for an exercise. Some shit's going down. I know it can't be... well I don't know what it is."

He could see fires coming from Oakland. *What the fuck is this? Am I really supposed to fire on our own citizens? The orders say clear the streets of Oakland. Permission to fire on our citizens. I can't remember ever hearing of rules of engagement that allow the taking of innocent lives, let alone innocent American lives.*

Sam saw a crowd of people running onto the bridge from the Oakland side. "I think we better close up," he said. "You too, Jones."

Jones coughed. "Ugh! I was really enjoying a bit of fresh air," he said mournfully.

Sam took a last look at Oakland, and then a quick look behind him at the barricades and retreated into the tank. He had noted that the marines were preparing to be attacked. It looked like they meant business. *Locked and loaded. Jesus… what am I going to do here. Am I really going to fire on American citizens. Can I do that?* He imagined being tried as a mass murderer. *You don't become a hero for harming innocents. There is such a thing as an illegal order. Should I declare this an illegal order and turn around? No.*

A few minutes later he watched on the monitors as the crowd reached the tanks and started running past them towards the barricades. Sam watched the rear-view monitor to see what the marines would do.

"Barry, you are clear on the ROE?"

Barry chuckled. "ROE is fuck 'em up."

Sam nodded. "That's about the size of it. But how do we tell the difference between the infected and …"

Gunfire erupted behind them. The marines had opened fire on the civilians. Sam's face went grim. "That's what the rules of engagement are, if in doubt take them out." He shook his head, not quite believing the situation.

Something caught his eye on the forward monitors. One of the civilians had just jumped on another. He saw black slime dripping from the attacker's mouth as it snarled and bit. *Well, that's what a zombie looks like in a movie.*

"Should we be lighting these up?" asked Barry.

Sam hesitated. "I'll use the MG."

He watched as one man wearing a suit and tie sunk his teeth into a woman in yoga pants. He aimed the machine gun at the man and gave a short burst of M80 rounds that tore the man, and the woman apart.

The driver brought the tank to a halt. "I can't go forward without driving over these civilians."

People started climbing over the tank. They began pounding on the outside.

"Jones…" began Sam, he wanted to order the driver to proceed forward, but he could not utter the words.

He saw the other tanks had stopped too. *It's instinctive, no one wants to kill innocents.* He remembered the Tank man of Tiananmen square. A whole column of tanks was stopped by one innocent man with two bags of groceries. *Later he was shot in some dark cell somewhere.*

The radio buzzed in his ear. He felt dizzy. He had to shake his head.

OVERLORD: "Alpha One, this is Overlord, over."

COMMANDER BUTCHEART: "Overlord, this is Alpha One, send your traffic, over."

OVERLORD: "Alpha One, despite current challenges, mission parameters require you to proceed forward. Disengage from current location and push towards objective, over."

COMMANDER BUTCHEART: "Understood, Overlord. Alpha One is Oscar Mike. Over and out."

"Jones…" Sam began again.

The sound of people pounding on the tank became deafening.

"I heard," said Jones and the engine revved, but the tank did not move.

"Jones!" shouted Liam.

"You have to go forward!" shouted Sam.

"Sir, I refuse to obey this order. It is not a legal order. I am not running over American citizens. I see children among them."

Sam was frozen. He watched the rear-view camera. The marines were obeying orders. They were cutting swathes of people down, but the horde was getting closer to them.

OVERLORD: "Alpha One, this is Overlord, over."

COMMANDER BUTCHEART: "Go ahead, Overlord. Alpha One listening, over."

OVERLORD: "Alpha One, I say again, you are to move forward and continue with the mission. This is a direct order. Over."

COMMANDER BUTCHEART: "Copy that, Overlord. Proceeding with mission. Alpha One out."

Sam took a deep breath. "Jones, just fucking go. The infected will reach San Francisco if you don't."

The engine revved again, but the tank did not move.

"Jones! Go!" Sam repeated.

The tank lurched forward a few feet then came to a halt.

Adrenaline pumped through Sam's system. "Jones!"

Jones just coughed.

"Jones, I am fucking ordering you to go forward."

Jones coughed again. Sam began to be concerned about him. In order to check on him he'd have to reposition the gun. He turned to Barry. "Five O'clock this fucker," he shouted.

The turret moved. "Liam, see what's going on with …" Sam saw something unusual in the hull ammo store. "Stop! What the fuck is that?"

Liam looked into the ammo store and saw some black liquid.

"That's not oil," said Liam.

Sam shook his head. "That wasn't there yesterday. Okay, keep moving the gun and then check on Jones."

The gun moved. Liam bent down to the cage door that separated the driver's section from the turret. "Jones?" said Liam.

Sam looked down at Liam just in time to see his eyes widen and his face turn white. Jones' face hit the cage door, his mouth snarling.

"Fuck me!" shouted Liam.

The gun moved cutting off access to the driver's area.

"How the fuck did that happen," said Sam. He looked through the periscope to see what was going on with the other tanks. One was ahead by a hundred yards but had stopped, the other was to their right. *I better let them know what's going on.*

A hiss filled the air from the radio. There was a garbled transmission. "…Alpha Two … Tango….returning…" It was the voice of Big Joe, the commander of tank two.

"Say again, speak slower," shouted Sam.

He looked through the periscope at tank two. It was veering right. *Are they turning back?"* The tank headed directly to the rails at the edge of the bridge. It did not stop.

"Joe!" shouted Sam.

The tank drove through the rails and off the side of the bridge.

Sam felt sick, he had to take a few deep breaths to calm his stomach. He could hear Jones snarling. *What the fuck do I now. I better report.*

COMMANDER BUTCHEART: "Overlord, this is Alpha One, over."

OVERLORD: "Alpha One, this is Overlord, send your traffic, over."

COMMANDER BUTCHEART: "Overlord, Alpha One is Tango Uniform. We have multiple infected on the hull; my driver is Whiskey India Alpha… infected. Alpha Two is in the drink. Require immediate assistance to RTB, over."

OVERLORD: "Alpha One, Overlord copies all. Standby for assistance, over."

Sam felt a bit better knowing that help was on the way. *They'll have to tow us back to base.* The snarling sounds from Jones were getting frantic. Sam felt like there was not enough oxygen in the air. He was sweating and felt dizzy again. He coughed and saw a small spray of black liquid hit the instruments in front of him. A deep chill ran down his spine as the radio crackled.

ALPHA THREE: "Alpha One, this is Alpha Three, over."

COMMANDER BUTCHEART: "Alpha Three, Alpha One, go ahead, over."

ALPHA THREE: "Alpha One, I'm looking at the big picture here. You've got to push forward, over. You've really got to push forward."

COMMANDER BUTCHEART: "Copy that, Alpha Three. We're really Tango Uniform…. Jones is sick. We're tits up. Alpha One out."

ALPHA THREE: "Fuck."

Sam looked down and saw Liam looking up at him frozen in fear. "You got it, don't you?" asked Liam.

Sam nodded. *How did I get infected? I was not bitten.* He felt an incredible surge of anger inside him, and he glared down at Liam and snarled. *I am turning into a zombie.* He thought about his parents, his girlfriend. He thought about his plans for a family. He closed his eyes and rested his head against the periscope.

We were sabotaged. Someone infected us before we headed out on this mission. There's a conspiracy. It's the only explanation.

He opened his eyes and stared out at the beautiful blue skies. He noticed Alpha Three's gun rotating until it pointed right at him. *What?* A sinking feeling settled on him and his last thought before the muzzle flash was … *of course…*

AMAND WILLARD –
THE CANYON

The Canyon

Amanda steered the Sprinter van, its headlights slicing through the inky blackness of the serpentine canyon road. Her fingers tensed on the wheel, knuckles whitening, as she navigated the relentless maze of twists and turns with a precision born of desperation. The silence inside the van was only broken by the occasional shifting of Bert in the passenger seat, handcuffed and eerily calm. His composure in the face of their grim situation set an undercurrent of unease curling within her, an unsettling counterpoint to the urgent roar of the engine and the quiet foreboding of the canyon around them.

A surprise awaited them as they rounded a bend—a crude roadblock, thrown together by a band of rugged, hardened locals. These were the infamous 'Canyon Critters,' who had a reputation for handling matters their own way. As the hulking forms of the Critters stepped forward to halt the van, their stern faces were bathed in the harsh, unflattering glare of the headlights, every line of wear and grime starkly defined.

Lowering the window with a shaky hand, Amanda pasted a tight smile on her face. "Good evening, gentlemen," she greeted, her voice a thin thread of cheer in the heavy, threatening silence.

Their penetrating eyes darted past her, latching onto the restrained figure of Bert in the back. A burly, heavily bearded figure, whose bulk seemed to fill the entire window frame, gestured towards him. "And what's his story?" he grunted, his gaze turning into a piercing stare.

The sight of the raw, inflamed bite mark marring Bert's leg seemed to be the visual validation of their nightmares. Amanda watched as a subtle, chilling transformation overcame their faces; eyes morphed into icy stones, fingers whitened around weapon handles, their stances taking on a deadly readiness.

"He's been infected," one of them pronounced, his voice a steel-edged decree.

Amanda's head whipped back and forth in frantic denial, her pulse hammering a frenzied rhythm against her ribs. "No, you're mistaken," she countered, a desperate undertone threading through her words. "It's not what it appears to be."

She could see they were not convinced.

"No, you have to believe me. I only handcuffed him out of an abundance of caution."

"And what reason do we have to trust your words?" the bearded man countered, his stare burrowing into Bert.

"Because I'm a medical professional," Amanda shot back, her voice steady even as fear snaked up her spine. "And that is a dog bite, not a human one. I can differentiate. Like I said, he's bound for precaution, nothing more."

The atmosphere grew tense as Amanda's words hung in the air, and the Canyon Critters traded skeptical glances. The cool night air seemed to hold its breath as they considered her plea. She felt beads of sweat start to form on her brow. Would they believe her? Or would they take matters into their own hands, as they were so known to do?

"He was bit last night, by a dog. I have my kid with me. I would not take any chances with my kid."

Slowly, doubt began to creep into the Critters' resolute expressions. They looked at Amanda, at Joshua and then at Bert, their brows furrowed in thought. Her professional assurance clashed with their primal instincts for survival.

The Critters talked amongst themselves. She could only hear a little of the back and forth of an argument. She heard a woman speaking. "East checkpoint barely held off. I think we'll know it when we get actual growlers on us."

Amanda could not hear the response as it was low and grumbled but she watched as they quietly deliberated amongst themselves, their hushed voices just a murmur against the wind rustling through the trees. She saw the bearded man glance back at her, then at Bert, his stern gaze softening slightly.

Then, after what seemed like an age, the bearded man sighed, nodded towards Amanda, and lowered his weapon.

"Alright," he finally grumbled, his eyes meeting Amanda's. "We'll trust your judgment, nurse. But know this, there are a lot of heavily armed folk in the canyon. If I were you, I would head straight on through to the other side without taking any detours."

The other Critters also lowered their weapons slightly. The blockade of bodies and suspicion that had seemed so impenetrable moments ago began to dissolve, allowing Amanda and her van to pass.

As they grudgingly moved aside, Amanda felt the taut knot of anxiety in her chest unravel. This minor triumph gave her a feeling of hope.

"Alright, nurse," the bearded man conceded, "but if he turns, it's on you."

With a nod of acknowledgment, Amanda rolled up her window and drove past the roadblock, her heart still racing. Now all she could do was hope that she was right about Bert's bite.

As the van hummed down the twisting canyon road, she flicked the radio back on, hoping for some good news amidst the dire updates. The announcer's voice filtered through the vehicle, filling the tense silence that had settled in the van.

"I'm afraid we have distressing updates from Oakland," the announcer began, his normally composed voice tinged with anxiety. "Reports are coming in that the tank crews dispatched to tackle the infection have...somehow...fallen victim to the contagion."

Amanda's grip tightened on the steering wheel, her knuckles whitening. The news hit her like a punch to the gut. *How could this be possible? Tanks should have been invulnerable...don't they have biological and chemical filter systems? How could they possibly be infected?*

"The Bay Bridge is now erupting in gunfire as marines attempt to keep the infection from spreading to San Francisco," continued the announcer. "The only way anything is getting past those marines is if they run out of ammunition."

The radio abruptly went silent. *That's weird,* she thought. *They were not finished with that news report.*

If the infection could reach a tank crew, who was truly safe?

A soft, insidious cough broke the tense silence left by the grim news report, resonating through the confines of the van. Amanda glanced in the rear-view mirror, her eyes falling on her two-year-old son, Joshua, nestled in the back seat. He was oddly quiet, unusually subdued; not even their tense encounter with the Canyon Critters had coaxed him into his usual lively chatter.

Consumed by concern, she guided the van onto a secluded spot off the main road, the gravel crunching under the tires and the quiet hum of the engine the only sounds in the still night. Unbuckling her seatbelt with shaky hands, she climbed into the back of the vehicle, her gaze never wavering from Joshua. Every instinct screamed at her to keep moving, to not expose them to the unknown threats lurking in the darkness, but her son needed her. And that overrode everything else.

His skin held an unnerving chill, a stark contrast to the moderate warmth of the night. The unhealthy pallor that tainted his once rosy cheeks sent a wave of fear crashing through Amanda. "Joshua, sweetheart," she murmured, her voice an uneven mix of forced calm and concealed dread. "Open your mouth, let mommy see your throat."

With what little strength he had left, Joshua obeyed. His small mouth parted in a feeble yawn, revealing not the expected pinkish hue of a healthy throat, but an ominous sight that froze Amanda's heart. Black, viscous ooze bubbled up from his throat, splattering onto Amanda's face as a violent cough wracked his tiny body.

An icy shock slammed into her, thrusting her into the harsh reality she'd been desperate to evade. This was the dreadful symptom, the irrefutable sign of infection. "Oh, God..." she whispered, the words barely more than a breath as the grim comprehension seeped into her consciousness. Joshua, her precious little boy, was infected.

She reached out and grabbed him, bringing him close and wrapping her arms around him in a smothering hug. She kissed the top of his head.

"Oh baby," she cooed.

Beside her, Bert recoiled, his hardened features twisted into a mask of pure horror that mirrored Amanda's own dread. His eyes,

170

usually so steady, were now blown wide, stark against the pallor that had stolen over his complexion. This was a man who had navigated life's harsh tides and weathered its stormy seas, but the sight of an innocent child gripped by the throes of the infection cut him to the core. The oppressive silence hung heavy between them, filled only with the harrowing echo of Joshua's labored breaths.

Slowly, she laid Joshua back and then wiped the black ooze from her face with unsteady hands, her heart aching as an uncompromising reality swept over her. She was a nurse, steeled in the crucible of combating disease and injury, yet this insidious infection rendered her utterly powerless. A stark terror took root within her—not only for Joshua, but for herself. The silent dread she had harbored for everyone in the face of this plague was now not a specter looming in the distance but a visceral, immediate truth. She sat back. "I…" she began. She shook her head, knowing she had no words. With a quiet resignation she reached over and unlocked Bert's handcuffs.

"You have more to fear from me, than I have from you," she said.

Bert put his hand on her shoulder. "So, what are you going to do now?"

Amanda stared at Joshua, her mind a whirlwind of fear and confusion. She was trained to diagnose, to treat, to comfort, but this...this was beyond her comprehension. She felt helpless, a feeling she despised more than anything else.

Only a few hours ago, Joshua had been his usual lively self. His laughter had filled their home, his energy infectious. Now, he lay still, his body racked with a mysterious illness, oozing black fluid from his mouth. A fluid she knew was a symptom of the infection ravaging her world.

As a nurse, she was used to being the source of answers, of reassurances, of hope. But now, she found herself plagued with questions, the weight of her fear threatening to crush her. How had Joshua contracted the infection? They had been careful, incredibly so. Was it airborne now, mutating beyond their understanding? Or had he somehow come into contact with an infected individual or object?

Maybe he had been exposed in daycare. Hadn't he mentioned others were sick there? Then there was Meredith's Daryl, who had obviously been infected. Just how contagious was this thing?

The most chilling question of all: was this infection a death sentence? Did every infected person eventually turn into one of those horrific creatures? The mere thought of Joshua, her sweet, innocent son, turning into one of them, was unthinkable. And if he was infected, didn't that mean she was too?

If he turned, she realized she could not end his reanimated form. She would rather be his first victim than his executioner. Harming him was…inconceivable.

What was she supposed to do now? Who could she turn to for help? How could she save her son from this unknown, deadly force?

Her medical knowledge was a weapon she had wielded with confidence throughout her career. Now, it felt like she was holding a blunt sword in a battle against a monstrous enemy. Yet, she knew she had no choice but to face this challenge head on. She had to figure out how to navigate this horrifying new reality, not just for her own sake, but for her son's.

This was a battle she could not afford to lose.

A long silence had filled the van as she contemplated her options. "I am not going to just assume that there's no hope," she said.

"That's the spirit, girl," Bert encouraged, his eyes gleaming. He was a fighter, he wasn't ready to give up, and that determination seemed to fuel Amanda's own resolve.

"Yes," she confirmed, her voice steadying as clarity began to replace her initial panic. "There's something I have. Zolga." She paused; her eyes clouded with realization. Her friend at the hospital had salvaged this experimental drug from the incinerator, understanding its potential. It was designed to combat the most drug resistant bacterial infections, ones that had started to rear their ugly heads with an alarming frequency at her clandestine free clinic.

Bert raised his eyebrows. "Zolga?" He paused, considering her words. "So, it's an antibiotic?"

"No, not exactly," she clarified. "Zolga is a gene therapy. It delivers a gene into the patient's cells. The gene it delivers is designed to fight multi-resistant bacteria."

Amanda couldn't help the excitement creeping into her voice. Could this be their lifeline? Could Zolga hold the key to fighting the infection?

Turning to the side, Amanda slid open a concealed compartment in the van. This was her secret stash, a collection of illicit prescriptions she had gathered over the years. Stored in an innocuous antacid bottle was the drug that might be their salvation—Zolga.

The problem with Zolga was the high percentage of patients who could not tolerate it. Whenever Zolga was administered a crash team had to be kept on constant vigil. It was one of the most dangerous drugs ever approved. It was for no hope situations.

She remembered denying it for use on Daryl because of the risks…but at that time, she did not know how ruthless the infection was and what dire creatures emerged when a patient lost their battle with it.

Her hands trembled as she picked up the bottle. She couldn't help but consider the magnitude of what she was about to do. It was a risk, a leap into the unknown. But then again, wasn't that the nature of desperation? She mused, her mind spinning, "History must be full of people like us, in desperate times trying desperate solutions." Looking at the small pills, she knew that their chances were slim. "A long shot is definitely better than no shot."

Unscrewing the bottle, she gently tipped a pill into her palm.

There was no way to know if it would work. It was a hail Mary pass. But in this desperate hour, she clung to that slim ray of hope, that chance for a miracle.

"Joshua, swallow this," she said and put the pill in his mouth.

He looked at it suspiciously. "Mmmm yummy," she said.

He swallowed, closed his eyes, and returned to sleep.

Have I just sentenced him to death? The way that black stuff hit me, I must be infected too. She then took a pill herself. *If it is a death sentence than I will join you my little Jo Jo.*

She closed her eyes for a moment and imagined infected versions of her and Joshua wandering through the canyon attacking hapless inhabitants, creating more infected. *I don't want to be part of the problem.*

What if the black stuff kills me, but not Jo Jo? What if the pill kills me, but not Jo Jo?

A thoughtful silence ensued, with Bert's gaze settling on Joshua. "How...when will we know if it worked?" he asked, his voice laced with anxiety.

Amanda's throat clenched at the question. "I honestly don't know, Bert," she admitted after a long pause.

Suddenly, she turned to look at him, her gaze piercing. "Tell me the truth now, were you bitten by a dog?"

"I swear," Bert nodded fervently, meeting her gaze squarely. "It was a dog."

Inhaling deeply, she managed a decisive nod. "It's only right...to act responsibly," she began, her voice laced with a stoicism that belied the turmoil within her. If she and Joshua were fated to morph into those horrifying creatures, they couldn't be allowed to add to the carnage. "We should be secured...handcuffed to the chair." She swallowed the lump in her throat, her resolve hardening. "We won't become another threat, another source of misery."

A bleak decision indeed, yet it remained their only safeguard against becoming the monsters they were striving to evade. Following Amanda's sobering directive, Bert set about the melancholy task of securing both mother and child to the chair. Each snap of the cuffs resonated with a heavy finality within the strained silence of the van. Bert's every movement was deliberate, measured with painstaking care—as though the tiniest misstep might topple the delicate balance they were desperately maintaining. He smiled a feigned expression of reassurance, but his hands trembled slightly, betraying the deep-seated fear lurking beneath the surface.

Once the task was complete, he retreated, his eyes anchored on Amanda and Joshua. A potent cocktail of dread, compassion, and impotence bled through his hardened exterior. The scene before him—a mother and her child shackled to a chair.

A heavy silence fell between them; words seemed redundant, powerless. Their collective hopes rested on the success of the treatment, on the slim chance of awakening from this macabre dream. As for Bert, he was sentenced to the sidelines, his heart burdened by the precarious nature of the forthcoming hours, a silent observer to their agonizing wait.

Joshua stared at Bert. Bert stuck his tongue out at him, making the little boy laugh. Amanda smiled. Bert looked at her. "You two are like angels," he said.

"Tell me a funny," said Joshua.

Amanda shook her head. She could not think of any jokes.

"Tell me a funny," repeated Joshua.

"Why did the pony lose its voice?" said Bert.

Joshua smiled.

"Because it was a little horse," said Bert.

Joshua laughed. Amanda chuckled. "You know, he didn't really understand that."

Bert gave Joshua a big grin. "I only know 25 letters of the alphabet—I just don't know y."

Joshua laughed again. Amanda shook her head.

"I'm so good at sleeping that I can do it with my eyes closed!" said Bert.

Joshua laughed and coughed. Amanda took a deep breath as she closed her eyes and gave Joshua a kiss on the head.

"I think we should go to sleep now," Amanda suggested, her voice barely above a whisper.

Bert nodded, his gaze drifting out the window of the van. "The horde will find us here. I need to move the van somewhere less conspicuous."

She nodded and Bert moved into the driver's seat, coaxing the van to life with a gentle turn of the ignition key. She watched as he navigated the winding labyrinth of canyon streets, his gaze vigilant, scrutinizing the unfamiliar surroundings for an inconspicuous haven. His eyes eventually settled on a small dirt road, barely noticeable off the main artery, its entrance draped in a curtain of overgrown vegetation suggesting long years of abandonment. Steering the vehicle onto the unpaved path, the van rustled a symphony against the untamed undergrowth, receding deeper into the welcoming solitude.

After a few more twists and turns, he found a suitable spot. A small clearing surrounded by trees, hidden from the main road. It was as good a place as any, offering some semblance of safety and concealment. He parked the van, killing the engine.

Silence descended upon them. As Amanda and Joshua settled in for the night, Bert took one last look at their surroundings. It wasn't much, but it was something—a tiny respite in the heart of chaos. And for now, that was enough.

"Goodnight," said Bert as he pushed the seat into a tilted back position.

"Goodnight," mumbled Amanda.

With a soft click, Bert switched off the van's headlights, plunging them into the comforting anonymity of darkness. Outside, the world was still, the hushed rustling of leaves and the occasional call of a night bird the only reminders of the life that once thrived in these parts. The air was heavy with a foreboding silence, as if the world was holding its breath, waiting for the dawn of a new day or the end of it all.

In the dim light filtering through the van's windows, Amanda was a study in resolve, even as she descended into slumber. Her eyes, though closed, bore the weight of the world. Her hands, now secured by cold steel, had once healed and comforted. Beside her, little Joshua slept soundly, oblivious to the horror that was slowly consuming them and their world. His innocent face, untouched by the ravages of their reality, was a stark contrast to the terror that loomed over them.

For now, all any of them could do was wait and hope—hope that the dawn would bring a miracle, not a nightmare.

PROFESSOR MARK PRESTON –
THE WHITE HOUSE

Whitehouse on War Setting

ncased within the fortified walls of the situation room, Mark Preston felt the weight of the President's gaze upon him. The President's aide, after conferring in hushed whispers, introduced him, "Remember, this is Professor Mark Preston, from the CDC, sir." President Mitchel's gaze hardened; the stern set of his jaw highlighted by the harsh overhead lighting.

"Ah, yes," President Mitchel murmured, his words slicing through the tense silence. "You're more in your element with lab coats and Petri dishes, not battle strategies and weaponry." The President's words carried a bitter sting, and Mark bristled, a sensation of unease creeping up his spine. His gaze fell upon the table strewn with classified reports and elaborate dossiers, each one a testament to the critical situation they faced.

"Your recommendation of deploying tanks was ill-advised. From here on, let's leave the military decisions to the professionals," the President continued, his voice icy. Mark's earlier plan, a desperate attempt to combine his knowledge of biology and the brute force of the military, had failed miserably.

"Are you a religious man, professor?" asked the President.

It was an unexpected question and momentarily took Mark out of his thoughts and into his memories. "I used to be. My wife and I would enjoy the services."

"Then?"

"If there is a God, sir, then we have fallen out." Mark's reply was soft. *I have seen what passes for God's work in the pediatric oncology wards, and...* The memory of his wife was too painful to revisit.

The President sneered at him. "So far, you have failed to come up with any actionable plan for this outbreak, and your military tactics have been disastrous...and now I learn even your spiritual life is a failure. A life of defeat...perhaps that is the fate for all men of medicine. You always lose that battle against death in the end."

The bitter taste of defeat lingered, magnified by the President's reproachful words, settled in his stomach like leaden weights. But even as he stood at the receiving end of the President's disappointment, Mark's resolve hardened. His eyes met the President's, acknowledging the reprimand but also holding an unspoken promise—he wouldn't back down, not while lives were still at stake.

"Those tanks were our best shot, Mr. President," Mark retorted, a ripple of frustration breaking through the professional veneer in his voice. "They had state-of-the-art anti-biochemical filters; they were designed to be impregnable, both to chemicals, infection and to physical intrusion, especially from unarmed assailants..." He paused, the word hanging heavily in the room, a grotesque understatement of the reality they faced. "...such as these...growling infected victims." His voice dropped to a near whisper, the term still sounding jarringly out of place in the grave environment of the situation room. His fingers clenched into fists at his sides, the gleam in his eyes revealing a fiery determination that refused to be extinguished. Despite the setback, he was far from admitting defeat.

President Mitchel nodded, his face grim. "Growlers, people are calling them. And yet, the infection breached their defenses. It's adapting faster than we can counter."

Mark dragged his fingers through his hair, a gesture of deep frustration and bewilderment. His usually neat locks now stood in disarray, much like his thoughts. "I can't say it evolved," he admitted, his gaze intense, lost in the uncertainty of their situation. "The truth is, we're still grappling in the dark. We don't fully comprehend what has transpired." His words, laced with discomfort, seemed to linger in the tense air, a stark admission of their shared fear and confusion.

The President emitted a derisive snort, his eyes hardened with resolve. "Exactly. We might be in the dark about the nature of this infection, but I'll tell you one thing I do understand," he declared, slamming his hand on the table for emphasis. "A tactical nuclear explosion obliterates everything in its path, infected or not." His words echoed ominously in the confined space, causing a murmur of shock among the present officials. "We'll reduce Oakland to ashes and then let the Marines sweep clean whatever remnants are left." His decision was firm, leaving no room for further debate.

The President's stern declaration triggered a flurry of whispers among his staff, their bodies huddling close around him, a living barrier between him and the dismissed academic. Disdain dripped from his icy gaze as it met Mark's. "You're dismissed, Professor," he stated tersely, the scorn in his voice clear as day. "This nation is at war. We don't have room for white-haired scholars in this battle." His tone echoed finality, his glare a silent command to leave the war room.

"The nuclear option is the only viable solution, sir. A thorough cleansing," chimed in a rigid military advisor, his uniform as starched as his unwavering belief in the plan. His face, hardened by years of war strategies and battlefield outcomes, held no trace of doubt. "It's the sole way to guarantee the containment of this infection."

With a vehement shake of his head, Mark shattered the growing accord. "You don't extinguish a bacterial outbreak with a nuke," he asserted with impassioned intensity, the fire in his eyes undimmed by the resistant room. "That's not the mechanics of disease control. You might just be igniting a disaster far more devastating."

A staff aide lightly rested his hand on Mark's shoulder, a silent echo of the President's terse dismissal. With a weary nod, Mark closed his eyes momentarily, shielding the world away. A heavy sigh slipped past his lips, carrying the weight of his disappointment and frustration. Then he pivoted and strode out of the situation room.

Exhausted from the draining encounter, he navigated the eerie quiet and dimly lit hallways of the White House towards his assigned cubicle. Each echo of his footsteps seemed to pound against his skull, echoing his own emotional turmoil. When he finally reached his small workspace, he sank into the threadbare chair, the comforting cradle of worn upholstery welcoming his weary frame. His head dropped onto the cool surface of his cluttered desk, the faint scent of old papers and sterile office supplies filling his senses. The steady hum of the overhead fluorescent light was his lullaby, lulling him into a deep, much-needed slumber within moments.

His dreams were plagued by a parade of disturbing images—throngs of the infected advancing with unholy speed, their lifeless eyes devoid of any humanity, tanks being swarmed over like children's toys, and the chilling finality of a nuclear explosion. Even in sleep, he couldn't escape the horror that had befallen the world.

He awoke with a start, the haunting remnants of his nightmares still lingering. The cubicle was bathed in the sickly yellow light of a dying fluorescent tube, casting long, distorted shadows that seemed to writhe in the corners of his vision. Mark's gaze fell upon his desk, scattered with research notes and a disarray of hastily scrawled hypotheses about the infection. His eyes traced the faint outline of a microscope in the corner, a reminder of his fight against an enemy that was too small to see but too large to comprehend.

He pulled himself upright, the weight of his mission pressing heavily on his shoulders. His reflection stared back at him from the dark screen of his laptop—a man out of his element, yet the only hope against an impending apocalypse. As his fingers hovered over the keyboard, the dire consequences of failure, the countless lives that depended on his success, churned in his gut like a physical force.

All I have to do is figure out how to fight the infected, persuade these morons to let the scientists analyze the pathogen, come up with a vaccine or a cure and then sell it to the idiot in chief.

And though the odds seemed insurmountable, he knew he had to press on. If not him, then who?

The ticking of the wall clock, the only other sound in the dead silence of the night, was a grim reminder of time slipping away. Every second counted in this battle. He had to find a solution, he had to save humanity, and he had to do it fast.

BILLY HALLSON – THE CANYON

Uncle Joe

Through the static hum of the truck's radio, Billy clung to the updates that trickled in. Each new broadcast painted a grimmer picture: the infection was galloping through the Bay Area like wildfire, outpacing all containment efforts. Oakland was lost, unreachable even by the might of tanks, and San Francisco teetered on the edge, kept afloat solely by the desperate tenacity of the marines. Now, the radio buzzed with anticipatory silence, the hollow pause before a Presidential address. Billy could almost feel the nation holding its collective breath, awaiting guidance in a world spiraling out of control.

As he steered his way through the canyon's winding maze, Billy felt an unsettling disconnection from himself, as if he was a passenger in his own body. The threat of violence hung in the air, a palpable presence that gnawed at his focus, scattering his thoughts and dulling his sense of direction. Darkness had swallowed the canyon whole, reducing the world to vague shapes and shadows that played tricks on his eyes. The unending web of side roads, each one a serpent's knot of twists and turns, pulled him deeper into disorientation, reflecting the chaos unfurling in his mind.

After a seeming eternity behind the wheel, a dirt road appeared like a long-lost friend amidst the night's obscurity. Landmarks jumped out from the darkness, each a beacon pulling him back from disorientation—an ancient tree stump twisted into gnarled forms by time, a boulder crowned with a vibrant quilt of moss, and the gentle murmur of a stream cutting through the silence. It was as though the canyon itself breathed a sigh of relief with him. Every muscle in his body uncoiled as a tangible wave of relief crashed over him, grounding him back to reality. He was on the right path, at last.

Just as Billy's tires began to crunch on the gravel of the driveway, the radio announcer's tinny voice punctured the silence, a dire herald, "Ladies and Gentlemen, President Mitchel is about to address the nation."

An icy tendril of apprehension snaked its way down Billy's spine, and he halted the truck, hands gripping the wheel tightly. The silence that followed was suffocating, as if the world itself held its breath. Then, the President's voice cut through the night—it wasn't just the voice of a man, but the echo of a nation's fears and determination, hardened by grim resolve.

"Ladies and gentlemen, fellow Americans, I am speaking to you on a matter of utmost urgency and grave national concern. The past few hours have been trying, filled with loss and fear. Our strength as a nation, as a people, is being tested like never before. And I want to assure you, we are responding to this challenge head-on.

Our response has been swift and decisive, but the threat we face is of a magnitude that necessitates drastic measures. The city of Oakland is now under the shadow of an unprecedented threat. The infection has spread rapidly, defying containment efforts, turning our friends and neighbors into creatures we can barely recognize.

Our best scientists, doctors, and military strategists have been working round the clock to devise a solution. It is with a heavy heart that I announce the necessity of an extreme course of action. In order to curb this infection, to protect our nation, and to ensure the future of our people, we will deploy a tactical nuclear strike on Oakland.

I understand the sheer magnitude of this decision and the inevitable consequences it brings. Our primary concern is to safeguard as many lives as possible. If you are within Oakland city or in the surrounding areas, I implore you, seek underground shelter immediately. Time is of the essence.

The blast radius of the device will be approximately seven miles, and anyone caught in the open within a range of about fifteen miles may experience severe burns. So, I repeat, seek shelter immediately.

The coming days will be hard, and the losses, significant. But remember, we are Americans. We endure. We overcome. This too shall pass.

God bless you all, and God bless the United States of America."

Thank God Uncle Joe has a bunker, thought Billy. *The geography of the canyon should offer some protection, though.*

His headlights slashed through the darkness, illuminating an odd spectacle that momentarily snatched his attention. Tucked away in the dense underbrush flanking the driveway was a van. Its presence was an anomaly, a jigsaw piece refusing to meld with the rest of the picture. He squinted, straining his eyes against the inky darkness as he eased his foot off the gas pedal, striving to pick out further details from this unexpected enigma.

This is definitely on Uncle Joe's property. He stopped the truck and got out.

Breathing as softly as possible, he edged closer to the van. His only weapon was his set of car keys, their cold, metallic edges pressing uncomfortably into his clenched palm. Swallowing hard, he tried to steady his voice, to mask the fear gnawing at his insides. "Anyone in there?" he called out, his words echoing in the silent night.

An eerie silence swallowed his words before the creaky van door abruptly swung open, revealing a man with his hands raised in surrender. "Don't shoot!" he implored, his eyes squinting against the harsh glare of Billy's headlights. His voice was raspy, etched with a desperation that echoed the tension of the night.

Billy surveyed him, a practiced eye taking in the stranger's frantic state and his disheveled appearance. The grime-streaked face, the wide, terrified eyes—telltale signs of a struggle for survival. "Is there anyone else inside?" he queried, his voice threaded with caution, yet underpinned by an inherent kindness, a humanity amidst the chaos.

There was a momentary pause, the man's gaze flicking anxiously back to the shadowy interior of the van. Uncertainty flitted across his features, hinting at concerns left unsaid. With a swallow that bobbed his Adam's apple noticeably, he finally responded, his voice shaking with barely concealed trepidation. "Yes," he admitted, the word hanging heavy in the night air.

"Name's Billy," he offered, extending a hand, despite the distance between them. "Who might you be?"

"Bert," the man responded, lowering his hands but maintaining a cautious stance. "Inside's Amanda and her little boy, Joshua. She's a nurse."

Billy's brow furrowed. "Did you catch the announcement?" he asked, his tone serious.

The question seemed to catch Bert off guard. "Announcement?" He looked genuinely confused.

"The President's gonna nuke Oakland," he revealed, the gravity of the situation heavy in his voice. "He said to seek underground shelter immediately. My Uncle has a bunker nearby, reckon we should head there."

Bert's silence stretched on, filling the space between them with an undeniable tension. Billy felt a surge of impatience. "What's the hold-up?" he pressed, anxiety knotting in his stomach.

Bert seemed to battle with his thoughts for a moment before finally gesturing towards the van. "The woman and her kid...they're infected," he confessed, his voice carrying a weight of sorrow.

Billy's breath stopped in his throat. The word 'infected' hung in the air like a specter, chilling his blood. The risk of being near those infected was a terrifying prospect, making his body tingle with an icy chill. But at the forefront of his mind, he saw a mother and her child, vulnerable and in danger. Could he, in good conscience, abandon them to face this nightmare alone?

I left the entire city in my rearview mirror because I felt I couldn't help, but these people...maybe...there again, the risk...

"Have they turned?" he asked.

Bert shook his head.

Then there's hope, thought Billy. "How long ago were they bit?" he inquired, his mind racing with the implications.

Bert shook his head again. "They were not bit, they just got sick."

How does this sickness work? This black stuff...is it a cause or a symptom? I don't know these people. They might shoot and rob me the moment I try to help. Jesus, Billy! What's the point of living if you turn your back on everyone you meet?

"There might still be hope, Bert," Billy began, a tentative optimism seeping into his voice. "There's a possibility that this infection has an airborne component to it."

Bert's eyebrows knitted together in confusion, his gaze full of doubt. "How can you be so sure?"

I didn't say I was sure, he thought. He ran his fingers through his hair, his mind racing back to the horrifying scene he had witnessed earlier. "I saw a woman turn... She wasn't injured, she was just eating lunch."

"And if it's airborne, so what?" asked Bert.

"I think it's worth considering, Bert," Billy said, an intense earnestness in his voice. "We've all been breathing the same East Bay air, haven't we? Perhaps some of us have a natural immunity? Perhaps getting this black… stuff, is not a death sentence. Maybe the body can fight it."

The glimmer of hope in Bert's eyes was almost painful to see. "You mean, some of us might not turn, even if we're bitten?"

Billy hesitated, not wanting to give false hope. "Well…everyone I saw that was bitten turned, so I'm afraid a bite might always be fatal. But the airborne particles... perhaps in smaller doses, we might stand a chance."

I'm just making this shit up as I go. I don't know what I am talking about.

Bert nodded, slowly taking in this new information. "The nurse...Amanda...she had some medicine. She and her son took it. I don't know if it'll make a difference."

"In times like these, we got to help each other. Don't you think?" Billy asked. He thought about everyone he had seen in the city, that he had felt he could not help. The teller in the bank, the people in the tunnel and the men at the roadblock. At any point he could have tried harder to warn them, or even offered to fight side by side with them. *Instead, I ran away.*

Bert nodded. "I sure do," he responded. "But you understand, it is a risk?"

"I understand," Billy responded, his voice barely above a whisper. His mind spun with the enormity of their situation. He cast a glance toward the van, picturing Amanda and Joshua huddled inside, their fate balanced on a knife's edge. "But listen, Bert...if there's even a sliver of a chance they can beat this, we can't afford not to take it. If they're above ground when that bomb goes off..."

Bert regarded Billy, a flicker of surprise lighting his weary eyes. He offered no objection, merely nodded slowly, his throat working as he swallowed. As he pulled open the rear door of the van, Billy ventured a glance inside.

Handcuffed to the passenger seat were Amanda and Joshua. They were huddled together, their faces pale and etched with fear. Amanda's eyes, bright despite her obvious exhaustion, were wide and cautious as they flickered between Billy and Bert. Joshua clung tightly to her, his small form shivering despite the warm night. The tangible fear emanating from them hit Billy like a physical blow.

Billy's gaze softened as he absorbed the disheartening scene before him: the mother and son, holding each other, fearful and helpless.

I am not sure what Uncle Joe will say, but I got to help them.

"Hey," he said, his tone an island of calm in the chaotic night. "My name's Billy. We're going to get you both to safety, alright?"

Amanda managed a feeble nod, a small spark of hope flickering in her dull eyes. Joshua, however, continued to stare at Billy, his wide, frightened eyes reflecting the harsh light of the van's interior. The innocence marred by terror was a sight Billy would never forget.

Billy swung his gaze back to Bert. "Unlock them," he commanded, his voice threaded with urgency. "Every second counts now."

Bert's eyes flickered with a brief struggle, weighing the risks, but the gravity of the situation won out. With a sigh, he retrieved the key from his pocket and moved to free the captives.

As the metallic clink of the cuffs echoed in the van, Billy shifted his attention back to Amanda and Joshua. "We're heading to a bunker owned by my Uncle Joe," he quickly explained. "It's close, fortified, and our best bet against the impending nuclear strike. Are you both capable of walking?"

Amanda nodded, her throat bobbing with a hard swallow, her determination evident despite her fear. "Yes," she replied, her voice barely above a whisper.

Billy mustered a small but reassuring smile. "Good. That's good. We need to move. Now."

Billy navigated the truck up the serpentine path towards Uncle Joe's house, the silence of the night unbroken except for the low grumble of the vehicle's engine. This tranquility was abruptly and violently shattered when a torrent of intense, stark white light flooded the vehicle. It was as if daylight had intruded upon the night, blinding in its ferocity. Shielding his eyes against the merciless glare, Billy felt his heartbeat accelerate into a thunderous rhythm.

The piercing light was not from a nuclear blast though, it originated from the direction of Uncle Joe's house, it was a powerful spotlight, a precautionary measure that his Uncle Joe had installed long ago. Billy could still recall the day his uncle had proudly demonstrated it, boasting about the spotlight's capacity to transform midnight into midday, a formidable deterrent against trespassers. His Uncle's words echoed in his mind now, an eerie prophecy as they faced this onslaught of the infected.

"What the hell," Billy muttered, instinctively throwing an arm up to shield his eyes from the blinding onslaught. He recognized this beacon as a sentinel of safety, marking the end of their treacherous journey. Yet, he was gripped by an unsettling realization—the challenge now was not the journey, but convincing the person who held the reins of that brilliant light that they were friends, not foes. The intensity of the light mirrored the severity of their plight, heightening the urgency thrumming through his veins.

"Uncle Joe! Turn off the damn light!" Billy hollered into the engulfing brightness, his voice a jagged shard of desperation cutting through the relentless hum of the spotlight. He desperately hoped his familiar tone would resonate in the ears of the operator. "It's me, Billy!" he reiterated, his words an echo in the quiet night.

"Who you got with you?" Uncle Joe's voice boomed back, rough as sandpaper yet cloaked in undeniable concern. Relief washed over Billy like a wave, the tight knot of worry in his chest untangling at the sound of that familiar timbre. His Uncle Joe—a man of few words, but each one weighted with wisdom and care. His voice was a rugged lighthouse amidst the chaos, a signal that they were not alone.

"I've got a man named Bert, and a woman with her kid, Amanda and Joshua," Billy called back, his voice steady despite the piercing glare of the light in his eyes. "Amanda and Joshua are ill, Uncle Joe. They're...they're infected." A prolonged silence stretched out from the other end, punctuated only by the relentless drone of the spotlight and the eerie cries of the infected, their mournful howls carried on the cool night breeze.

"Infected?" Uncle Joe's voice bounced back, the undercurrent of concern crystal clear.

Billy took a deep, shaky breath. "Yes, Uncle Joe," he confessed. "But they haven't turned. They weren't bit. They might just get better. We're here seeking refuge in your bunker. I don't know if you heard the announcement about the bomb, but time isn't on our side." A tense beat of silence stretched out, the weight of the decision hanging in the air. Then, almost as a sigh of relief, the spotlight's unforgiving glare faded away, replaced by the soft, inviting illumination of the porch light.

"Billy, you always were a softie," said Joe. "But you need to harden your heart. You need to be practical. You can't bring an infected in, it's too dangerous."

"They have handcuffs. We can keep them restrained until…well, until either they get better or…they don't."

Billy could only watch the dimly-lit silhouette of Uncle Joe in the distance, his sturdy figure paused at the edge of the porch light. He could practically feel the older man wrestling with the decision, the heavy weight of it hanging in the air between them. The regular hum of the floodlight was a steady heartbeat in the silence. The occasional distant cries of the infected seemed to underscore the urgency of the situation, an eerie soundtrack to their grim reality. Billy knew his uncle was a pragmatic man, hardened by years of dealing with life's challenges, but this was an agonizing decision. Choosing between potentially compromising the safety of his refuge or turning away a desperate family facing certain death was a choice no man should have to make.

As the silence stretched on, Billy found his hope dwindling. He knew his Uncle Joe too well—the man's practicality, his willingness to make the hard choices for the sake of survival. As much as he wanted to believe otherwise, he felt a sinking sensation in his gut. He understood, logically, that allowing an infected mother and child into the bunker was a risk, a dangerous gamble that could compromise the safety of everyone else inside. But the understanding did nothing to ease the dread pooling in his stomach, the knowledge of the fate that would befall Amanda and Joshua should they be turned away.

Uncle Joe's voice cut through the cool night air, rough as sandpaper, but its hardness couldn't mask the undercurrent of concern. "Alright, get in. But make it quick," he ordered. The gruffness of his words betrayed an attempt to maintain control, a veneer over the worry gnawing at his composure.

Relief washed over Billy as he heard Uncle Joe's consent. "Thank you, Uncle," he whispered, more to himself than anyone else. Quickly, he turned to Bert. "Let's get them out and get inside quickly," he said, already unbuckling his seatbelt.

Navigating the final stretch of the rough-hewn path, Billy was beset by a whirl of conflicting emotions. Relief, like a long-awaited exhale, for having found refuge, yet a deep-seated apprehension prickling under his skin. Their temporary sanctuary was but a small lull in the storm. The weight of their grim reality bore down on him, a reminder that the darkness of the night was pregnant with threats yet unseen.

Under the harsh glare of the porch light, they approached Uncle Joe, with Billy in the lead. Joe, a silhouette against the softly lit backdrop of his house, held a formidable shotgun trained on them. Billy raised his hands in a placating gesture, trying to calm the tension. "They weren't bitten. They weren't bitten," he repeated, his voice steady despite the unnerving sight of the weapon. "They might not turn. They've taken some medicine."

Joe looked at the woman and little boy. "Are you sure they are okay with being restrained?"

"Absolutely," Billy responded without hesitation, his voice firm. But even as he answered, he couldn't help but feel a pang of guilt seeing the fear etched on their faces. He turned to look at Amanda and Bert. They gave reluctant nods, their eyes as wide as saucers, glistening with fear under the porch light. Yet, amidst the fear, there was a glimmer of understanding—they were acutely aware of the knife-edge on which their survival balanced.

"Good," Uncle Joe grumbled, the tight lines around his eyes easing just a bit as he slightly lowered the shotgun. However, his weathered finger remained firmly near the trigger, ready for any sign of a threat. "It's purely a precaution, y'understand. This darned disease... we don't know the first thing about how it spreads. Until we get a grip on that, we're playin' it safe. Y'all will remain restrained till we're sure you're no threat to us." His voice was gruff, underpinned by a firmness that underscored his seriousness. His gaze, though hard, held a touch of regret—the restraint was a necessary cruelty in the face of an unthinkable threat.

Amanda turned her gaze to Billy, her eyes wide and shimmering with questions and unspoken pleas.

"We're really grateful," Amanda said.

Billy could only return her look with a sorrowful, apologetic expression. His heart twisted in his chest. *I can't believe we're going to keep a toddler handcuffed.*

This bleak reality of their new world allowed no room for empathy to cloud judgment. Trust had become a premium they could scarcely afford, and survival took precedence.

Suddenly, the once tranquil, ivory expanse of the sky was overwhelmed by a blinding burst of white, transforming the peaceful night into a spectacle of intense luminosity.

Holy shit, it's the nuke.

PROFESSOR MARK PRESTON –
THE WHITE HOUSE

Whitehouse Prepares for Siege

✳

Stirred from his semi-conscious state, Mark felt the world rocking slightly as if he were on the deck of a ship. He blinked open his bleary eyes to see his young intern, his face etched with a mix of worry and excitement, looming over him, gripping a manila folder in his trembling hands.

"Professor Preston," the intern stammered, a note of reverence edging into his urgency, "We've sequenced the DNA of the bacteria. The report's right here." He extended the folder, its corners crinkled from his nervous grip, towards the awakening scientist.

Already! This is crazy fast. Suspiciously fast, actually.

With heavy eyelids, he accepted the folder, his eyes flicking back and forth as they scanned the executive summary. "Derived from Deinococcus Radiodurans," he muttered to himself. His breath hitched as the implications began to take form. "This bacterium...it's a radiation survivor...even thriving within nuclear reactors." His pulse raced, his surprise making the room feel suddenly very small and quiet.

The implication of his discovery sent a shiver down his spine. He shot a glance at his intern. "How long have I been asleep?" he asked hurriedly.

The intern shrugged. "I'm not sure, Professor. I wasn't here when you nodded off. There's more, sir, on page six."

With a sense of growing unease, Mark quickly flipped to the indicated page. "The bacteria is merely a carrier...the actual pathogen is a modified adenovirus housed within the bacteria. Jesus Christ," he breathed.

The intern's face wrinkled in a mix of worry and confusion. "Is...is that a significant detail, professor? Should we be worried?"

Mark's mind was racing, trying to untangle the implications of this revelation. "Significant?" He looked up, his eyes meeting the intern's. "An adenovirus is tiny; it could bypass most biofilters and masks."

"And that's not all," he continued, frantically flipping through the rest of the pages. "An adenovirus can be modified to carry any sort of genetic payload. This particular one has been engineered to disrupt the neural networks in the brain, causing the infected to lose all sense of self-preservation and turn aggressive."

There is no way the CDC completed this analysis so quickly. What does that mean? Someone, somewhere, already had this information ready to go, and they are just feeding it to me now...how do I even know this is accurate? Maybe

I am getting misinformation. No, it fits what we've been seeing. I will have to find out how we did this analysis so quickly, but that can wait. First, I need to think about the implications of this dual action pathology.

Sinking back into his chair, Mark was overwhelmed by the magnitude of the discovery. The bacteria was merely a Trojan horse, shielding and transporting the real weapon to its unsuspecting victims. The adenovirus was the epitome of biological warfare—minuscule, readily spread, and terrifyingly versatile. The full horror of the situation struck him, leaving him feeling like he'd been punched in the gut.

He turned to his intern, his expression hardening into one of grave resolve. "We're not simply dealing with a pandemic—we're up against a meticulously crafted biological weapon. If the tanks have been breached...it implies our existing containment measures have failed spectacularly. We've been blind, addressing this from entirely the wrong perspective." He noted the intern's stricken expression, the color draining from his face at Mark's grim revelations.

"The President is in the dark about the true nature of this bacteria—its insusceptibility to radiation. If they unleash a nuclear weapon, it won't annihilate the infection, but rather, invigorate its proliferation due to the blast wave. The resultant shockwave would send it soaring into the atmosphere, leading to a large-scale dispersal event. It won't just be a local disaster; it'll be a global catastrophe." Mark jumped up from his chair, a surge of frantic energy coursing through his veins. "I must intervene—I have to stop them!"

"But Professor," the intern protested, "do you really think the President will listen to you?"

"I have to try," he replied resolutely. "It's not just Oakland at stake here. It's the whole world."

Mark dashed through the labyrinthine corridors of the White House, his mind buzzing with the dire implications of his discovery. However, as he skidded around a corner and the grand oak doors of the Oval Office came into view, he came to a sudden halt.

Standing in his way were a pair of stern-faced Secret Service agents, their dark suits practically blending into the shadows. Their expressions were unreadable, their posture unyielding.

"Hold it right there, Professor," one of them said, his hand instinctively moving towards the firearm holstered at his side. "The President is in a critical meeting. He cannot be disturbed."

"But this is urgent!" Mark insisted, his voice echoing down the grand corridor. "It's about the nuclear strike. It will make the situation worse, not better!"

The Secret Service agents exchanged a glance. Clearly, they were not used to dealing with such outbursts.

"We'll pass on the message," the other one said, a hint of impatience creeping into his voice. "But you need to calm down, Professor. Panic won't help anyone right now."

Mark's heart sank. He knew he couldn't afford to waste any more time. With the fate of an entire city, potentially the world, hanging in the balance, he had to get through to the President—and fast.

"Mr. President!" he shouted as loud as he could.

His shout echoed through the grand corridor, drawing startled glances from nearby staff. One of the Secret Service agents lifted his hand to his ear, receiving a message via his earpiece. He nodded, a curt, almost imperceptible gesture. Within seconds, a quartet of Marines materialized from a side corridor, their crisp uniforms contrasting starkly against the opulence of their surroundings.

The lead Marine, a towering figure with a stern gaze and a jaw set in determination, stepped up to Mark, coming uncomfortably close. Mark could feel the warmth of the man's breath against his face as he spoke in a voice that was at once authoritative and alarmingly calm.

"Follow me, sir."

Mark felt a surge of desperation. Gathering all his strength, he shouted at the top of his lungs, "Mr. President, the bomb will spread the infection across the entire world!"

His words echoed through the grand corridors, resonating with a chilling urgency. For a moment, all movement seemed to freeze, and heads turned towards the source of the outcry.

However, the Marines surrounding Mark didn't flinch. They maintained their steely expressions, undeterred by his desperate plea. Without a word, they hoisted Mark from the floor. His feet barely touched the ground as they marched him through the dark depressing hallways of the White House, their stride unrelenting, carrying him farther and farther away from the President's office and the pivotal decisions being made there.

AMANDA –
THE CANYON BUNKER

Oakland Bomb

"The bomb's dropped!" Joe shouted.

As Uncle Joe's warning reverberated through the air, reality descended like a shockwave over the group. Billy, Bert, Amanda, and Joshua all turned towards the horizon, their eyes widening in horrified awe as they took in the sight. A gigantic mushroom cloud was blossoming against the twilight sky, a sickly orange glow that was both fascinating and terrifying. The world was on fire, and the shockwave was advancing towards them.

Billy was the first to snap back to reality. "Inside! Now!" he yelled, pointing at the bunker entrance. There was no time to process the shock, no time for goodbyes. Survival was all that mattered now. He grabbed Amanda and Joshua by their hands, propelling them towards safety.

Amanda didn't need any coaxing. Gripping Joshua close to her, she ran with all the strength she could muster. Her heart pounded in her chest like a drum, each beat echoing the seconds that stood between them and certain death. She could hear the roar now, an ever-increasing thunder that drowned out everything else.

Uncle Joe, his usually calm demeanor replaced by an urgent panic. "Faster!" he barked; his gaze fixed on the oncoming shockwave. It was a race they couldn't afford to lose.

Bert was last in line, muttering what Amanda assumed was a silent prayer, as he sprinted towards the bunker.

Joe led them through the house down into the basement and ushered them to the inch thick steel bunker door.

They plunged into the bunker just as the world outside began to shake. Billy and Uncle Joe threw their weight against the heavy steel door, desperation lending them strength as they forced it shut against the onslaught.

The moment the bunker door groaned to a final close, the world outside convulsed in a maelstrom of raw power. The blast wave's thunderous outcry was a monstrous cacophony that echoed menacingly through the bunker's concrete shell and into the very marrow of their bones. The sheer, unbridled force of the explosion hurled them to the ground in a chaotic sprawl of limbs. The bunker, their sanctuary, seemed to shudder and tremble in sympathy with the tumult outside, and within its cold, austere confines, the group was forced to confront the immediate, overwhelming reality of their situation.

As the initial surge of terror ebbed and the deafening roar mellowed into a distant, ominous rumble, Amanda clung to Joshua.

Her body instinctively curved around his smaller frame, offering a physical barrier between him and whatever threats the world might offer to her child. *Normally Jo Jo would be playing, laughing, or crying. His silence is breaking my heart. Poor thing has no energy. He's fighting for his life.*

The bunker lapsed into a suffocating silence, punctuated only by the group's ragged, tremulous breathing. They had weathered the immediate danger, yet as the thunderous echoes of the explosion waned into the haunting silence of the night, they were confronted with an unsettling uncertainty: what horrors awaited them once they dared to emerge from their steel haven?

Within the bunker, they were isolated from the world beyond, ensconced in a fortress of solidified concrete and unyielding steel. Time appeared to be suspended as they endured the enduring tremors. Then, just as abruptly as it had erupted, the cacophony ceased. The vibrations diminished, the resonating din vanished, leaving behind only the rhythmic echo of their respirations within the restrictive enclosure.

Uncle Joe was the first to shatter the ensuing quiet, his voice nothing more than a hushed utterance. "We're safe now," he murmured softly. Yet, his statement failed to ease the collective anxiety.

Amanda pressed Joshua to her and felt his cold forehead. She knew that people outside were battling against the outbreak, but here in the bunker, she and her little boy were having their own battle, and she had no idea if they would win.

"Alright, everyone," Joe announced, his voice echoing off the concrete walls. "This is our haven now. Let me give you the grand tour."

Amanda stared at him in disbelief. "A nuclear cataclysm just occurred outside, and you're getting straight down to practicalities?"

"That's Uncle Joe," said Billy, as if that explained everything.

The distraction of a guided tour through their new surroundings was a welcome break from the intense emotions of the past few minutes. Uncle Joe led them through the bunker, showcasing its impressive survival features.

He pointed to a neat stack of plastic boxes sitting on a row of wooden shelves. "Food supply," he stated in a gruff voice, "Enough for a few months if we ration properly." His eyes flicked to Joshua, adding softer, "Got some stuff for the kid too. Nothing fancy, but it'll keep him going."

Amanda wondered what he meant by 'stuff for the kid', and why he had thought to store it.

Their water needs were met by an advanced purification system. "Every drop of water we use is filtered and reused. It's how we'll manage to stay hydrated for as long as we need to be down here," he explained as Amanda observed the system closely. The idea of recycling water with these three men made her grimace. "We'll only use the recycler if the well becomes tainted," he added, to Amanda's relief.

In one corner was a medical station, stocked with first-aid supplies. As a nurse, Amanda felt a sense of relief at the sight. Her quick examination made her realize the supplies had been well thought out.

Lastly, Joe showed them the sleeping quarters, a row of sturdy metal bunk beds lining one wall of the bunker.

"We'll figure out how to provide privacy for you," Joe said to Amanda. "I'll rig up a curtain at the end there."

Bert sat down on a bunk, his gaze went to Amanda and then to Joshua.

Billy put his hand on Joshua's forehead and a look of obvious concern appeared on his face. He ruffled the boy's hair, but Joshua didn't respond.

Joe cleared his throat in a way that instantly filled the room with tension. His gaze stayed on Amanda and Joshua. There was an apology in his eyes, but also a resolution that Amanda couldn't deny.

"Look," he began, his voice heavy with a discomfort that belied his tough exterior, "I don't want to darken the mood any further, but there's one more thing we need to address."

Amanda knew instantly what he was referring to and she tightened her grip on Joshua.

"We...we need to implement the precautions we talked about, Amanda," Uncle Joe continued, his gaze never leaving hers. "Until we know for sure that you and Joshua are going to be alright...I'm sorry, but you understand why you need to be restrained, don't you?"

It was the inevitable reality she had been dreading, the looming possibility that she could turn into one of those things. The memory of that black ooze coming out of Joshua's mouth returned to her in vivid detail, a horrible reminder of the unknown they were dealing with. Uncle Joe was right, of course. It was a necessary precaution, a harsh reality of their new world. But that didn't make it any easier.

"Yes," she finally answered, her voice barely above a whisper. "I understand. It is the right thing to do, and I will help."

Joe retrieved some thick ropes and a couple of surgical masks from one of the storage lockers. He tried to give a comforting smile, but the situation felt too grave for any real comfort.

"Alright, Amanda," he said in a gentle but firm voice. "Please sit on the chair and extend your hands forward. We'll tie you and Joshua separately, but close enough so you can comfort each other if you need to. And at night, we can move you to the bunks."

Amanda followed his instructions, feeling an increasing sense of dread as she sat and extended her hands. Beside her, Joshua was silent, watching with wide eyes as Uncle Joe began to secure the ropes around Amanda's wrists. The knots were firm, the ropes digging slightly into her skin, but not too tight to cut off circulation.

Next, Uncle Joe moved over to Joshua, the ropes in his hands. "This won't hurt, buddy," he said in a voice much softer than Amanda had heard him use up to now. Joshua simply nodded, his little hands trembling slightly as Uncle Joe tied them in the same manner he did with Amanda.

What must little Jo Jo think? she wondered to herself.

With the ropes in place, Uncle Joe held up the surgical masks. "Just a precaution in case it's airborne," he explained, helping them put it on. The masks were slightly too big for Joshua, but Joe managed to adjust it to fit as well as possible.

Confined by bindings and a mask, Amanda felt an alien sensation creep over her. Shutting her eyes, she tried to coax her anxiety into submission. The threat they faced had evolved, no longer solely a lurking external menace, but potentially a dangerous enemy within. Yet in the face of this compounded fear, their only option was to wait and place their faith in the power of the medication.

She started feeling claustrophobic. The mask made her conscious of her breathing, then she wondered how much air there was in the bunker. Was there enough for five people? She suddenly realized how small the bunker's rooms were. The grey concrete walls were just too close. She closed her eyes and took some deep breaths.

Get a grip, Amanda. Get a grip.

In the oppressive silence, the hum of the bunker's life-support systems was a relentless undercurrent. The rhythmic hum was soothing and indicative of safety, and yet it had taken on a haunting note. It was a grim lullaby that spoke of the horror outside and the unknown within. It was a world away from the comfortable hum of the city they had known.

She looked down at Joshua. His little face, innocent and oblivious to the potential danger his own body might harbor, was peaceful in sleep. She tightened her grip on his small hand, which was the only contact she could make with him. She yearned to cuddle him, to make him know she was present, protecting him. She would do everything in her power to protect him, even if it meant facing her own potential transformation. The maternal instincts within her roared defiantly against the fear that attempted to consume her. She drew on this strength and resolve, knowing she would need it in the days to come.

And yet, amid the dread and anxiety, she knew a fragile hope held them together. The hope that they might find a way to survive this. The hope that the medication would work, that they would not succumb to the horrifying fate that potentially lay in wait. It was a fragile thread in the dark abyss, but it was the only thing they had to hold onto in the face of the unknown. As each second ticked by, the suspense grew, leaving them in a tense limbo that strained their nerves. Each heartbeat, each breath became a testament to their determination to live, to endure whatever came next.

PROFESSOR MARK PRESTON –
WASHINGTON D.C.

The Empty Oval Office

A soft voice pierced through the veil of Mark's fitful sleep, "Professor Preston?" Blinking open his eyes, he slowly lifted his head from the haphazard pile of papers and scientific paraphernalia cluttering his desk. A young woman, dressed in a crisp military uniform, was standing rigidly in the doorframe, her face all but familiar.

"Yes," Mark croaked out, his voice raw from fatigue and countless hours of relentless work.

"The Situation Room requests your presence, sir," she stated, maintaining her formal composure. Her words cut through the silence of the lab, resonating with an urgency that jerked Mark back into alertness.

Mark blinked in surprise. "Really?" He was taken aback. It had been barely twelve hours since he'd been unceremoniously escorted away from the Oval Office, cut off mid-plea. His protestations against the nuke had fallen on deaf ears, and he'd assumed he'd been effectively blacklisted, destined to be frozen out of any further discussions.

It was a perplexing turn of events. But if they were willing to listen now, he wouldn't waste the opportunity. Scrambling to gather his things, he followed the messenger towards the heart of power, the Situation Room.

Traversing the all too familiar corridors to the Situation Room, his thoughts spiraled. The launch of the nuclear weapon was an immutable fact, and the disastrous consequences it would yield were an impending certainty. Yet, amidst the looming dread, a glimmer of hope sparked within him—he could still, perhaps, sway the trajectory of events.

They had made their decision hastily, under immense pressure, and without understanding the full implications of their actions. Mark nurtured a glimmer of hope: maybe they had now realized the magnitude of their mistake and were finally ready to listen, to let science and reason rule their future decisions.

His urgency mounted with each step. He had to make them grasp the enormity of their actions, the vast danger now unleashed. He had to guide them through the minefield they'd created, help them contain the fallout.

We need to treat this as both a military and medical emergency. The infected can potentially be treated if they haven't turned. Those who are bit can have limbs amputated if it is caught within a few minutes… what else can we do. We can have mask mandates to slow down the airborne aspect…but will people accept that? It doesn't matter if some reject the masks as long as others comply. It's a numbers game from here on. Now I wonder what the R zero rate is … He began to contemplate the mathematics of the infection.

With a mind full of ideas and determination hardening his resolve, he steeled himself for the impending meeting. Now wasn't the time for hesitation or doubt. He would marshal every ounce of his knowledge and experience to guide them through this crisis.

As he neared the situation room, the two Marines on guard snapped to attention. They shared a brief, knowing glance at his approach, then one of them extended a hand, twisting the doorknob. The weighty door opened, unveiling the fervor of activity within the Situation Room.

The room was bathed in a soft glow from screens and lamps that flickered across the walls. The persistent murmur of urgent discussions wove through the room, punctuated by the steady hum of the state-of-the-art electronics.

The Situation Room was alive, as it always was, with ceaseless activity. Yet, an undercurrent of tension gave the room a charged atmosphere. Staff members moved with hurried precision and hushed. Faces were taut, eyes darting, brows furrowed in deep thought. The room's heart, a large central table, was a sea of maps, documents, and the ghostly glow from numerous laptop screens. This spectral light painted the room's occupants in shades of uncertainty.

Inhaling deeply, Mark crossed the threshold. The door shut softly behind him, enclosing him in the room's intense atmosphere.

As he advanced towards the central table, a pathway opened through the busy throng, all conversations halting, all gazes shifting in his direction. This was his moment, his opportunity to exert influence over the unfolding crisis. His determination solidified; he would not squander it. He only hoped it wasn't too late.

President Mitchel wore a broad smile. "Hey Mikey boy!" he said jovially.

For a moment Mark was confused. *Mikey boy? Is he referring to me? Well, I am not going to correct him, he'll forget my name in a few minutes anyway.*

President Mitchel's eyes gleamed with anticipation. "Our helicopters are nearing Oakland as we speak. Soon, we'll have live footage of the situation. The world will see the effectiveness of swift, decisive action." He paused, glancing at Mark. "You too will witness what happens when we let the military take control, Mikey boy."

Mark nodded, but inside, his mind was racing. The President's casual tone, the use of the nickname—it all felt uncomfortably discordant against the backdrop of the looming crisis. Yet he reminded himself, he wasn't here for pleasantries. His role was to dissect the reality of their situation and relay it in the most unvarnished, scientific terms possible. The President's levity would not deter him.

"Thank you, Mr. President," Mark responded, managing to produce a thin, polite smile. Each word was carefully chosen, an act of balancing on a thin rope. Internally, his mind was a whirl of calculations and potential scenarios. "I'm here to offer my expertise and guide us through this crisis as effectively as possible."

President Mitchel responded with a hearty chuckle, his hand landing heavily on Mark's shoulder. "That's the spirit, Mikey boy!"

Gathering his composure, Mark began in a controlled tone, "My advice, Mr. President," he paused, ensuring he had the room's full attention, "is that we instruct the helicopters to maintain a substantial distance from the area. The agent causing this infection isn't your run-of-the-mill pathogen."

Mark took a moment, allowing his words to sink in as he swept his gaze around the room. The once jovial atmosphere had noticeably cooled, giving way to a tense hush. "Our adversary," he continued, "isn't a typical pathogen. Instead, it's a modified adenovirus that's found refuge in a bacterial host – Deinococcus Radiodurans. A bacterium infamous for its unparalleled resilience, capable of withstanding extreme temperatures and even radiation."

For a moment, silence lingered, letting Mark's chilling revelation echo in the room. President Mitchel's once beaming smile faltered, the light in his eyes dimming momentarily. Then, with an almost mechanical effort, he stretched his lips into a smile again, struggling to hold on to the veneer of joviality he had projected.

"I must admit, the speed with which the CDC has performed its analysis is… astonishing. Beyond credibility really," said the President.

Well, he is right about that.

"The CDC is highly motivated and working round the clock," said Mark.

"Still…" said the President. His jovial tone had vanished, replaced with a caution that was uncharacteristic of him. He leaned forward, gripping the edge of the table tightly. "So, you're implying..." he began, each word carrying a heavier weight than the last, "...the nuclear blast might have...spread the infection?"

Did I imply that? Maybe he's not as dumb as I thought.

Mark's nod was solemn, his gaze steady on the President's. "Yes, sir, that's exactly what I'm suggesting. The blast wave, the cleansing fire you spoke of, it could have aerosolized and disseminated the infection on a scale we have yet to fathom," he explained. His voice dropped lower; the next words weighted with grim potential. "And the helicopter crews...if they've entered the contaminated airspace, they might already be infected."

A heavy pause fell upon the room, every breath held in collective anticipation. President Mitchel fixed his gaze on Mark, the silence stretching taut between them. Finally, he sighed, the vibrant smile that once graced his face now resembling a taut, strained grimace.

"Mikey boy, you have a real knack for dampening spirits," President Mitchel retorted, his voice laced with a hint of annoyance. "Just...find a seat. And hold back on the apocalyptic warnings, will you?"

Apocalyptic? That's the appropriate word, Mark thought.

With a respectful nod, Mark complied, "Yes, Mr. President." As he lowered himself into his seat, his mind was a tumult of anxiety and resolve. The implications of the information he had just imparted hung heavily on him. It was painfully clear that his challenge went beyond just providing scientific insight—he would have to navigate the evolving political intricacies and find a way to guide these leaders through the unfolding disaster, whether his counsel was welcome or not.

The room dimmed as the enormous main screen came to life, a live feed from a patrolling helicopter overtaking the wall-to-wall display. It was a shocking panorama of the devastation, a cruel tableau of what once was Oakland city center. The vibrancy of the metropolis was extinguished, replaced with a desolate expanse of scorched earth and fractured skyscrapers, an apocalyptic landscape etched into stark relief.

A collective intake of breath resonated through the room as the camera widened its focus, laying bare an alarming ring of fire that was ferociously expanding from the epicenter. At first glance, it appeared to be a repercussion of the nuclear assault, a lethal fringe delineating the outer limits of devastation. But as the lens tightened, zooming in for a closer examination, the harrowing reality emerged with heart-stopping clarity.

There was fire. Lots of fire, but it wasn't just fire. It was an unending wave of infected individuals, thousands upon thousands of them, all aflame. The infected, or 'zombies', or 'growlers' as they were commonly referred to, were sprinting away from the city, their burning bodies leaving trails of smoke. The sight was both mesmerizing and horrifying, like a portal into hell.

The room descended into a stunned silence. This wasn't just a disaster—it was a nightmare made real.

As the helicopter continued to hover at a distance from the searing spectacle, the camera lens was suddenly besmirched with droplets of an opaque, thick substance. Like an abrupt blight, the black ooze appeared, blotting the screen with disconcerting splotches and veiling the harrowing scene below.

The pilot tried to veer away, but the contamination had already claimed its ground. The dark liquid blossomed across the screen, each smear a grotesque stroke in a real-time abstract painting of horror.

The jovial mask President Mitchel had been wearing until now faltered, succumbing to the horrific spectacle. The room was saturated with a silence so profound that the only sound was the unsettling crackle of static from the deteriorating feed on the screen.

President Mitchel's gaze swiveled towards Mark, his eyes flickering with a storm of embarrassment and resentment. But just as swiftly, he reined himself in, ironing out his features into a stern, authoritative mask. "Clear the lens," he commanded, his voice slicing through the room's silence. His stare, cold and accusatory, remained fixed on Mark. A silent rebuke—a spiteful blame cast onto the scientist for the disaster unfolding before them, despite the stark warnings Mark had given.

"Professor Preston," Harold Dern, the President's chief of staff, cut in abruptly. His face was taut with restrained anxiety as he asked, "Just how do we fight this infection?"

"Deinococcus radiodurans," Mark began, "is like a microscopic super soldier. It's incredibly tough and can survive in the harshest conditions due to its unique physiology and cellular structure..."

President Mitchel snorted. "Use English, Professor, you aren't going to impress anyone here with mumbo jumbo,"

"I'll put it in layman's terms, Mr. President," Mark said, his gaze unflinching. "This bacterium is a microscopic Houdini. It's built to escape death even in conditions that would obliterate most life forms. This resilience is what makes it a tough adversary, but understanding its survival tactics could also guide us in finding a way to combat it."

Seeing the President's gaze narrow, he quickly added, "To effectively combat this infection, we'll need to explore novel methods to break down its defense mechanisms and then neutralize it. Traditional methods won't work."

"Be specific," said Dern.

Mark was not sure what specific defenses he could recommend. "Well... being infected with the bacteria does not mean you will turn into those... I am just going to use the word zombies."

Dern leaned forward; his hands splayed on the table. "That is a sliver of hope, yes, but we need more, Professor. We need a course of action. What's the next step? What do we do now?"

Mark exhaled slowly, collecting his thoughts. "I don't have all the answers yet," he admitted. "For example, I have no idea how it spread to other cities so quickly. I can only assume that it was spread deliberately, perhaps pouring this bacteria into the water supply." He noticed an officer nodded, and then whispering to an aide. "The more we know, the better we can respond. But let's start by avoiding any more use of nuclear weapons. We need to be studying the pathogen's behavior, its spread pattern, and the environmental factors influencing it. This will help us formulate a more comprehensive response."

I need to give them some good news, something to give them hope.

"Some individuals will possess a natural immunity to the bacteria, their bodies capable of mounting a defense. However," Mark paused, the weight of his next words hanging heavy in the room, "in the case of a bite, the virus is released from the bacteria. This virus is extraordinarily infectious. Virtually all bite victims will succumb to it...unless the bite is located on an extremity and they're willing—and able—to amputate it swiftly."

"And..." said Dern.

"We must arm the population with immunity against the bacteria," Mark said, his voice resolute. "One way to achieve this is by developing a benign version of it. Neutralize the airborne threat. I'll immediately assemble a team to get to work on this." He paused, glancing around the room, "It won't be cheap, and it won't be quick. And once we have a vaccine, the next challenge will be convincing people to take it."

President Mitchel exhaled deeply, his brow furrowing. "There's a vocal segment of the population that'll resist vaccines, you know."

"We could introduce it into the water supply," Mark proposed.

His suggestion was met with a look of horror from the President. "That would be political suicide. I'd never win another election."

Mark countered sharply, his gaze unwavering. "Mr. President, if we let this infection rampage unchecked across the country, you might not have a reelection to worry about. Think about it, it practically destroyed an entire city in a day. What do you think it can do in a week, in a month, in a year?"

An expression darted across the President's face—fleeting, but Mark could have sworn it was one of triumph.

"But how do we deal with...the zombies themselves?" Dern's voice was strained. "Can we douse them with some sort of antiviral agent?"

President Mitchel echoed his concern, nodding vigorously in agreement. Mark paused, looking at each man in turn, his face grave. "No," he said finally. "There's only one thing that will stop them." He let the words hang in the air for a moment before adding, "Bullets. Lots of bullets. Bullets hitting them in the head."

A uniformed general, sitting at the table, chuckled. "Well, this zombie apocalypse chose the wrong fucking country. We got trillions of bullets, and we have more guns than we have people. Those creatures never made it across the bay bridge because we had a few thousand marines and a few million rounds of ammunition."

"Bullets," said President Mitchel. "We certainly have enough bullets."

"Consider this," Mark replied, leaning forward, his voice grave. "There are approximately eight million people in the Bay Area. Let's assume ninety percent of them become infected by the bacterial cloud we inadvertently dispersed. That cloud is now on its way across the country, ready to spawn tens of millions of these...zombies. Each one of those creatures will serve as a new point of contagion, exponentially escalating the crisis. Within a week, that cloud of pathogens will reach every nation on Earth, and they will all be fighting for survival."

Mark paused to allow them to digest this idea. "As for bullets. In Iraq, our military expended 250,000 rounds of ammunition for each successful kill, and they didn't have to aim for the head. I am not much of a shot myself, but I think even a marine will find it hard to pull off rapid head shots against a sea of eight million sprinting, growling, monsters."

As Mark's words echoed in the suddenly quiet room, an unsettling chill swept across the occupants. Each syllable was a drumbeat, every sentence a grim prophecy. Outside, beyond the thick, reinforced walls of the Situation Room, the world was turning into a nightmare, a deadly stage where the rules of life and death were being rewritten with each passing moment.

The large screen continued to display the disconcerting and now silent live feed from the helicopter, the lens smeared with the grotesque infection. The once vibrant cityscape was now just a smoldering ruin, a testament to the havoc the infection had wreaked in such a short span of time. The flickering, distorted images served as a sobering reminder of the immense challenge they were up against.

Mark found himself under the weight of several pairs of eyes, each one reflecting a cocktail of fear, disbelief, and anticipation.

President Mitchel shifted uncomfortably in his chair, his gaze lingering on the haunting imagery on the screen. His previous air of joviality had vanished, replaced by a stern facade.

As the gravity of their situation hung heavily in the air, the question on everyone's mind remained unspoken: What happens next?

Chapter – Clapp Spring Bunker

SAMANTHA WINTERS

Bunker Corridors

The screen displayed an ominous mushroom-shaped inferno dominating the Oakland skyline, painting the worship hall with a surreal, fiery hue. Struck dumb by the sight, Samantha's eyes widened to their limits, glued to the apocalyptic spectacle that unfolded before her. The words "What is..." escaped from her lips in a shaky whisper, her mind reeling, unable to grasp the full extent of the disaster that had befallen her city.

The Prophet sprang to his feet, his countenance lit with an ecstatic fervor. He thrust his hands upwards, magnetically pulling everyone's attention towards him. "Behold, my brothers and sisters," he boomed with an awe-struck reverence, "this marks the genesis of phase two. Praise be to the Lord!" he roared out, his voice echoing within the confines of the worship hall.

The hall reverberated with the resonant chorus of the congregation, their voices merging into a single mighty echo that mirrored the Prophet's proclamation. "Praise the Lord!" they chanted, the fervency of their belief saturating the air with an intense, energy. Samantha could feel the waves of their collective zeal washing over her, stirring an unsettling mix of awe and apprehension within her.

In the aftermath of his passionate proclamation, the Prophet seemed to deflate. The charismatic armor he wore in front of his disciples began to crack, revealing beneath it a man visibly worn by the day's extraordinary events. He turned his attention towards Samantha, his gaze piercing in its intensity.

An uncanny shiver of discomfort traced a cold path down Samantha's spine under his scrutiny. Yet, as abruptly as it had come, the intensity in his eyes flickered out. He shook his head as if dispelling an unwelcome thought.

"My children, forgive me," he projected, his voice resonating in the cavernous expanse of the room. "The burdens of this day have taken their toll. I must retreat and seek restorative solitude. Use this interlude to meditate, to ready your hearts and minds for the trials that the coming nights will undoubtedly bring."

His eyes met Samantha's, within them she thought she detected a flare of anger, swiftly followed by a glint of cunning, as if he held a secret about her yet unknown to her. She had the feeling of being a chess piece in his grand game, strategically positioned, while the next move was hidden in the shadows of his knowing gaze.

He turned and left, walking as if the weight of the world were on his shoulders.

Something about his words sparked unease in her. *What am I supposed to do now?* The thought reverberated through her consciousness, underpinning the silent dread that had claimed squatter's rights in her soul. Her eyes strayed back to the screen, its ominous luminescence serving as the room's sole beacon, casting phantasmal silhouettes that danced and warped around the room. She felt the chilling touch of isolation and the oppressive atmosphere of the cult's underground bunker.

With the Prophet's abrupt exit, her mind catapulted into frenzied activity. She needed to breach the silent barrier that separated her from the world beyond, to sound the alarm bell that would draw the authorities' attention. The weight of this responsibility bore down on her, an invisible load threatening to crush her resolve. But she couldn't— wouldn't—let it immobilize her. She had to take charge, had to devise a plan. Failure was simply not an option.

Her gaze swept the room covertly, her mind churning with strategies. Tools for communication or a link to the outside world, these were her lifelines now. She needed an edge, a means to broadcast her plea for assistance.

With the absence of the Prophet, she realized she had the opportunity to roam and explore a little. She saw a young woman exit a door that had mirrors and sinks behind it. *Ah, a restroom*, she realized. She immediately seized the opportunity. Perhaps in the privacy of a stall she could attempt contact with the outside, though she doubted her little transmitter would work in an underground bunker.

She slipped out of her seat and quietly, nonchalantly, headed to the door. Pushing it open, her eyes had to adjust to the bright lights inside. An older woman was standing in front of the mirror. Samantha smiled at her, but received a cold disdainful look, as if she had committed some awful crime.

Whoa what's that about, she thought as she walked past the lady and entered a stall. She immediately took off her backpack and fumbled for the secret pocket where the transmitter was. In seconds she had it on her lap and adjusted the screen. The old lady was still outside so she knew she would not be able to start communicating straight away. She just wanted to test that she had reception.

The device lit up and went through a wake-up process. She waited to see how much of a sat-signal she would get. She knew she would not get five bars, but the device would still work with four or three or even two.

The old woman was still outside.

A few more seconds passed then the words "No Signal" flashed on the device. It was the result she expected but it was still crushing. She knew she would have to find another way to communicate. She took a few deep breaths to quell her feeling of isolation and claustrophobia.

She put her device back in its secret pocket, flushed the toilet and exited the stall. The old lady was standing at the sinks and gave her a withering look, even shaking her head.

Jesus weirdo, what's wrong with you?

The old lady never took her eyes off Samantha as she walked up to the sinks. Samantha quickly washed her hands and exited.

Her eyes returned to the looming screen, its haunting imagery casting a harsh, unwelcome glow over the room. But in its spectral light, Samantha saw a lifeline. It was a beacon, transmitting images from the outside world into their underground fortress. Somewhere there was some kind of communications or a nexus of technology where those signals were coming into the bunker, so maybe, just maybe, if she could find it, she could get her signal out. This thought gave her a glimmer of hope, a fragile thread of a plan beginning to form.

She cast furtive glances at the Prophet's disciples around her, their faces illuminated by the sickly pallor of the screen's light. Did any of them harbor doubts, a secret defiance against the Prophet's domination? Or were they all irrevocably ensnared in his persuasive grip? The odds seemed stacked against her, but she knew she had to gamble. The stakes were simply too high.

As she observed, she also began to hatch a plan. She would have to convince them she was with them, fully devoted to the Prophet's cause, while secretly working to reach out to authorities. It was a daunting task, layered with risk and uncertainty, but it was the only option she had. She steeled herself, ready to play the role of a lifetime in the theatre of the Prophet's apocalyptic drama.

A sudden touch on her shoulder jolted her from her thoughts. Startled, she turned to see Bethany, her expression brimming with regret and a faint trace of fear. "I apologize, Samantha," she began, her voice barely more than a whisper, "I didn't intend to startle you. I was tasked with guiding you to your sleeping quarters."

Samantha smiled. "Wonderful," she said in an overly enthusiastic tone. "Perhaps you can show me round the whole bunker. I will serve the Prophet better, if I know all the facilities here."

"Oh yes, I'd love to," Bethany gushed.

Under the intense, sterile glow of fluorescent lights, Bethany took the lead, guiding Samantha through the labyrinthine network of the bunker. Her lively chatter filled the corridor, bouncing off the hard, unyielding concrete that surrounded them, the echo lending an eerie undertone to their exploration.

"The bunker is a wonder," gushed Bethany. "It has everything we need here. There is a games room for the men, and a knitting and sewing room for the women."

Seriously?

Bethany pointed to a closed door. "There's a bar and smoking room for the men, the Prophet likes to share cigars after dinner. There's an ultra-modern laundry room for the women."

Yay!

They descended several flights of stairs, and the tour continued. There was a library. "Strictly for men!" said Bethany earnestly. There was a large worship hall, with several rows of seats for men, smaller seats for boys, and an open space where women, girls and infants could appreciate the Prophet's sermons.

239

At one point they stopped at a door with a simple lock and two armed guards. "That's the Prophet's chamber," Bethany announced, her voice dropping to an awestruck whisper. Her eyes were wide with a mix of reverence and fear.

"Only a select few have ever stepped foot inside," she continued, pausing for a moment as she let the significance of her words sink in. Samantha noted the hushed reverence in her voice, the deep respect she held for the Prophet. The heavy door was mute, revealing nothing of the secrets it might hold beyond. The air of mystery surrounding the Prophet's chamber made Samantha nervous.

"I am told he has a secret room in there that only his most trusted wives get to see," gushed Bethany in a whisper.

Wives? Plural? Of course. That was not in the literature.

Guiding Samantha further into the complex, Bethany led her to the next stop of the tour—a room whose function was immediately apparent even before Bethany uttered a word. Encased behind a door replete with intimidating locking mechanisms, lay an impressive armory.

Through a reinforced glass window in the door, an extensive collection of firearms and melee weapons were on display. Each piece appeared impeccably maintained, their gleaming surfaces lined up in an orderly fashion on rows of spotless shelves. Shotguns, rifles, handguns, and a myriad of sharp-edged instruments lay in wait.

"We have to be prepared for anything," Bethany said, her voice crisp and even. Her nonchalant shrug belied the gravity of the room's contents. This was a cult on a war footing against the rest of the world. Samantha found herself staring a moment too long, taken aback by the raw reality of their situation, and quickly forced herself to move on, following Bethany down the echoing corridor.

Next, Samantha was led to a large room, its doors swinging open to reveal a sight that momentarily dispelled the sense of dread that had taken root in her. Before her lay an Aladdin's cave of survival, brimming with a cornucopia of supplies. Industrial shelves, towering like city skyscrapers, were laden with orderly rows of canned goods. Colored labels advertising beans, soups, fruits, and an eclectic variety of other pantry staples painted a rainbow of relief amidst the stark, utilitarian gray of the bunker's walls. The sight was a warm blanket of reassurance in the cold reality of their situation, a tangible promise of sustenance amidst uncertainty.

Beyond the cans, she noticed crates filled with plastic water bottles, their transparency revealing the life-sustaining fluid within. Elsewhere, stacks of other essentials such as medical supplies, blankets, clothing, and even toiletries were arranged in a meticulous, methodical manner, their strategic organization a testament to the thoroughness of the preparation.

"We have enough provisions to last us for years," Bethany announced, her voice imbued with a hint of pride. She swept a hand toward the vast expanse of supplies, a smile playing on her lips as she watched Samantha's eyes take in the extent of their preparation. Samantha could only nod in response, her mind racing with the implications. Their survival was not just hoped for, it was planned, down to the last canned pea.

How long have they been planning for the apocalypse?

They entered a part of the bunker that had far fewer people wandering around. The sound of their footsteps bounced off the walls, their echo magnifying the sense of isolation within the bunker. They came to a halt in front of a door different from the rest. This one was marked with a sign painted in bold, crimson letters. 'Off Limits' it read, stark against the gray door.

Bethany gestured at the door with a wave of her hand, her voice dropping to a lower pitch. "That's the science lab," she informed Samantha in almost a whisper, her eyes darting strangely. Samantha felt Bethany was hinting at things unsaid and secrets untold.

She didn't elaborate further and they didn't linger. She turned on her heel and briskly led Samantha away, but not before Samantha noticed the sophisticated security system that secured the door. It was apparent that whatever lay beyond that door was of significant importance to the Prophet. Only he and a select few, she presumed, were privy to its secrets. She filed this information away in her mind, an intriguing piece of the larger puzzle.

Bethany guided Samantha towards another unassuming door, its appearance just as mundane as the rest. "That's the IT room," she stated, her hand vaguely gesturing towards it. "Full of computers and all sorts of technical stuff. But we're not allowed in there, either. The Prophet says men are more suited to understanding and using technology."

Samantha nodded, as if in full agreement. She masked both her disgust and her interest, keeping her face neutral and her response casual. Internally, however, her thoughts were racing. The IT room; that could be her salvation. If she could find a way into that room, she might be able to make contact with the outside world. She wouldn't need her transmitter, she would just need access to a computer with internet. *I am sure they keep this room well protected; they don't want their faithful talking to people in the real world.*

She offered a nonchalant nod, commenting, "You're really well-prepared here, aren't you?" She hoped her remark came across as an innocuous observation. Underneath her calm exterior, she was alert and plotting, her focus zeroing in on the key to her escape.

As they continued the tour of the bunker, she couldn't shake off the aura of disquiet that hung heavy in the air. The concrete walls seemed to whisper secrets, the echoes of hushed conversations resonating in the eerie silence. Everywhere she turned, she was greeted by secured steel doors and unyielding locks, symbols of an enigmatic world she was desperate to decode.

In the background, the hum of the bunker's generator reverberated like a monstrous heartbeat, a constant reminder of the artificial life sustained within these subterranean depths. She wondered about the complexity of the bunker's infrastructure, about the vast web of wires and cables hidden behind the steel-clad walls.

Samantha realized that Bethany was both a guide and a gatekeeper, an essential key in her quest for escape.

Her thoughts went to her family. Were they safe? How could she ever get back to them? Were they worrying about her? She feared for her own life, but it felt like the worst thing about her death would be the pain she brought to her family. *So many things to worry about.* She tried to push those thoughts from her mind.

A strange thought struck her. In a world gone mad, a bunker full of canned beans, locked doors, and veiled secrets was her new reality. It all seemed surreal, ludicrous even. How did this happen? She remembered a documentary she'd seen on the Jonestown massacre. Innocent people were led step by step into a death trap secluded in an African forest. Here she was in a doomsday bunker. *History repeats,* she thought. Somehow, she was a player in a high-stakes game, the rules of which were as murky as the shadows that danced in the bunker's corners. With a silent vow to herself, she decided that she would uncover the secrets this place hid, expose the veiled truths, and find her way out. It was not just self-preservation, she wanted justice done against these people for the nightmare they had released. A nightmare she knew had only just started and was about to get much, much worse.

AMANDA WILLARD

Joe's Bunker

In the icy grip of the pre-dawn hours, the bunker stood in sterile silence, a bubble of calm amidst the storm. On the other side of its fortress-like, steel-reinforced walls, the world was succumbing to a nightmarish descent into chaos, a dystopian hellscape offering no promise of escape. Yet, within the bunker's austere confines, a frail mirage of normality persisted, an unlikely haven sheltering its occupants from the unspeakable horrors that stalked the world above.

Amanda tossed and turned on her impromptu bed, ensnared by the ruthless claws of fitful sleep. Nightmares, which were once rare intruders disturbing her peaceful slumbers, had now become her relentless tormentors, serving up vivid and terrifying replays of the world before and the horrors that it had morphed into. Her dreamscape was a theatre of the macabre, staging ghastly scenes of terror, populated by the beloved faces she had lost and the memories of a world that had faded into oblivion.

She awoke, the rhythm of a throbbing headache reverberating through her skull. Her attempt to rise was met with protesting aches coursing through her limbs, compelling her to drop onto her knees before she could gradually elevate herself. Shuffling over to the bathroom, she braced herself in front of the mirror. The reflection that confronted her was a horrifying distortion of the woman she once was. Her skin bore a sickly, pallid hue and her once vibrant eyes had become vacant milky-white orbs. A viscous, black liquid trickled from the corners of her mouth, a chilling contrast against her pale skin that evoked a shudder of revulsion.

She attempted to summon a scream, to let loose a plea for help, but the sound that wrenched itself from her throat was a grotesque, inhuman snarl. Panic welled up within her like a tidal wave, crashing against the shores of her sanity, rapidly succeeded by a piercing stab of despair. The realization chilled her to the bone—she was morphing, transforming into the very horror they'd been running from. It was the relentless process of her humanity being stripped away, replaced with the monstrous mutation of the infection.

Rage gripped her. A fury she knew would only be sated by burying her teeth into any living human she could find.

Her scream reverberated throughout the confines of Joe's bunker, a bone-chilling symphony of dread that shattered the serene stillness of the pre-dawn hours. In the blink of an eye, the soothing embrace of sleep was violently cast aside, supplanted by the frantic urgency of survival. Every soul within the bunker stirred, rudely yanked from slumber, senses heightened and primed for a potential confrontation. A sudden dance of shadows and hurried whispers filled the previously calm spaces, every person grappling with the fear of what Amanda's horrifying cry could signify.

Stirred from the clutches of her nightmare, Amanda sat up abruptly in her bunk, her breaths coming in ragged gasps. She tried to move her arms but found her hands still bound to the sides of the bunk.

Joe was the first to get to her side, the usual rigidity etched on his weathered face softening at the sight of her trembling form. His gaze held a potent mix of relief and concern as he took in the fear that glittered in her eyes, a clear indication that she wasn't a victim of the infection. Close on his heels, Billy and Bert made their entrance, their grip on their makeshift weapons white-knuckled, their eyes darting around the room in a frantic search for any potential threats. Each creak, every shadow, seemed to intensify their vigilance.

Joshua began to cry, his tiny body shaking with the intensity of his fear. The echoes of Amanda's scream still reverberated around the room.

It took a moment for the tension to ebb, for the men to lower their weapons, for Joshua's cries to quiet into shaky breaths. Amanda looked at her trembling bound hands, her mind still caught in the terrifying dream. *I am not one of those monsters*, she told herself, the taste of bile and fear lingering in her mouth.

It was just a dream. Yet, as she met the wary, watchful gazes of the men around her, she couldn't shake off the feeling that it was a premonition. A horrifying glimpse into a future she desperately hoped to avoid.

For a moment, the bunker was filled with a tense silence, the air thick with unvoiced questions and uncertainties.

Bert dropped to one knee, gently cradling her handcuffed hand in his. His brow creased as he observed, "Your hand is warm, that's a good sign."

With a gentleness that belied the hardened survivor he was, he lowered her mask and asked, "Can you open your mouth for me?"

She nodded, opening her mouth wide. She squeezed her eyes shut, unable to stifle the fear that laced her thoughts. If there was no improvement by now, then the chances were dwindling.

A moment of silence stretched between them before Bert finally broke it. "It's all clear," he declared, relief evident in his tone.

He turned his attention to Joshua, his voice softening. "Hey buddy, can Uncle Bert take a look in your mouth too?"

Rubbing the sleep from his eyes, Joshua obediently opened his mouth. Bert leaned in, his eyes narrowing as he inspected the young boy. After a moment, he straightened and grinned. "He's in the clear too."

Joe expelled a shaky breath, his shoulders sagging with relief. "That's good news. I suppose it means, if you can avoid getting bit, there's hope for survival." He knelt down and released both of them. "I really don't think I could have watched another little one die."

Amanda tilted her head in puzzlement. *Another little one die? Did he lose a child? Is that why he hides in the middle of nowhere? Hiding from a past too painful to face.*

The lingering tension from Amanda's nightmare scream was abruptly displaced as Billy's voice cut through the silence. "We've got a problem," he declared, an urgency in his tone that had them all turning towards him.

He led them to the storeroom and picked up a large plastic bucket labelled 'Survival Food.' At that moment Amanda noticed Billy was wearing ridiculous looking striped pajamas, she felt a quizzical smile twitching at her lips—a fleeting moment of levity in their dire situation. She returned her attention to the bucket he was holding just as Joe, his face serious, strode over to investigate. Billy held out the bucket, presenting its contents for all to see. It was a sight that instantly wiped the smile off Amanda's face.

Inside the bucket was chaos—torn packets strewn amongst decomposing food, its foul stench now permeating the room. Worst of all were the writhing maggots that infested the mess, a sickening testimony to the food's decay.

"Damn it," Joe cursed, his voice barely above a whisper as he surveyed the ruined food supplies with a sense of despair. He raked a hand through his hair, a gesture of helpless frustration. "I bought dozens of these buckets of survival food off the net, foolishly trusted in its promise. I checked one of the buckets and it was fine." His voice was thick with self-reproach. "Who can really vouch for its quality until you're cornered, when you're banking on it for

250

survival...Damn it all!" His last words echoed in the stark room, a bitter testament to their dire predicament.

"Not every bucket is in this bad a shape but... enough to cause an issue," said Billy.

The stifling silence of the dimly lit bunker was punctured by Billy's worried voice. He cast a concerned glance towards Joe, anxiety carving deep lines across his usually stoic features. "Joe, I have a ton of food in my truck, but that damn blast...Could it have messed up my truck?"

Amanda looked on, her eyes trailing to Joe who appeared deep in thought, his hands instinctively sifting through a dusty box secluded in the room's corner.

"It's not the blast you should be fretting over, Billy. It's the radiation." Joe's voice reverberated within the claustrophobic confines of the bunker, yanking Amanda from the pit of anxiety stirring in her gut. Her gaze fastened onto the small, rectangular device he extracted from a box—a Geiger counter, she realized. "Our current radiation levels hover around a safe 0.01 millisieverts. Outside, though..." His voice trailed off, leaving the statement ominously unfinished.

"And there are the growlers outside," added Bert.

Radiated growlers, thought Amanda with a shudder.

"And there will be fires from the nuke," added Joe.

"Growlers and radiation versus starvation," said Billy.

"Radiated growlers on fire," mused Amanda. "We could wait for the radiation and the fire to abate," she added.

Joe shook his head. "The fires probably haven't spread to the canyon yet and the radiation is going to go up a lot before it starts to come down. All the radioactive material in the air is going to start coming down like snow. No, if we don't want to starve, we have to go out now, deal with the dead, and transfer the food before it gets too irradiated."

"Really?" Bert's question hung in the air. "So...we are thinking about moving the food from the truck?" He glanced around the room, meeting each pair of eyes, including Amanda's. She felt a lump form in her throat but said nothing. *Joshua needs to be fed.*

Joe nodded, walking over to a capped pipe. He held his device up to it. "Before we decide, let's get a reading on the outside air." He unscrewed the cap, and Amanda watched his eyebrows raise slightly. "Well, it's higher, but not lethal. If we're exposed for an hour, it'd be equivalent to four chest x-rays."

"Is that safe?" asked Bert.

"Not really," said Joe.

"Not really," said Amanda at the same time. "But we don't really have a choice."

Joe nodded. "Okay, then it's decided. Everyone but Amanda, gear up. We're making a run for the truck." His words filled the room with a newfound determination, creating a plan out of the chaos.

"Wait, what?" said Amanda.

Joe shook his head. "It could get quite physical out there. I'm not a sexist but you wouldn't stand a chance against the average growler, and it'd be better if someone stayed with Joshua."

This isn't about sexism, she thought. *This is about survival.* She looked at Joe. He was from a time when men opened doors for women. It was sweet really. She nodded her acceptance.

"Wait," she said. "What guns do you have?"

Joe chuckled. "Don't worry, I got enough guns for everybody. I have a forty-five magnum, Dirty Harry special, blow a head clean off, like old Harry used to say. We'll see if any of those zombies feel lucky."

"Do you have anything quieter?" she asked.

"What, don't like the sound of a magnum?" Joe quipped, amusement twinkling in his eyes.

Amanda shot him a pointed look. "Guns make noise, Joe. Noise attracts attention. Attention we don't want. If we're going out there, we need to be as quiet as possible."

Joe scratched his head, giving her a thoughtful look. "Well, I do have a couple of locked breach twenty-two Rugers. We could use those. They're pretty quiet."

Amanda nodded. "That's a start. Remember, we're trying to avoid those creatures, not picking a fight." She tried to inject some levity into her voice, hoping to ease the tension. The last thing they needed right now was panic.

Joe shuffled into the back room. "I think I'll take the magnum as a backup though. And Billy can have a shotgun, in case shit goes sideways out there."

"Yeah, as a last resort," said Billy. "And because I am a terrible shot."

"True," said Joe. "Does everyone know how to shoot?" he added.

They all gave him a "Are you serious?" look.

"Well," said Amanda. "Joshua could probably use a few lessons."

The group chuckled and looked over at Joshua who was looking bleary eyed from his bed having heard his name.

As the tension gradually dissipated into a mixture of light humor and determination, they each began to focus on their personal preparations. The Rugers were brought out from their storage, their matte black finish and substantial weight inspiring a measure of confidence.

Bert took one of the Rugers, and seemed quite content with it.

Billy inspected the shotgun handed to him, his gaze serious. He'd always been comfortable around firearms; his uncle had made sure of that when he was young. He had hoped never to have to wield one in self-defense. No matter how many lessons his uncle had provided he had never become a good shot. He had a tendency to tense up and close his eyes when it came time to pull the trigger.

In contrast to the men, Amanda found her eyes drifting towards Joshua. She watched as he struggled to stifle a yawn, the remnants of sleep still evident on his face. The light-hearted chuckles earlier did nothing to erase the worry etched deep within her heart. *Joshua is just a little boy, not yet ready to bear the weight of this new world's brutal realities. One day he would have to be. In the meantime…* the feeling of love for him overwhelmed her for a moment. *The power of a mother's love,* she thought. *I would do anything for him.*

Meanwhile, Joe examined the radiation meter, his forehead creasing with thought. Its readings held a significant bearing on their expedition's success. Despite their attempts at levity, the sobering reality of their situation was never far from their minds. Every action they took, every decision they made, hinged on the brutal truth that their world had changed beyond recognition, and they were just trying to survive in it.

Amanda felt a pang of guilt. She knew they had asked her to stay behind because she was a woman, and less likely to be able to survive a hand-to-hand fight with the growlers. She knew someone needed to stay with Joshua and she was the natural choice, but she did not want to be a burden. She wanted to carry her own weight. Billy and Joe had been incredibly generous allowing her to come into the bunker, when she might have been infected.

The smart thing to do would have been to leave me and Jo Jo outside. If they are to survive this new world, they are probably going to have to learn to be less kindhearted and trusting. Now they're going to go outside and battle radiated growlers on fire, and in some sense of chivalry they think it right to leave me inside. This will not end well…

BILLY

Growlers in the Canyon

*F*uck, thought Billy. *I really do not want to be doing this.*

The growlers he had met had been terrifying. Their ferociousness, strength, and single-minded murderous intent had provoked in him one and only one instinct, and that was to get away as fast as possible, not to engage and attempt to fight.

Perhaps the time of running away all the time is over. Now we have to fight to survive.

The foreboding door to the bunker stood heavy and unyielding before them, a final barrier between the relative safety of their subterranean sanctuary and the ominous world beyond.

He pushed the door open a sliver and peered out. The basement was intact, and there were no growlers.

He closed the door again and, in the stark, artificial light of the bunker, he took in the men beside him. Joe, a natural leader despite the grim toll of their situation, was a study of stoic resilience. His gaze held a steely determination, his stature unyielding despite the tension. But Billy, who had known Joe since childhood, could see the faint tremors of worry in his stoic exterior, the slight tightness in his grip. Underneath the mantle of bravery, he was fraught with fear. But his fear was well-masked, hidden beneath layers of strength and resolve, a beacon for the rest of them.

Contrasting the steady façade of Joe was Bert, the street-hardened survivor. Though shabby and rough around the edges, Bert had a raw grit about him that belied his unassuming appearance. He may be a few years older, but his frame was taut with apprehension, his breaths shallow and irregular. His hands shook almost imperceptibly, but there was a fierce resolve in his eyes. *This is a man who has had to fight for food before*, Billy thought. This world might have been a nightmare to others, but for Bert, it was just another layer of the hard reality he had always known.

Turning his gaze inward, Billy had to confront the stark reality of his own preparedness. His physique, a testament to years of comfort and sedentary work, left much to be desired in this new world of survival and brute force. He was overweight, his muscles unfamiliar with strain, and his mind untrained in the dance of violence that had become the rhythm of their existence. A heavy sigh escaped his lips, and he could taste the bitter tang of fear in the back of his throat. His fingers clenched, nails biting into his sweaty palms. As he stood there, on the precipice of an unknown fraught with danger, a sobering thought crept into his mind. This terrifying reality was going to be his crucible, one that would either shatter him or forge him anew.

The weight of the shotgun slung across his back and the cold presence of the knife at his side were foreign to him, physical embodiments of a reality he'd never envisioned. The shotgun, he was aware, was given to him because, as Uncle Joe had once offhandedly remarked, even an inept shooter couldn't miss with a shotgun. A testament to his lack of experience and skill.

As Billy persuaded the door wider, a tangible shroud of tension thickened, pressing down upon the room with a weight that squeezed the breath from their lungs. Each man was an island, locked within his own thoughts, fortifying his spirit against the grim spectacle of the ruined world just beyond their haven. The hush of dread was underscored by the spectral menace of the growlers—unseen monstrosities, their identities only suggested by their ominous name, capable of erupting into a terrifying frenzy the instant they dared breach the bunker's threshold.

Nodding with determination, Billy led the way, Joe and Bert on his heels.

They crept up the stairs, opened the door. Joe's house was missing its windows but the walls were upright. There were signs of charring but not an all-out fire. Perhaps the blast wave had snuffed out fires, he wondered.

Chunks of plaster littered the hallway.

The realm outside was now a charred and hollow echo of its former self, twisted by the apocalyptic kiss of an atomic bomb. There was little light. The world was painted with a palette of black and grey.

The desolate silence that clung to the air was punctuated by the distant, sinister growls of creatures that now laid claim to the ruinous landscape, lending an eerie symphony to their encroaching dread.

Well, there are definitely growlers nearby.

His foot met not familiar terrain, but a wasteland. It was forever scarred by the atomic horror that had befallen it. The sky above brooded ominously, its canvas smeared with the grey smudge of ash-laden clouds.

From it, a spectral snowfall of fallout began its descent. It coated their desolate surrounds in a chilling, ghostly white.

Joe lifted the Geiger counter, the device's steady clicking growing more rapid as the radiation level climbed. "Nine millisieverts," he said. A shiver of dread ran through Billy.

"We should minimize the time we spend out here," said Joe.

"Well, I wasn't planning a picnic," said Billy.

He led the way towards his truck, each step crunching ominously in the carpet of ash. The truck was charred and a little twisted but, aside from the paint job, it seemed to be intact.

A guttural growl cut through the eerie silence, turning them all to statues in the fallout haze.

"Keep moving," Joe hissed, his eyes hardened with resolve. "We need that food."

Summoning his courage, Billy grappled with the stubborn rear door of the truck. The rusted metal screamed against his efforts, a grating screech in the lifeless air. Then, with sudden defiance, it wrenched free, crashing open with a resounding clang that seemed to reverberate through the ghostly landscape like a hellish dinner bell summoning demons.

A pair of hardened glares, sharp as daggers, landed on him from Joe and Bert.

Billy mouthed a silent 'sorry', regret knotting in his gut.

He gently climbed into the truck, and as quietly as possible started passing boxes of supplies to the others.

Their initial venture ended with a successful return to the bunker, arms laden with much-needed sustenance. Amanda immediately set about sorting through their spoils.

However, the second outing bore a harrowing shift in mood. Billy, the last to re-emerge from the bunker, was met with an abrupt monstrous growl echoing across the desolation, a lone figure emerged from the ashen veil of fallout—a growler.

God, that's huge, thought Billy. *It must have been a professional body builder or wrestler or something.*

In the dim, gloomy light, the creature was more monster than human, its skin mottled and veiled in ghostly white ash. Its clothes were smoldering. Upon spotting them, it unleashed a chilling roar and charged toward them.

A spike of ice-cold fear coursed through Billy. His hands, guided by primal instinct, reached for the shotgun strapped to his back. However, the biting cold and his trembling fear conspired against him, causing his fingers to slip. The weapon clattered uselessly to the frost-bitten ground.

Bert and Joe, however, managed a quicker response. Their Rugers sparked to life in the pallid light, belching fire at the rampaging beast. Their hurried shots were wide of the mark, the bullets merely skimming the monster and doing little to halt its terrifying advance.

Billy muttered a curse, his hands clawing the frozen earth for his dropped weapon. Before he could reclaim it, however, Joe's gun roared again. This time, the lead found its mark, burrowing into the monster's skull.

The behemoth stumbled, its chilling advance abruptly halted. It collapsed onto the snow-dusted ground, the guttural growl that had fueled their terror dying in its throat. The silence that followed its fall was heavy, haunted by the lingering specter of the threat just extinguished.

Finally, Joe broke the silence, his voice barely more than a hoarse whisper. "First one...up close," he managed to croak out, the raw terror in his eyes mirroring their grim reality. "Absolutely fucking terrifying."

Bert shuddered, his gaze riveted to the unmoving monster. "Not my first, but damn that was a big one. They...they don't seem real," he rasped, disbelief creeping into his voice.

"They're real enough," Billy retorted, his tone edged with grim determination. "We need that food, fast. No cavalry's coming for us."

Joe nodded, his eyes mirroring the heavy truth of Billy's words. "Billy's right," he said, his gaze flitting back to the truck. "Back to work, then."

The next load was uneventful.

The first hint of dawn clawed through the gloom, painting the ashen landscape with a ghostly glow as they ventured out for what they hoped was their final haul. They emptied the truck and headed toward the house. Billy, arms laden with supplies, twisted around to face his companions, a smirk of satisfaction tugging at his lips. But his triumph froze into dread as he took in the sight before him.

Shit, it's another one.

A growler had materialized out of thin air, its grotesque visage basked in the morning's eerie light. Its mouth gaped open, oozing a foul black liquid, and it charged towards Bert with a predator's swiftness, its silence only adding to its terror.

Joe's reflexes snapped into action. His Ruger spat fire into the pre-dawn silence, jolting his arm with the recoil, but the bullet merely nicked the creature, doing nothing to hinder its relentless advance.

It's so easy to miss a running target, especially when you have to hit the head, Billy realized. He felt a surge of adrenaline. The world seemed to slow down around him as he drew his shotgun. He steadied his shaking hands, aimed and squeezed the trigger. The weapon roared, the deafening echo ricocheting off the desolate surroundings.

The buckshot landed true, detonating the growler's head in a grotesque eruption. The creature's lurching momentum stuttered, and it toppled onto the ash-laden terrain, a lone twitch signaling its final farewell before it fell into stillness. Black sludge seeped from its form, a macabre parody of blood, the inky rivers streaking across a snowy canvas.

Billy stood frozen, gasping for breath, his heartbeat a wild drum against his chest. He glanced towards Joe, whose solemn nod spoke volumes, and then to Bert, who gazed with a blend of horror and disbelief at the monstrous corpse at their feet.

A wave of growls and roars, primitive and chilling, shattered the eerie silence. The once tranquil woodland was now echoing with the nightmarish serenade of the infected, their dreadful hunger cries permeating the dawn-lit air.

"Holy hell, back inside, NOW!" Joe bellowed, his voice slicing through the sudden bedlam.

They scrambled to gather the last remnants of the food, their movements frenzied and desperate. The very air seemed to vibrate with the impending threat of the infected, their snarls and hisses growing louder and more frenetic with each passing second.

Billy, his arms laden with supplies, stumbled, cans tumbling from his grasp with a resounding clatter. The others, too panicked to reprimand him, helped him up.

"Sounds like thousands of them," shouted Joe. "They're close and they're coming right for us."

An enraged horde of infected broke from the cover of the trees, charging straight at them. They were of all sizes. Some were huge men, some were no more than children. Some seemed unaffected by the blast wave, others were smoldering or on even on fire. Some were naked, their clothes torn from them by the blast, others had clothes shredded. One appeared to be wearing body armor.

Damn it! Billy's mind screamed. His hands scrambled to retrieve the shotgun he'd dropped. With a thunderous roar, a gargantuan growler lunged, its milky eyes fixated on him.

"Damn! Damn! Damn!" Billy's voice echoed his internal panic. His gut clenched in terror as his trembling hands lifted the shotgun, loosing off two rounds. The first slammed into the creature's gut, inciting a ferocious roar but barely slowing its charge. *Headshot*, his mind screeched, a silent reprimand. The second shell sheared off a portion of the growler's skull, a fountain of black replacing the missing mass. It crumpled into the dust without a sound. Yet as it fell, another growler launched itself from behind it, covering an impossible distance to collide with Billy's chest, toppling him backwards.

The shotgun, now wedged sideways, was lodged in the new growler's open maw, its gruesome face inching closer to Billy's. Black, viscous ooze coated the creature's teeth, droplets splattering onto the gun and then onto Billy's face.

The infection!

The horrifying prospect of transformation ignited a spark of fury within him, fueling a surge of strength. With a primal roar, he managed to overturn the growler, pinning it beneath him.

Realization dawned on him instantly—his exposed back was a fatal mistake. Yet, his position granted him the advantage of

265

leveraging his weight against the growler's gnashing teeth via the gun's barrel.

He glanced over his shoulder to see Joe and Bert engaged in a frantic firefight, their targets dropping one by one. But one growler slipped past their defenses and lunged towards him. On instinct, he rolled once more, the captured growler beneath him bearing the brunt of the new attacker's assault.

A sudden spark of insight flared within Billy—the knife strapped to his side! Abandoning the grip on his firearm with his right hand, he unsheathed the blade and drove it deep into the first growler's skull. It stilled instantly. The newcomer, momentarily disoriented from the roll, had managed to right itself. Now on all fours, it skittered towards him with renewed ferocity.

He yanked at the blade embedded in the fallen growler's skull, but it held fast. Abandoning the knife, he snatched up the shotgun, fingers wrapping tightly around its cold grip. The trigger yielded nothing but a hollow click. He pulled again—another futile click.

His heart seemed to stop with the sudden realization—he had no defense but his fists and feet, and he knew that was not going to be enough.

Frantic, he kicked out as the growler clamped onto his foot, its teeth tearing a sizeable piece from the shoe's sole. It spat out the rubbery chunk, its grotesque hands clamping onto his jeans and tugging itself closer, gnashing and snarling, spittle speckled with that damned black fluid.

The noise of gunfire continued to crack through the air, Bert and Joe putting up a valiant fight. But it was a losing battle—the gunfire was acting as a beacon, drawing more and more of the creatures from the surrounding woods. Billy could see it—they were fighting a rising tide. A tide that was about to engulf them.

He felt the growler's weight bearing down on him as it fought against his efforts to keep it at bay. His legs were trembling, the strain evident as he put every ounce of his strength into repelling the monster. Out of the corner of his eye, he saw Bert and Joe teetering on the brink, their situation desperate.

And then the dreadful click of Joe's empty gun echoed in his ears. Out of ammo. Out of time. Out of options. The realization hit him like a punch to the gut. They weren't going to make it. Not against these odds.

From out of nowhere, the deafening crack of gunfire echoed from a fresh direction. Billy's eyes widened at the sight of Amanda, dual-wielding handguns, mowing down the growlers around Joe. Her stance was unwavering, her aim deadly precise. A lifeline in the chaos.

The growler grappling with Billy gave a ferocious push, the strength of it threatening to crush him. But just as his strength wavered, the creature's head suddenly erupted, scattering remnants of blackened gore. Billy, wide-eyed, looked to Amanda, her gun still smoking. *Goddamn, she's a hell of a shot.*

Pulling himself to his feet, Billy took in their slight reprieve. The growlers were still coming, their ghastly noises cutting through the air, but for now, they had a moment.

"Grab the supplies!" Amanda's shout echoed through the ash-covered landscape, her hands swiftly reloading her guns. "I'll cover you!"

Their eyes met, a silent agreement passing between them. The men holstered their weapons, their hands now preoccupied with grabbing as many supplies as they could. Their task was clear—get to the bunker, no matter what. Amanda was their last line of defense.

A screech from the right side of the house warned of the next arrival. Billy could see this growler had been a young woman. It still had a purse around its neck. It was wounded, half its left leg was missing, but it hopped forward snarling.

Amanda shot it. Growls were now coming from all sides. Billy's hands began to shake from the effort of carrying the supplies. He entered the house and staggered toward the bunker door.

"Alright, Amanda, get back to the bunker now," Joe shouted.

She fired three more shots and then retreated inside the house.

She walked backwards and when a growler appeared she fired. Billy looked back in time to see its head explode in a black mist. *Damn, she's good,* he thought. The infected were pouring into the house and Amanda was shooting them as fast as she could until she fired her last round. When she turned and ran.

She was the last to enter the bunker, casting one final glance at the encroaching horde behind, before slamming the heavy door shut behind her.

She and Billy leaned against the door panting.

"Don't worry," said Joe. "Nothing's getting through that door."

Amanda nodded slowly. "Yeah… and we're not getting out; not for a long time."

Joe nodded. "And the world will be very different when we do."

Billy realized their world had drastically shrunk, confined to the cold concrete of the bunker. The door, once an ordinary piece of metal, had now become the boundary line between life and the horrors of the post-apocalyptic world that lay beyond it. His sweaty palms felt cold against the icy steel as he fought to regulate his breathing.

Amanda stood next to him, her eyes wide with adrenaline. Despite the high stakes, her hands were steady, the echo of her last round firing off still haunting the stillness of the bunker. The hollowness of the empty chamber, a stark symbol of their dwindling resources.

Joe was pacing the length of the room, the raw intensity in his eyes a mirror to the harsh reality.

"I just hope we have enough supplies to last until the fallout has subsided," Joe said.

No one replied. Everyone had to come to terms with their precarious position.

"Not every one of those plastic buckets of food was spoiled," said Amanda.

Everyone looked at her. "Goddamn!" said Billy.

"But it's still good we got the extra supplies. Who knows how long we have to stay here," she added.

An eerie silence settled over the bunker, the only sound being their shallow breaths, attempting to suck in oxygen from the stale air.

They had survived for now, but the question loomed in the air—how long before their luck ran out? Each noise, each echoing growl from beyond the door, was a chilling reminder of the fight that lay ahead. The world they would eventually emerge into was drastically different, infected by fear and death. And it was waiting for them.

Chapter – Clapp Spring Bunker -
The IT lab break-in

SAMANTHA WINTERS

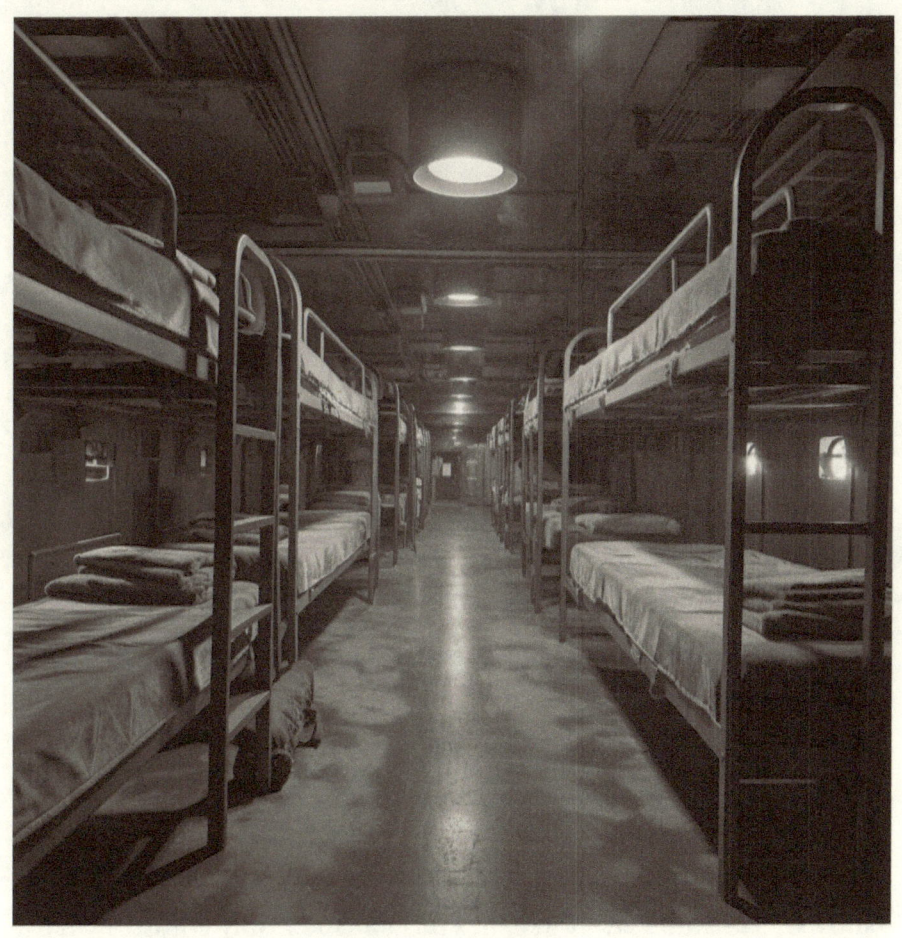

Women's Dorm

The clocks lining the bunker walls announced the arrival of nighttime, though within the windowless confines of the underground compound, day and night blurred into an indistinguishable continuum. In this subterranean world, it was the unbending rhythm of schedules and chores, not the sun, that dictated the passage of time.

Samantha Winters found herself sequestered within the women's dormitory, adhering to the curfew which fell an hour earlier than the men's. This was not a mere custom but a rigid rule, a mandate enforced ruthlessly under the stern gaze of the guards.

Her narrow bed provided scant comfort, she had been given a thin blanket, incapable of holding back the creeping chill of the concrete surroundings. With silence descending like an oppressive shroud, Samantha lay awake, her thoughts her only company in the isolating gloom.

While her body lay motionless in the impersonal gloom, her mind was a whirlwind of restless thought and anticipation. She was like a coiled spring hidden under a façade of restful sleep, each second ticking closer to her moment of action.

The men's quarters echoed with the distant sound of laughter and conversation. She clung to each sound, dissecting its significance against the backdrop of her impending act. The low hum of masculine voices floated down the sterile hallways, punctuated by the occasional clink of a glass or the dull echo of boots against the unforgiving concrete.

The men will have to go to bed soon, she knew. *Then I'll have to wait for them to settle before I act.*

Gradually, the noise of the bunker ebbed away, supplanted by the soothing, soporific hum of a subterranean world settling into nocturnal rest. She meticulously catalogued each rhythmic snore, each rustling whisper of fabric against cold concrete as bodies shifted restlessly in fitful sleep. Even after the final echo of retreating footsteps had been absorbed by the oppressive silence, she held herself in check.

She knew the stakes—one misstep and catastrophe would descend. The certainty of this lent an edge of hyper-alertness to her senses, the surrounding quiet not a comfort but a battlefield she had to navigate.

An interminable stretch of time ebbed away while she remained motionless, her gaze fixed on the invisible ceiling of her lightless cocoon. Once she was certain that a sufficient silence-heavy hour had smothered the last vestiges of life outside her quarters, she began her careful dance with destiny. As silent as the shadows she shared the room with, she slid the threadbare blanket from her body, every sinew taut with anticipation.

The cold floor beneath her bare feet was a jarring reminder of the reality she was mired in, sending a frisson of goosebumps crawling up her legs.

She ghosted through the half-lit labyrinth of the bunker, each careful footfall a hushed whisper against the backdrop of the bunker's pulse. Her memory of Bethany's earlier tour served as her guiding star, as she danced through the maze, a delicate ballet of urgency and caution. The chill of the air made her skin prickle, but it was the frosty tendrils of fear weaving around her resolve that kept her hyperaware of her surroundings.

A whisper, slicing through the oppressive silence of the bunker, caused Samantha's heart to falter mid-beat. "What are you doing out of bed?" The voice was faint, yet it resonated like a thunderclap amid the hushed stillness.

Samantha whirled around, adrenaline flowing. There stood Bethany, the dim light casting an ethereal glow on her face, illuminating a mix of youthful excitement and a dash of playful wickedness.

Hmm, her loyalty is obviously to the Prophet, but she's out of bed too. She obviously wants a little adventure.

Samantha held a finger to her lips, signaling for silence. "I need to check something in the IT room. I just need to know what's going on in the world," she whispered.

Bethany's eyes sparkled with excitement. "Ooo, that sounds fun! Can I come with you?" she asked, her voice filled with anticipation. Despite the gravity of the situation, Samantha couldn't help but be amused by Bethany's naivety. Perhaps, with Bethany by her side the risk would be reduced. If caught they could claim to be naughty little girls having an adventure. *The men of the cult think women have feeble immature minds, maybe I can play on that. I can't really tell her no; she might alert people.* "Of course, you can come, but let's be quiet."

Bethany responded with an energetic nod, her face splitting into a wide, infectious grin.

Together, they navigated the bunker's winding corridors, their path illuminated by sparse, dimmed lights. Samantha felt an icy thread of anxiety weave through her nerves. Bethany was an uncalculated factor in her ad hoc plan, but the time for second-guessing was past. The only way was forward.

As they neared the IT room, the distinctive murmur of active computers reached her ears, punctuated by the soft click-clack of fingertips dancing over a keyboard. A cold knot of apprehension formed in her stomach. *Someone is still working, way past curfew.* An unexpected complication. She turned towards Bethany, her expression a mosaic of worry and frustration.

Yet, Bethany seemed unfazed. "That's probably just Barry," she dismissed casually, the mere mention of his name casting a mischievous twinkle in her eyes. "He's one of the Prophet's sons, and he kind of fancies me. I'll just send him off on a cocoa run. We've had little rendezvous after hours." She paused, her eyes pleading, "But you have to promise to tell me what's really going on outside. I'm dying to know if the Miami Marlins made the playoffs."

Samantha's mind reeled at the stark contrast of their perspectives. Amid the bunker's damp walls and the looming threat outside, Bethany clung to the ordinary— baseball scores and teenage crushes. A pang of realization hit Samantha. Maybe it was this sliver of normalcy that kept Bethany from spiraling into despair. She nodded in affirmation, prompting Bethany to set her plan into motion.

Samantha hid behind a corner as Bethany headed into the IT room. After some soft whispers and giggles Bethany and Barry emerged and headed towards a break room.

As stealthy as a shadow, Samantha emerged from her corner. Cautiously, she advanced towards the IT room. A swift, tense glance down the vacated corridor confirmed she was indeed alone.

Upon entering, she found herself cocooned within a crammed hub of technology. Bathed in the spectral glow of numerous monitors, the room hummed a continuous electronic symphony, serenading the otherwise silent space.

She gravitated towards the most commanding workstation. Barry had left it unlocked, its multiple screens flickering like the eyes of an electronic beast. Its setup was alien compared to what she was accustomed to, but she adjusted, her nimble fingers traversing the foreign terrain of the keyboard. Within minutes, she managed to launch an internet browser.

Now she had to remember the instructions her handler had given her. *It has to be an anonymous session.* She started the session, her fingers deftly typing in the address of a secured, encrypted messenger site. She connected, her heartbeat skipping a beat as her handler's online status flickered on her screen. Relief washed over her, cutting through the thick fog of tension.

"SitRep?" her handler's message popped up on her screen, stark and demanding against the bluish glow. Swallowing down her anxiety, she began typing, "In cult's bunker, underground at Clapp Spring. Need help. Urgent. We are underground. I cannot use transmitter."

"What are they up to. Details?" The curt reply came almost instantaneously, feeding her apprehension. "They are orchestrating the events in Oakland. They possess a vaccine, and an advanced science lab," she relayed, each word typed carrying a weight of its own.

The reply from her handler was immediate and precise. "This is consistent with our suspicions. We believe what we need resides within their science lab. Your extraction will only occur once you have procured samples of the bacteria, the vaccine, and a vial of the virus for analysis. This is imperative. Find a way into that lab."

Bacteria and virus?

Her handler then gave her a series of technical terms to look for on the labelling of the tubes and vials.

This is crazy, they're asking too much of me. "You have to get me out," she typed.

"Negative. Not until you have secured what we need," came the response.

"But if you raid the place, you'd get everything in the lab," she typed.

"Negative. They would destroy everything the moment they detect us. You have to get these samples and keep them safe. The world depends on it."

"This is crazy. Why would you use someone like me, with no training? Why wouldn't you just storm this place. Something doesn't make sense here. Explain it to me."

"Samantha. You are right, more right than you know, but my hands are tied. One day I hope to explain it all to you. But for now, you must do what I ask."

Oh Goddamn! She desperately just wanted to be saved. She knew she had no choice, and she knew she did not have much time before Barry and Bethany would return from their cocoa run.

"I don't have the access code," Samantha typed back, her pulse racing.

Her handler responded swiftly with a series of alphanumeric characters. "Heed my warning—your inoculation should guard against the bacteria, but the virus is a different story. Exercise extreme caution. Do not, under any circumstances, break that virus vial. It is extremely infectious, yet highly delicate outside of its host

278

bacteria. It will perish within seconds if not inside a host, and we need it viable. Do not compromise that vial."

Samantha took a deep, shaky breath, the gravity of her mission settling like a rock in her stomach. This was even more perilous than she'd thought. She exhaled shakily, her fingers hovering over the keyboard. "Understood," she replied, adding, "However, acquiring the samples will take time. Security is high."

"It needs to be tonight. The event is happening already. Ensure it's done," came the stern instruction. "Trust no one."

Samantha felt her pulse throb against her temple. *Trust no one. Who would I trust?* The complexity and danger of her mission just escalated exponentially. She realized they were not going to help her unless she had what they needed. She would have preferred to have time to observe and plan.

"Understood. It will be done," she assured, logging out of the messenger platform. She paused, her hand resting on the keyboard as she took a moment to center herself. Every decision she made from here on out held incredible weight—it could bring her a step closer to averting a global catastrophe, or unwittingly accelerate it. The high stakes of her mission were enough to drown her in anxiety, yet she knew she had to remain calm and focused. There was no room for error.

She cautiously eased the door open, padding softly towards her dorm. Suddenly, a door down the corridor creaked open and Barry stepped out, his gaze fixated on Bethany. His back was turned to Samantha, providing her with a precious window of opportunity.

279

As Barry began to swivel around, Bethany spotted Samantha from the corner of her eye. With an impulsive quickness that took Samantha by surprise, Bethany reached out, cupped Barry's cheeks and pressed her lips against his in a sweet distraction.

Grateful for the unexpected aid, Samantha seized the moment, and turned the corner, continuing her stealthy journey towards the dormitory.

With every step Samantha took, her heart threatened to reverberate out of her chest. Despite the cacophony inside her, she meticulously maintained an even pace, suppressing her breaths to the faintest whispers, tuning into the resounding echo of Bethany's laughter and Barry's astounded exclamations that lingered in her wake.

Hidden from their view, she hastened her steps, navigating the ghostly silent passages. The sound of her own footsteps softly rebounded off the stark concrete walls, amplifying her anxiety. As she passed the monotonously uniform doors, her nerves thrummed with a nervous energy, a reminder of the perilous path she was treading.

Gently nudging her dorm door open, Samantha slipped through the crack, carefully pulling it shut without a sound. Relief flooded her, washing over the tight knot of stress in her chest, as she leaned back against the door.

While her mission was nowhere close to accomplished, she was, for now, tucked away from immediate danger. Collapsing onto her narrow bed, the enormity of her task loomed ominously above her.

Breaking into a highly secured science lab, procuring lethal samples, and then smuggling them out; the very thought was daunting.

Her thoughts swirled in a whirlwind, pulling her gaze up to the ceiling as the dorm's oppressive silence seeped into her. But amongst the tumult, Samantha's resolve was unwavering: the dawn would usher in a day that promised to alter everything.

Moments later, the dorm door creaked open as Bethany slipped in, a gleeful rub of her hands conveying her exhilaration. "That was so thrilling," she whispered, barely able to contain her excitement. "So, how are the Marlins faring?"

A jolt of surprise ran through Samantha. She had completely overlooked the Marlins amidst her mission. "The playoffs have been postponed because of...well, the situation in Oakland."

"That's awful," said Bethany.

It's as if the apocalypse you guys have unleashed might be slightly inconvenient for you. Does everyone here really understand what is happening? Did they know it was going to happen? Did everyone actually help bring about this catastrophe? Bethany is upset that the playoffs were postponed!

The dry chuckle that escaped Samantha was barely audible. "Yeah, it certainly is," she responded, her mind miles away from the subject of baseball. "Let's try to get some rest. We have a long day awaiting us tomorrow."

Bethany expelled a melodramatic sigh but acknowledged with a nod. "Alright then, goodnight, Samantha," she murmured, leaving her alone in the dorm.

The faint echo of Bethany's receding footsteps dissipated into the stillness. Samantha was well aware that sleep wasn't a luxury she could afford at this moment. Her destination was the lab.

An adrenaline-fueled surge dispelled the lingering fragments of tiredness from Samantha's body. She sat upright, scanning her surroundings to ensure her solitude.

It's time for another nighttime venture.

She eased herself from her bed, her steps a muted whisper against the cold floor as she advanced towards the door. With cautious precision, she eased it open, stealing a glance into the eerily still corridor. The artificial illumination threw distorted, lengthy shadows against the bare walls, but there was no hint of any stirring life.

As she stealthily traversed the corridors, her mind replayed the path to the lab she had memorized. With every step, her senses were attuned to the subtlest of sounds, the faintest ripple in the silence.

Footsteps alerted her to the presence of people approaching from around a corner. She looked around and saw a door she thought led to a stairwell, but when she opened it, it was a storage closet. There was just enough room for her to step inside, ease the door closed and wait for the footsteps to pass.

There is too much that can go wrong, she thought, gritting her teeth and trying to calm herself. When the corridor was silent again, she emerged.

She was acutely aware that her imminent actions were not only perilous, but potentially disastrous if discovered. However, the potential fruits of her risky endeavor vastly outweighed the threats. Success was not just a personal goal, but a necessity for the countless victims of the outbreak.

What choice do I really have? I know exactly what the Prophet will do to me. Consent is not something I think this cult believes in. The memory of the Prophet's hand on her thigh made her snarl.

The imposing metallic door of the lab loomed large in her path, the stark sign of 'Off Limits' seeming to mock her audacity. This was the threshold. Inhaling a deep, steadying breath, she entered the code provided by her FBI handler, and nudged the door open.

As she stepped across the threshold of the lab, an enveloping tranquility consumed her. The sterile luminescence of fluorescent bulbs cast a steady glow over the various tools and instruments, each one precisely arranged in a hushed orchestra of endeavor.

Cabinets of glass housed enigmatic vials and beakers, their contents a mystery. Her gaze darted across the room, methodically surveying for the refrigeration unit alluded to by her handler.

As she made her way further into the lab, she inadvertently knocked over a test tube holder. Her heart leaped into her throat, but with a swift motion, she managed to catch it just before it crashed onto the floor, but as she caught it her head banged against the corner of a table. Her breath came in ragged gasps as she realized just how close she had been to alerting anyone nearby. She set the holder back in its place and rubbed her eyebrow where she had hit it on the table. She saw a small smudge of blood on her hand.

An open wound isn't exactly what I want in a lab full of biohazards.

Tucked away in the remote shadows of the lab, a towering metallic door stood sentinel. Adorned with cautionary signage and symbols of hazard, its intimidating presence was impossible to overlook. As realization dawned on her that this was the refrigeration unit, a wave of apprehension washed over Samantha.

To her relief there was no lock, so she pried it open carefully.

Inside the refrigeration unit, rows of meticulously labelled samples stood in formation, their contents shimmering with a myriad of hues that oscillated between beguiling vibrancy and disquieting darkness. Samantha's eyes danced over the labels, her mind a whirlwind of tension as she hunted for the trinity of items she needed.

Her gaze settled on the vaccine first. The vial was filled with a transparent liquid that caught the sterile light, reflecting it back like a beacon of hope. Its seeming simplicity belied its profound significance. With a careful hand tempered by the weight of its importance, she secured it in her bag.

Next, her eyes were drawn to the bacterial sample. Its vessel housed a substance as black as midnight, a light-devouring specter that hinted at its malevolent potency. With an acute sense of caution, she lifted the vial, ensuring the lethal brew within remained undisturbed. Once nestled in her bag, she felt a ghost of relief—two down.

Her final prize, the virus sample, lay ominously under the shadow of the biohazard symbol. Its container seemed to encase an ethereal void, the contents hidden from sight but their threat, she knew, was real. A shiver traced its way down her spine, her fingers quivering as she carefully extended her hand to claim it.

Suddenly, she noticed a red light flashing from a panel on the wall. Below the light there was a camera she had not noticed. *Had that light been flashing this whole time?* Her heart leapt, a surge of adrenaline rushing through her. Was it an alarm? Had she triggered some security measure? Was someone watching her... or maybe it was automatically recording. She hastily stowed the vial in her bag, her eyes never leaving the blinking light. All she knew was that she needed to get out of the lab as fast as she could.

Tomorrow night I will ask Bethany to help me get into the IT room again. I'll tell her the playoffs might be reinstated.

The bunker's corridors seemed to stretch out in an unending labyrinth before Samantha as she navigated her way back to the safety of her dorm. Each flickering overhead light sent a jolt of anxiety through her, causing her heart to flutter like a trapped bird in her chest. The echo of her own footsteps seemed to taunt her in the silent, oppressive halls, their sound a stark testament to her clandestine mission. In the midst of this tension, a newfound resolve began to solidify within Samantha.

Damn them all for making me do this. For making the world suffer this horror. I'll bring them down...all of them, she thought fiercely, the cold determination steeling her nerves. An afterthought softened the edge of her wrath. *Except Bethany. I'll make sure she's rewarded for her bravery.* She shook her head. *One thing's for sure, I am not going to take any more orders from the Feds, and I am not going to let the Prophet touch me, and I am going to make it out of here or fucking die trying.*

Her mind raced with a new rhythm, one of purpose, as she crept back into her quarters. The bed beneath her felt as cold and impersonal as the bunker itself, yet her exhaustion outweighed her discomfort. Despite the looming uncertainties and fears, an unusual tranquility washed over her. Her eyes shut, but sleep was elusive— she was too wound up, her mind teeming with thoughts.

"Samantha Winters," a voice punctuated the darkness, shattering her momentary peace.

She bolted upright as the room was suddenly bathed in harsh, unyielding light. Squinting against the sudden glare, she discerned the imposing figure of the Prophet, flanked by his menacing entourage.

As the Prophet advanced, his silhouette stretched and distorted against the piercing light, instilling an aura of looming dread. Samantha instinctively raised a hand, shielding her eyes from the brutal illumination. "It is time for you to play your part in our endeavors," his voice rang out, cold and commanding, slicing through the silence of the room.

PROFESSOR MARK PRESTON

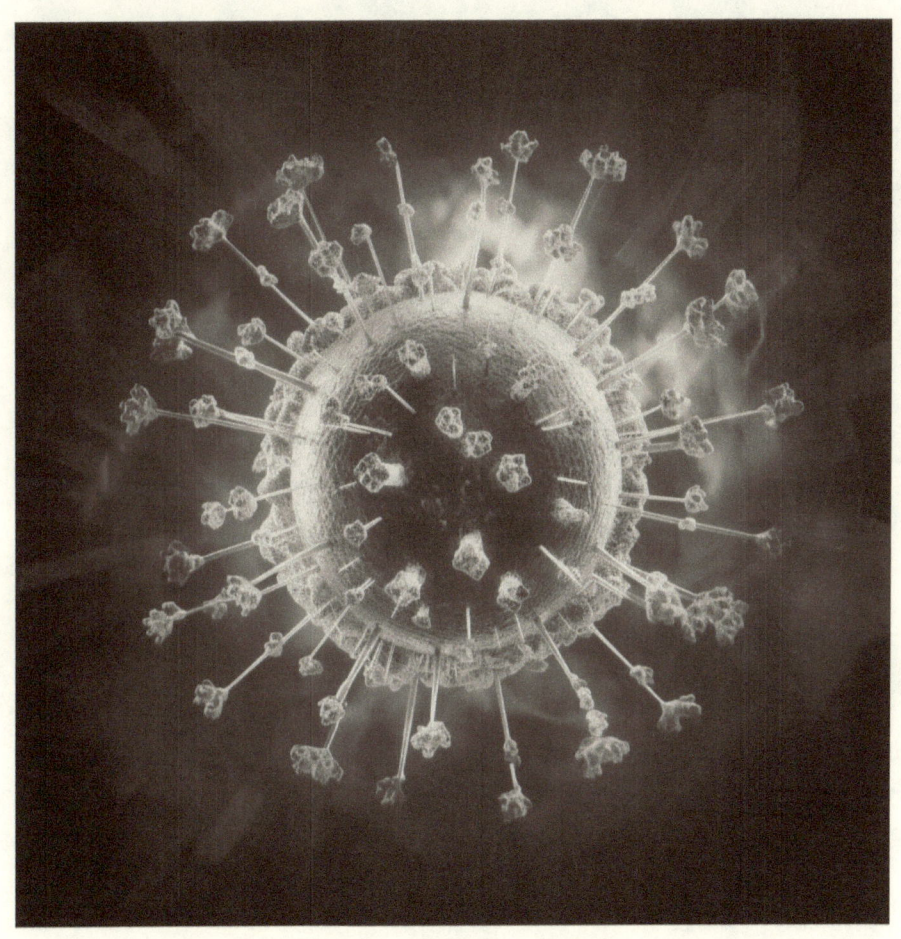

Virus

The President was seated at the rich mahogany desk of the Oval Office. To his left, stern military officers huddled, their uniforms crisp and somber. To his right, serious-faced members of the cabinet congregated, along with Professor Mark Preston. The room was filled with a quiet tension, the silence only broken by the occasional hushed whisper or the soft click of a camera being adjusted.

Mark was trying to control his breathing, he felt like he was beginning to hyperventilate. *I just want this speech to be over*, he thought. *The people should be listening to the advice of scientists.* He knew that science had fallen out of favor in many parts of the country; the Covid pandemic had seen to that. *Just don't politicize this, Mr. President. Just tell them to stay inside until the cloud of infectious bacteria has passed. Tell them to restrain those who get sick. Tell them to wear masks...*

The director motioned a countdown with his hand and then pointed at the President.

The lens of the camera was pointed directly at the President, the red recording light began to blink. Behind it, a large monitor loomed, its screen filled with the live feed of the room. Technicians were a quiet flurry of activity, their attention focused on the equipment.

Seeing his image displayed on the monitor, Mark became acutely aware of the millions of eyes that would be on him. A wave of self-consciousness washed over him, and he adjusted his bow tie, his mind a whirlwind of anticipation as the President began to speak.

"My fellow Americans, we have all been shocked by the developments on the west coast. My thoughts and prayers go out to all who have fallen to this scourge upon our beautiful country.

It is at times like these that a frightened nation turns to their leaders for protection, and it is my humble task to provide that protection. We are sending the full might of the American military to suppress this uprising of the undead.

I know this is an election year, but given the intensity of this crisis, I must require a small delay in the voting process. We need people to be focused on their families, not on some silly self-promoting politicians. Democracy at times like these is not your friend. What the families of America needs, is a strong hand unhindered by the vagaries, whims and fancies of an easily misled and misinformed electorate.

Now let us examine the cause of this disaster. It is no accident that it began in California, the most liberal, the most anti-family, the most immigrant friendly of our states. Our scientists have confirmed that the pathogen behind this outbreak was brought to our nation by illegal immigrants."

A picture of a pretty young woman appeared on the screen. She appeared to be Latino, was wearing jeans, a brown pack strapped to her chest and pastel green shirt. In the picture she was in a wilderness setting, perhaps hiking.

"This young woman, an illegal, and forgive me, I know the looney left don't like us calling them illegals, but that is what they are… this Samantha Winters, broke into a research lab, stole the pathogens and released them in a restaurant in Oakland."

Pictures of Samantha stealing pathogens appeared on the screen.

"This is what happens when you invite the devil to supper.

I have always stressed the need for family values, for good family values. Some of these ultra left-wing radicals allow all faiths, even those of terrorists who wish to bring this kind of disaster upon us.

Our scientists led, by Professor Preston here…"

The President pointed at Mark whose mouth was open in shock and he was still staring at the picture of Samantha on the monitor. When he realized the President was pointing at him, he closed his mouth and tried to look normal, which resulted in an uncomfortable flitting of expressions.

"… have determined that they can develop a vaccine, but it may take many weeks. In that time the threat will spread across the nation.

In this time of emergency. I take full command. Every member of our armed forces will descend upon the infected until they are purged from our land. We will also take into custody anyone who cannot prove their God given right to be in this blessed nation.

Make no mistake. We brought this on ourselves by having open borders, and open minds. Satan entered our borders and entered too many of our minds. God has shown us that the liberals are wrong, and in his compassion, he is wiping them from the face of this nation. Praise God! God Bless America!"

The transmission ended. Mark let out a long breath that he hadn't realized he was holding. *He is a looney toon.* Mark remembered the President on his campaign trail; he appealed to the evangelicals. He had talked about the end of times, but Mark had thought he was just pandering to his base. *He didn't tell the people what they needed to know to survive. What kind of fascist state does he want to create? The only thing he got right in that transmission, is that it's going to take a long time to develop a vaccine, and in the meantime a pathogen laden radioactive cloud is going to visit every lung in the country.*

Chapter –
Clapp Spring Bunker – Caught

SAMANTHA WINTERS

The Bunker Has Issues

Samantha found herself seated on an unyielding steel chair, alone at the center of a harshly lit stage. The relentless glare of several spotlights was trained on her, blinding her and turning the rest of the room into a nebulous darkness, full of shapeless shadows that teased her strained eyes. She felt as though she was caught in the jaws of an intense, relentless spotlight, an unwilling star in some macabre spectacle.

The ruthless lights sculpted her into a starkly outlined figure amidst an ocean of shadows, leaving her painfully exposed to the hidden onlookers. Attempting to shield her eyes, she found the lights too abundant, too relentless, to escape. Their invasive heat clung to her like an unwelcome embrace, provoking beads of sweat to trace down her skin and her clothing to cling to her form in a sticky embrace. The discomfort served as a raw, incessant reminder of her vulnerability under the piercing spotlight.

Yet amidst her disorientation, Samantha fought to steady her breathing, to harden her resolve. She refused to allow the startling severity of her surroundings to skew her off course. Her adversaries might have orchestrated this daunting stage, but she vowed not to let them manipulate her role. She was not a mere puppet in this grotesque play; she was a warrior; she would fight until there was no breath in her body. If they expected her to be compliant, they were in for a surprise.

The space beyond the blinding light was a dark abyss from which the Prophet's voice, chilling and condemning, boomed.

"We require your complete confession," he pronounced, his words weaving a tale as malevolent as it was fabricated. It rang through the silence, a frosty dagger of accusation designed to pierce her resolve.

Samantha responded, her voice carrying the tint of genuine bewilderment, "Confession to what?"

The Prophet's voice came again, slick with a chilling conviction. "You stole the bacteria and emptied it into the water supply in Oakland, California. You put it in the drink of an innocent white woman in a restaurant. Confess."

Her denial was instinctive and vehement. "What? I did no such thing!" Her protest reverberated off the unseen walls of the room, absorbed by the engulfing darkness.

"Well," the Prophet replied, his tone shifting, now laced with menace, "we are going to need you to confess to it anyway. We can do some...very, very unpleasant things to you, you know."

The implication was clear and unambiguous, and hung in the air like a poised guillotine.

Samantha's mind buzzed, caught in a dizzying whirlwind of fear and confusion. Should she delay, linger in the hopes that the FBI would storm this uncanny nightmare and right the wrongs? But even as the thought crystallized, a chilling comprehension crashed into her, turning her veins to ice. The FBI was complicit. Those she'd trusted for rescue, considered her allies, were entangled in this grotesque puppet show. Or at least, some malignant entity within the Bureau was. The meticulous mission, the grand staging—it had all been an elaborate deception, casting her as the architect of the outbreak. As if standing on a pulled rug, she teetered at the precipice of a chasm, filled with dread and uncertainty. There would be no cavalry. She was unequivocally alone.

Out of the corner of her eye, she glimpsed a door, standing unguarded to her right. A possible escape route, but her heart sank as she contemplated the attempt. There were big men in the interrogation room. She knew she could not physically fight her way out of the room, and even if she did, there was an entire bunker full of devotees to deal with. *And the bunker is sealed shut.*

The Prophet's voice reverberated throughout the cavernous chamber, a deep rumble akin to thunder heralding a tempest. "The only remaining question," he declared, his tone laden with a chilling threat, "is whether you'll play the part of the docile damsel, or force me to acquaint you with the compelling influence of my pliers."

Somehow, I have to survive. People need the vaccine. People need to know who is behind all this.

Bethany emerged from the curtain of glaring lights. "There's no use resisting, Samantha," she said, her voice holding an edge of mockery. "Don't oppose our Lord's chosen messenger in this realm."

"Bet...Bethany?" Samantha's voice faltered, a brittle whisper in the harshly lit room. Shock was a frozen lance through her chest, turning her words into a gasp. "You...you were part of this?"

A smirk slithered onto Bethany's lips, as cruel as it was self-satisfied. "Did you truly think that the gullible, sweet Bethany would abandon the divine path for ephemeral temptations with a boy?" Her laughter, malevolent and victorious, rebounded off the sterile walls, the cold echoes stabbing into Samantha's already frayed nerves, deepening the sense of betrayal that gnawed at her.

Samantha swallowed hard; she knew she was ensnared in a perilous dilemma. The unforgiving room encased her with the Prophet, a colossal figure whose stony countenance bore the mark of relentless determination. At his flank stood six unwavering minions, their formidable physicality further magnified by their absolute fealty to the man they revered as their spiritual guide. Their blind obedience made them volatile, undecipherable. A cold realization gripped Samantha: there would be no room for negotiation or compromise with such zealots.

Tears welled up, but she pushed them down. She knew that even if by some miracle she could get out of the room, she was inside a sealed bunker, on an island.

Samantha glanced to the camera, the blinking red light staring back at her like a demon's eye. Abruptly, the stark, dull walls of the room sprung to life, as the flickering image of President Mitchel began to manifest on the flat surface behind her.

"Is our Pandora ready to spin her tale?" The President's voice echoed in the room, steeped in derision and chilling certainty.

"It's all a lie, Mr. President," shouted Samantha. "The cult are the ones behind the whole outbreak!"

The President laughed. "I know, I know. But even so… we need you to confess. You can do it with or without your toenails. It makes no difference to me."

Samantha's mouth fell open in disbelief. *The President is in on this too!* The treacherous thought rattled around in her mind, amplifying the surreal horror of her predicament.

The Prophet sauntered into the blinding luminescence, his ominous silhouette stark against the harsh light. "We require your confession for the world to witness, a narrative wherein you, not us, are the puppeteer behind this outbreak," he dictated, his voice seeping with dark amusement. "Time is a luxury we do not have, my dear. After all, our esteemed President has a nation to govern." As his cruel intentions spilled out, a wave of dread crashed over Samantha, tightening its icy grip around her.

The President sneered. "We developed the perfect tool to spread the one true word of God. Those who believe will be vaccinated against the bacteria that harbors the virus. Those who defy will soon fall victim to either the bacteria or the growlers."

"So, let me make sure I've got this straight," Samantha fired back, venom and fear knitting a furious edge into her voice. "You, Mr. President, and the rest of your deranged followers ignited this unholy pandemic, razed democracy to the ground, all to seize unchallenged control with your religious brainwashing. You're not just monsters. You're the living embodiment of evil itself."

A deep chuckle reverberated from the spectral figure of the President. "You ought to show more respect to your elders, Miss Winters. Especially when speaking to my own flesh and blood, my brother."

"Your...brother?" Samantha's gaze flicked between the two men, the stark reality sinking in as she noted the uncanny familial similarities.

Exhaling a sigh, the Prophet remarked, "Our father couldn't resist temptation. So, yes, we're half-brothers. We had our close calls with the press, believe me."

"Judgement is the society's favorite pastime, isn't it?" the President chimed in.

"Religion will do that to people," added Samantha disdainfully.

"Religion will be humanity's salvation!" the Prophet roared. He stepped into the light's harsh glare, brandishing a pair of formidable pliers ominously before Samantha.

"Yes, we did engineer this disaster to usher in a new age—an age under our rule, where our faith guides the masses. The unchecked freedoms of the present age are a disgrace in the eyes of God."

Abruptly, the door to the room swung open and an underling stepped in, whispering urgently into the Prophet's ear. His gaze swiveled onto Samantha with a newfound intensity.

"Bethany observed you slipping our stolen property into your pack, yet it appears to be missing. What did you do with it?" he interrogated.

Samantha's eyes darted towards the open door, a spark of audacious hope igniting in her chest. "Looking for this?" she retorted, her voice laden with a feisty sarcasm. Her hand slipped into her pocket, fingers closing around the cool glass of the virus vial. In a single, fluid movement, she withdrew it and, with a defiant glare at the Prophet, hurled it towards his startled face.

The vial collided with the Prophet's cheek, exploding into a spray of shards upon impact. A shocked howl filled the air as he clutched his bleeding cheek. The room fell into disarray, a perfect distraction. Seizing the moment, Samantha moved with quick, calculated steps towards the small camera perched on a nearby table. Her fingers closed around it with a sure grip, and with the lens aimed at her pursuers, she bolted towards the tantalizing promise of the open door.

Behind her, a shrill scream cut through the chaos, its horror resonating in Bethany's voice. "It's the virus!"

She'd weaponized their fear and the ensuing chaos would be her cover. Bursting into the corridor, Samantha found herself thrown into the midst of the cult's hive-like activity. Among the sea of startled faces, her gaze caught Doctor Evers and Nathan, the guard, standing frozen amongst the flurry, their faces mirroring the shock and dread rippling through the crowd.

"Emergency! The Prophet's injured—he needs help!" she called out breathlessly, successfully feigning a panicked urgency.

A ripple of confusion clouded their faces before being swiftly replaced by alarm, and they charged past her, rushing to the Prophet's aid. Once they vanished into the interrogation room, Samantha sprinted away.

The unfamiliar labyrinth of the bunker stretched out around her, but uncertainty wasn't a luxury she could afford.

As she whipped around a corner, she caught her breath, realizing her frantic pace would draw attention. With an effort, she forced herself to slow to a brisk, but seemingly unperturbed, walk—the perfect façade of a cult member going about her business. Inside, however, her heart thudded like a wild drum, begging her to run.

A voice boomed over a speaker system. "Medics to the media room!"

Inside, she repeated to herself like a mantra, "Keep it cool." The buzz of angry voices reached her from the corner she had just turned, their tone spiked with hostility.

"Where is that bitch!" Bethany's voice rang out over the speakers.

An unadorned door to her right sported a crude icon of a staircase, a beacon of hope in the chaos. Without a second thought, Samantha flung it open and threw herself into the stairwell, her feet pounding the metal steps in rapid succession. She cleared three flights in a blur, her fear fueled by the escalating uproar from the floors beneath. The stairwell terminated at a nondescript door, reached just as the cacophony of the stairwell door below exploding open filled her ears. Panic threatened to unravel her, yet she fought it back, taking a steadying breath as she cautiously nudged the door open to materialize in the cavernous expanse of the worship hall.

A wave of relief washed over her; she knew where she was now. She cast her eyes on the formidable blast doors, her mind reeling. But there was no key, no visible mechanism to operate them. She needed a moment to figure it out, but with every passing second, the bunker was growing more alert to her escape.

She stared at the insurmountable obstacle before her, her mind racing to piece together a plan. Suddenly, a blaring alarm echoed through the hall, the red light flashing a warning. The worship hall transformed into a chaos of running figures, their panicked shouts intermingling with the alarm. The clock was ticking faster than ever, and she had to make a move.

With determination in her eyes, Samantha carefully extracted the memory card from the camera, sliding it into the sanctuary of her pocket. Now she had concrete proof of the plot that had ensnared the entire world. Accompanying the irrefutable evidence was the valuable vaccine, a precious weapon against the bacterial host carrying the lethal virus. She held within her hands, quite literally, the potential salvation of humanity.

She hoped she had not been too close when the vial shattered, exposing her to the deadly virus. She understood that the vaccine she possessed was targeted at the bacteria, not the virus it harbored.

Dwelling on the 'what ifs' would lead her nowhere, she realized. A glance around the chaotic worship hall confirmed her next course of action—the armory. Amidst the confusion, she would find her way there. Armed with more than just evidence and a vaccine, she might stand a chance at escape, and possibly, at exposing the perpetrators of this horrifying apocalypse.

She tried desperately to recall the blueprint of the bunker, the twisting corridors appearing as an unintelligible labyrinth in her mind. As she deliberated, a wave of panic swept through the crowd, amplified by a chorus of terrified screams, "Infected!"

A man armed with a handgun shouldered past her, his face etched with fear. The chilling, inhuman growl of a zombie echoed through the grand chamber, freezing her blood and sending the crowd into further disarray. They scattered like frightened animals, several of them brushing past Samantha in their frantic escape, just as the Prophet appeared at the entrance, his usually serene countenance warped into a horrifying mask of primal hunger.

The gun-bearing man aimed his weapon at the Prophet, his hands trembling. Then his eyes widened in fear and disbelief. "No, not you!" he cried out. "I can't shoot God's messenger!" His agonized proclamation echoed through the hall, a chilling testament to the blind faith of the followers.

The Prophet's response was swift and brutal. He lunged forward, sinking his teeth into the man's neck. The man's screams reverberated in the hall before he collapsed, dropping the gun.

Seizing the moment, she snatched up the gun and took off, not daring to glance back.

As she rounded the corner, she collided with a tableau of grotesque horror. A young man lay sprawled on the floor, body convulsing in agony as bloodcurdling screams filled the air. Above him, a figure hunched over, relentlessly tearing into his entrails.

The figure lifted its head at Samantha's approach, and she recognized the monster: Bethany. The woman she'd once known was now a terrifying apparition, her eyes transformed into a milky void, her mouth slick with a sickening black liquid. With a feral roar that echoed off the bunker walls, Bethany turned her full attention to Samantha.

The virus moves so quickly! Is it the direct exposure?

Panicked, Samantha aimed the gun in Bethany's direction, her finger instinctively squeezing the trigger, but the gun refused to comply. *The safety!* her mind screamed. With adrenaline-fueled dexterity, she flicked the safety off just as Bethany lunged towards her. Her finger tightened on the trigger, releasing a bullet that found its mark squarely between Bethany's eyes. The grotesque figure jerked mid-leap and crumpled to the ground, lifeless once more.

"Who's the bitch now?" Samantha retorted, her voice echoing in the deadly silent corridor.

A man careened around the corner, clutching his arm and screaming, his terror-filled eyes wide with pain. "I've been bitten, I've been bitten!" His voice echoed off the cold, sterile walls of the bunker. Samantha recognized him as either Nathan or his twin brother John.

"Nathan?" she called out tentatively. "We need to amputate that arm before the infection spreads." *Or in a few minutes you will be part of the problem.*

Upon hearing Samantha's words, Nathan froze, his face contorting with horror. His eyes bulged in their sockets, and his mouth gaped open in a silent, petrified scream.

A girl ran around the corner closely followed by an infected man who pounced on her bringing her to the ground. Two more infected rounded the corner and charged at Samantha and Nathan. Nathan curled his upper lip and launched himself at them.

"Run!" Nathan shouted at Samantha.

She immediately scrambled away trying to ignore the screams and sounds of flesh being ripped. She understood she was running back towards the Prophet, but it was the only direction not blocked by the infected.

She saw an elderly man open a door at the end of the corridor, his eyes scanned the scene before him, and he turned and ran. She headed for the door and as she got there, she saw the far end of the corridor being swarmed with a dozen or more zombies. She went through the door and closed it behind her.

There was a lock on the door, and she twisted it just in time because the door handle rattled. Someone was trying to get through, it was a girl who screamed and then there was the thumping sound as a series of zombies hit the door and presumably devoured the girl.

She knew she had lost track of where she was. Everything was chaos. She did not know where the infected would be.

Blood seeped under the door. Samantha took a step back and bumped into someone. She turned around and saw the white eyed, black mouthed, snarling face of the Prophet.

PROFESSOR MARK PRESTON

Oakland Lights

Mark was in an uncomfortable cot in his White House office. His body ached for rest, pleading with him through the physical fatigue that gnawed at his bones. Nevertheless, sleep remained a cruel tease, offering fleeting moments of respite amidst hours of tossing and turning. So, when an intern abruptly nudged him awake, his foggy mind waged a fierce battle to claw its way out of slumber's clutches.

"The girl, she's been caught!" stammered the intern, his words tumbling out amidst a quake of anxiety.

Stuck in the groggy no man's land between sleep and wakefulness, Mark grappled with the revelation, managing a confused, "Who are you talking about?"

The intern swallowed hard, the gravity of his message evident in his gaze, "Typhoid Mary. The girl who allegedly sparked the outbreak."

Mark's eyes snapped open, the haze of sleep instantly vanishing. "Samantha Winters?" He bolted upright, the weariness in his eyes replaced with a spark of alertness.

"If they have her, we could learn so much. She must know something about who is behind the infection," said Mark.

Affirming with a vigorous nod, the intern continued, "The story is, she was seeking refuge with a group of devout Christians. They initially offered her sanctuary, but after witnessing the President's address, they took her into custody."

"That was unexpectedly swift," Mark commented, pulling himself into a sitting position as the intern thrust a piece of paper into his hands. It was a photograph of a girl seated on a stage, a scene of interrogation.

"That's her, mid-interrogation," the intern pointed. "The President is watching the interrogation live."

On a more detailed look, the photograph struck Mark as off. "This is odd," he mused, his brows knitting together in confusion. "She's dressed exactly as she was when she supposedly stole the pathogen. Even her hair, and that raw gash on her eyebrow— identical to the security footage. This must have been snapped minutes after the theft. Are they planning to transport her here?"

"No, the President has commanded her immediate execution," the intern revealed.

"What!" A surge of disbelief washed over Mark, punctuating his usually calm demeanor. "He can't possibly have the legal authority to do that," he countered, his words carrying a trace of incredulity.

"Why would he even consider such a reckless step? There's a plethora of information she might possess. It strains credibility to think she pulled off this disaster on her own. What lab did she raid? How did she know what to take? How did she know what it would do? Why was it created in the first place?"

"The President described her as the most perilous individual alive," the intern said.

"That's preposterous! She's a young woman, barely in her twenties, for heaven's sake!" Mark exclaimed, frustration simmering beneath his usually calm demeanor. He stood up, the photograph clutched in his hand. "She couldn't have the expertise to design this pathogen, and what motive could she possibly have to instigate such a widespread outbreak?"

Driven by a new sense of urgency, Mark swiftly collected himself. "Where can I find the President? It's imperative that I persuade him against the execution. There's so much information we can glean from her; her objectives, any possible accomplices. This could be our best shot at unraveling this crisis."

"I think he's in the situation room, having breakfast," the intern informed him. They rounded a corner, the intern glancing nervously at Mark. "The nuclear strike turned out exactly like you warned—it escalated the spread of the infection, just like adding fuel to a fire."

The intern paused, gathering his breath before continuing, "Outbreaks are popping up all over the place—Arizona, Nevada, Oregon...Mexico's even reporting cases now." His voice dropped to a whisper, fear leaking into his words. "The President's called in the military, not just to deal with the infected and growlers, but to control the uninfected, to impose martial law. He sent a lot of marines into the Oakland area."

"And then what happened?" Mark's question pierced the silence.

"We...we lost all contact with them," the intern stammered, fear fraying the edges of his voice. "But, we should have a drone sweep over the area soon."

Mark took a big sigh. The implications were alarming. The need to confront the President had escalated from pressing to downright critical.

The guards flanking the situation room door sized up Mark with wary glances, yet dutifully swung the door open at his approach. As he crossed the threshold, the room buzzed with tense energy. The President, hunched over a sprawling map littered with blood-red pins marking infection hotspots, was the epicenter of this anxiety storm. Dern, his chief of staff, was engaged in a hushed, fervent conversation with him. A host of uniformed officers and secretaries were scattered around the room, their faces etched with the same grave concern.

"Mr. President," Mark began, striving to keep his voice steady amid the pressing tension.

President Mitchel swiveled to face him; his weary eyes mirrored the heavy toll of their dire circumstance. "Mark, what drives you to my doorstep at this hour?"

"Samantha Winters, sir," Mark said, drawing a sharp glance from the President at the mention of her name.

"What about her?" President Mitchel questioned, a discernible edge creeping into his voice.

"She's pivotal. She may be our solitary lead to decoding this pathogen and untangling the enigma behind its deployment."

The President frowned, "She's to be executed. I've made my decision, Mark. She's too dangerous to keep alive."

Mark clenched his jaw, struggling to keep his rising anger at bay. "She's just one small girl. Sir, the necessity to question her is paramount. We must dissect the machinations of this catastrophe—the rapid proliferation, the identities of any co-conspirators...We might even unearth a method to neutralize the pathogen directly from its creator."

A glance passed between Dern and the President, suggested a shared, hidden knowledge. President Mitchel's face contorted into a cruel sneer. "That wretched girl deserves nothing less than death. My people...our people, have endured unbearable torment. They deserve to witness justice, to see the perpetrator meet her rightful punishment."

"Isn't justice also about finding the truth?" Mark countered, his voice laced with challenge. He swallowed, the tremor in his voice betraying his anxiety. "I have concerns about the video, sir...the one of Samantha stealing the pathogens."

The President's glare fixed onto him, icy and unyielding. "Go on."

"She had a fresh wound on her forehead in the video," Mark began cautiously, "but the same fresh wound was visible when she was shown being interrogated live."

The President folded his arms, his demeanor unflinching. "Your point?"

"My point, sir," Mark said, forcing himself to meet the President's gaze, "is that the timelines don't match up. The interrogation happened today. If her wound was still fresh during the interrogation, it implies she must have stolen the pathogen after the outbreak had already started."

Dern retorted, a dismissive edge to his voice, "Maybe she's just a slow healer."

Mark shook his head, meeting the chief of staff's gaze with a determined look. "That's not how human physiology works, sir. The uniformity in her appearance, the identical fresh wound...it strongly suggests the possibility that Samantha Winters might have been set up."

"Set up?" President Mitchel burst into a mocking laughter, the sound echoing through the cold, silent room. "And who would do such a thing?"

Mark clenched his fists at his side, swallowing hard against the dryness in his throat. "I...I don't know, sir. But we can't ignore the anomalies. There are inconsistencies that we need to address before we pass judgment on her. I think someone with a lot of power has orchestrated this whole outbreak, and they would love to see her dead rather than talking."

312

"Mark," the President hissed, his voice dipping low and holding an undercurrent of threat, "are you insinuating a conspiracy within the very heart of my administration?"

Mark held his ground, maintaining his eye contact with the President's icy stare. "I'm suggesting that we're operating with an incomplete narrative, sir," he returned assertively. His posture rigid, conveying a resolve that wouldn't be easily shaken. "Proceeding with Samantha Winters' execution without proper due process would be a grave distortion of justice. Even more so if we are about to murder an innocent woman."

Silence fell like a shroud over the room. Each individual seemed frozen in place, even their breaths held hostage by the weight of Mark's words. The only audible sound was the quiet humming of the air conditioning, the normally insignificant noise now unnaturally loud.

A thought hit Mark, like a divine enlightenment. *Oh my God! Maybe the President is behind the outbreak.*

President Mitchel's gaze bore into Mark, the glint of suspicion in his eyes magnifying in the uncomfortable quiet. Their standoff felt like a tautly pulled wire, any additional pressure threatening to snap the fragile balance.

The static atmosphere was abruptly pierced by the hesitant voice of an officer. "Sir, we have a live feed coming in from a drone patrolling Oakland."

A flicker of relief washed over the President's face, a subtle shift in his hardened features. His lips curled into a tight smile, his words flippant as he grasped the lifeline to divert the conversation. "Oh, excellent. Now we can witness the effects of a regiment of marines against a swarm of mindless zombies."

"Did the marines have biochemical gear?" asked Mark.

The President's eyes widened.

The screen flickered to life with the drone feed, revealing a hauntingly desolate Oakland from a bird's eye perspective. Streets lay vacant, the lifeless buildings were mere husks of their former vitality, and vehicles sat abandoned in disarray. A steady rhythm sounded in the charged silence of the room: the anxious drumming of President Mitchel's fingers on his chair armrest. His gaze, along with everyone else's, was riveted to the unfolding scene on the screen, each of them anticipating the unseen horror that lay ahead.

The drone trudged forward, its camera methodically scanning the forsaken landscape as it closed in on the location of the marine regiment. Gradually, indistinct shapes morphed into the recognizable silhouettes of marines. Yet, their normally disciplined stances had given way to an unsettling disarray—their movements sluggish and uncoordinated, more akin to a shamble than the trained strides of military personnel.

"Zoom in on Bravo leader," Dern's voice cleaved the silence, his gaze fixed on a figure slightly distanced from the rest. The room collectively held its breath as the screen homed in, the image briefly pixelating before sharpening into horrifying detail.

Bravo leader's once stern countenance was now a grotesque parody of humanity. His eyes, now vacant and ghostly white, were set in a pallid skin networked with unnatural black veins. His rifle hung neglected from its strap, his helmet tilted in a carelessly odd angle, unveiling the true extent of the monstrous transformation. The gasps in the room were audible as the full revelation hit home—their men had fallen prey to the same nightmare they had been sent to eradicate.

A heavy silence descended on the room again. No one dared to breathe, let alone speak. The marines, the nation's elite warriors, were now part of the undead legion. Their rifles and guns reduced to mere ornaments, their body armor serving no purpose other than a chilling reminder of their past.

"We sent in the marines, and now the zombies have body armor," Mark finally said, his voice echoing ominously in the quiet room.

"Things were not meant to unfold this way," the President murmured, a hollow tone lacing his words.

Drawing in a steadying breath, Mark gathered his thoughts. "The pathogen was spread by the explosion," he said, attempting to maintain an objective tone. "In due time, it will start to settle down. But until then, we must instruct everyone to remain indoors. They should wear masks if possible. The winds have carried it eastward, sweeping across the nation. The United States is on the brink of experiencing outbreaks from coast to coast."

"All brought to us because of this damn Samantha Winters creature," President Mitchel muttered, resentment simmering in his voice.

Mark opened his mouth to object, to stress, "No, it was the detonation…"

But Dern interrupted him sharply, "Enough! Get out!" He spun toward the guards. "Escort him out immediately."

Mark exited the situation room, his thoughts buzzing like a swarm of bees, each one stinging with urgency. His mission now was clear, as troublesome as it might be. He needed to unravel President Mitchel's belief that Samantha Winters was the root cause of this catastrophe. He was unsure of her role in the pandemic, but he knew it was vital to talk to her. *She must know something important… in fact,* he realized, *that is why the President is so eager to have her killed.*

He traversed the labyrinth of White House corridors, his heart gripped by fear. At last, he reached the sanctuary of his office and collapsed into his chair, the old leather groaning in sympathy with his exhaustion. His gaze fell on the wilderness of documents sprawled on his desk, an untamed forest of graphs, data, and reports that he had been decoding just hours ago.

Each curve, each spike, each plummeting line on the graphs was a silent scream, an accusation of worsening circumstances. His eyes absorbed the chaotic symphony of lines, an unsolvable riddle that only seemed to deepen under President Mitchel's misguided policies. The feeling of powerlessness seeped into his veins, like he was battling a tidal wave with a flimsy shield, the immense pressure threatening to shatter his resolve.

He was yanked from the abyss of his thoughts by the intruding rhythm of footsteps. Lifting his gaze, he found two figures in tailored suits, but their military training shone clear in their rigid posture and alert eyes.

"Dr. Peterson," the taller of the two initiated, his voice seeping through the room like a chilling draft, echoing the unmistakable command of authority, "we've been instructed to escort you from the White House."

Mark's eyes widened. He darted glances between the pair. But their faces were as impassive as stone statues, offering no comfort or clarification.

"I...Excuse me?" the intern stuttered, his voice barely above a whisper. "On whose orders?"

"The President's," the second man cut in, his voice indifferent, the words dropping from his lips like stones, as though he had mastered the art of delivering such disheartening news. "And you will have to accompany Professor Preston."

The intern grabbed some items from his desk.

A sensation of cold dread coiled in Mark's stomach, akin to swallowing a chunk of ice. Banished from the White House, while the nation danced on the knife-edge of the most menacing crisis in its history. The thought was as surreal as a warped nightmare, yet it was sinking into him, cold and unyielding.

He rose slowly from his chair, the scraping sound echoing hollowly in the room. He moved about his office, gathering the fragments of his research, each paper a testament to countless sleepless nights and relentless efforts. The men stood by, silent

317

sentinels with eyes that traced his every movement, an air of patience belied by their vigilant gazes.

He fingered the dog-eared pages of his notepad, pausing on the hastily scribbled equations and theories.

His eyes traced the familiar surroundings one final time, lingering on the coffee-stained table, the stack of reference books on the corner shelf, the sight of Washington monument visible from the window. The room, once his bastion of thought and discovery, was now a symbol of loss and change. Uncertainty gnawed at his insides, a relentless rodent threatening to chew through his resolve.

Mark knew he needed a new plan. As he was escorted down the expansive corridor, his mind was already weaving a new strategy, a game of chess against invisible opponents. The portraits of past Presidents on the walls seemed to eye him with questioning gazes as if asking, 'What next?' And he silently promised an answer, not to the frames on the wall, but to himself and the nation he vowed to save.

Outside the White House, he was put in a car. The men navigated the winding streets of the city, each turn taking Mark and his intern further away from the heart of civilization and closer to its discarded periphery. The car slowed to a halt at the entrance of a landfill, a graveyard of man's excesses, veiled under the cloak of night. Piles of refuse stood tall, rising like grotesque monoliths, transforming the wasteland into a haphazard city of waste.

Why have they brought us here?

Under the pallid glow of the moon, the discarded remnants took on an eerie life. Shattered televisions were like dismembered robots, stripped washing machines resembled empty tombs, and decomposing food waste appeared as colorful mosaics of decay. The metallic scent of rusted iron clashed with the rotten odor of waste, tainting the air with a smell that made Mark's nostrils flare in distaste.

A foreboding chill slithered up Mark's spine as he stepped out of the car, the gravel crunching defiantly under his weight. He scanned the desolate scene, his eyes reflecting the grim landscape and his heart mimicking the heavy thump of the car door shutting behind him. The landfill, a monument of neglect and oblivion, seemed to resonate with his current status—discarded, overlooked, but brimming with unacknowledged potential.

Mark felt a knot of unease tighten in his stomach as he absorbed the stark reality of his surroundings. His eyes fell on his intern, a look of trepidation visible in the young man's eyes. Mark swallowed hard, steeling himself against the overwhelming sense of uncertainty.

The men exited the car. They dragged Mark and the intern along with them, their firm grips inescapable. One of the men produced a gun, the sheen of its metallic surface catching the light and throwing lurid shadows around. Its appearance sent an icy shudder through Mark.

They positioned Mark and the intern before them. With the lights behind them the executioners formed grim silhouettes against the backdrop of the landfill.

They definitely intend to kill us.

"You can't...you can't do this!" Mark's voice fractured the silence, the desperation in his tone seeming to bleed into the night air. His protest hung heavily in the stillness, sinking into the pit of ignored pleas.

Then, like a banshee's wail, the piercing shrill of a ringing phone cut through the air. The voice on the other end reverberated in the open air, unmistakably President Mitchel's. Mark strained his ears to catch fragments of the conversation.

"Mr. President, I swear on my life, my lips are sealed," Mark begged. "At least spare my intern, he's so young, an innocent!" Desperation seeped into every syllable.

A response crackled through the line, chilling him to his marrow. The President's orders, rendered all the more harrowing by the deceptive calm of his tone, echoed in the open space, each word a death knell. "People who do not believe in God, and that I am His mouth on earth, are not really people at all, they are empty shells sent here by God to test us. They have no souls, they only have the façade of humanity, not the divine spark, they do not really feel, they are soulless...Execute them..."

Two gunshots thundered through the landfill, their resonance shattering the oppressive silence, the sound bouncing off the skeletal remains of forgotten junk. But instead of Mark or the intern meeting their ends, it was the men in suits who slumped to the ground. Their bodies hit the gravel, not with the dramatic thud Mark expected, but with an almost balletic surrender to gravity.

Mark spun around to witness a sight that defied all his preconceptions. In the moonlight, the intern stood with a gun still smoking in his hand. The quiet, unassuming shadow who had mirrored his steps since the beginning of the outbreak had just become their savior.

"I am agent Carl Rutger," he declared, adding a layer of authority to his persona, the title rolling off his tongue with a level of comfort and certainty that left no room for doubt. "I am not with the CDC. The role of the intern was just a cover. I am a recent graduate of Quantico."

"FBI?" Mark stammered, his mind struggling to catch up with the swift turn of events, the surprise making the question sound more like a weak exclamation.

Carl merely nodded, his features steeling in the stark illumination, the soldier within him now visible amidst the tumultuous field of betrayals.

"How does an FBI cadet end up playing an intern in the midst of all this?" Mark demanded, his voice a cocktail of incredulity, fear, and a begrudging hint of admiration.

Carl inhaled deeply, as he tightened his grip around the weapon. The pistol was no longer just an instrument of defense but a badge of his true identity. "The FBI has been trying to piece together a series of mysteries. We needed eyes and ears on the inside, to sift through the chaos and gather intel." He paused, locking eyes with Mark. "So, I was planted as your intern—a ghost in the system, unnoticed yet vigilant."

"But you were in the White House! You went through the Secret Service's most vigorous vetting."

Carl smiled. "Yeah, the FBI does the vetting for the secret service."

"Oh… Oh!"

Carl's gaze drifted from the lifeless bodies to Mark, his eyes carrying the weight of grim revelations. "We're still piecing together a jigsaw of deception and conspiracy. But one thing is clear: the President is implicated, and Samantha Winters could be the key that proves it."

Mark exhaled a breath he hadn't realized he'd been holding, the air shuddering out of his lungs as he slumped against the car. His mind was a cyclone of thoughts.

"I knew we need to get to Samantha," he muttered, more to himself than Carl, his words dissolving into the crisp night air.

Carl nodded, his affirmation firm and determined. "The most important thing is that we suspect the architects of this outbreak are in league with the President and… they've developed a vaccine. Our latest information is that Miss Winters has secured the vaccine to the host bacteria."

"That's fantastic but … how do we locate her?" Mark asked.

"We actually know where she is," said Carl.

"You do?"

Carl nodded. "She's with the Phoenix cult, on an island on the west coast. We had an operative inside the cult helping her and feeding us continuous updates."

Mark's hand sliced through the air in a frustrated gesture. "So, the FBI just needs to mobilize its forces, go get her, and the vaccine, and we can vanquish this outbreak."

"The FBI is under the control of the President. Most agents are still loyal to him. There are a few that I can trust and those few cannot launch a rescue mission. She is being advised to make her own way out. We will rendezvous with her on the mainland."

Mark sighed in frustration.

Carl muttered. "In truth … it's probably too late. She's probably already dead. But we will try to meet her and figure out what dirt she has on the President, and hopefully get the vaccine from her. In the meantime, I need to get you somewhere safe. Given the nature of the pathogen, the outbreak will hit the east coast within two days."

"How do you know so much about the pathogen?"

"We have been picking up pieces of the mystery for the last eighteen months. That's how I was able to feed you the details of the pathogen so quickly. We've had people inside the Cult of the Phoenix for the last three months. I will give you the full story when I know you are safe."

"Safe?" Mark echoed, a touch of skepticism seeping into his voice as he looked at Carl. "You've already laid it out—the outbreak is coming. Where will be safe? We need to be taking action. We need to … we need to get the word out about the President. We need to get people wearing masks and we need to find the vaccine. I am not going to hold up somewhere."

Carl studied him, his gaze seeming to dissect Mark's resolve. "The outbreak…it's a ticking time bomb we can't defuse. We need you in the aftermath, to be the voice of science and reason, a beacon of hope, if you will, amidst the ruins. You're with me on this—we'll navigate this chaos together. But we need to make tracks before the President sends more enforcers when these two fail to report back."

As they prepared to retreat from the desolate landfill, Mark found his voice again, "Do we have any allies in this nightmare? Anyone who can assist us in finding Samantha?"

Carl's nod was steady and assured. "We do. We've got a handful of agents already sifting through the shadows. Plus, a few influential friends who haven't fallen prey to the President's deceit. They're our eyes and ears, our hope in this pandemonium."

Mark cast one last glance at the lifeless bodies of the men who had intended to end their lives. The grim reminder of the stakes they were playing with. Their survival wasn't just a personal triumph. It was a signal flare in the storm, the first defiance against the President's authoritarian regime. He knew in his heart this was just the beginning, the start of an uphill battle against a political

Goliath, the dawn of a rebellion that was as much about survival as it was about truth.

Clapp Spring Bunker –
Samantha Winters

Leah

"**H**oly shit!" Samantha gasped, her back slamming against the unyielding door. The gun seemed like an alien extension of her hand, gripped with a white-knuckled intensity. A primal echo within her yelled to fire, but her fingers wouldn't answer the call. It wasn't fear alone anchoring her hand. It was something else, an intangible dread that strung her veins with ice crystals.

Her eyes locked with those of the Prophet—a pair of alabaster orbs stripped of any human sentiment. All she saw was a spectral apparition, hollowed of empathy and humanity. His lips, tar-black with viscous fluid, twisted into a perverse smile that sang a chilling symphony of malice. The magnetic leader, the persuasive voice she once knew, was gone. In his stead stood a being, twisted by hunger, not for power but for something far more chilling.

And then, amid the horrifying reality, Samantha found her resolve. The cult was a lie. The Prophet was a monster. Her survival instincts roared to life, drowning out her fear.

She regained control of her trembling hand and shot the Prophet in the chest, making him stagger back.

She seized the moment to run past him, hearing his growls receding behind her and a small surge of hope welled up within her.

Finding herself in a narrow, dimly lit corridor, she began to formulate a plan. The layout of the bunker was intricate, a labyrinth of tunnels and rooms that could easily confuse those unfamiliar with its design. But she had not wasted her time in the bunker, she had been studying the bunker's layout, creating a vague mental map in her memory.

She remembered the armory and mentally pictured the route she needed to take. She raced towards the door to the stairs, but an infected girl suddenly lunged toward her. Instinctively she shot the girl in the forehead. The head exploded and the zombie collapsed. Three uninfected cult members ran by. Samantha was about to open the door to the stairs when a thought occurred. She looked down at the dead zombie and her eyes saw a glint of metal. She reached down and removed a hairpin.

A sickening growl echoed behind her, compelling her to whirl around. A zombie, sluggish in its gruesome march, emerged from a side room, its vacant gaze not yet tethered to her.

She steadied the gun, her finger poised on the trigger. With a sharp intake of breath, she squeezed—only to be answered by a hollow click. Cursing under her breath, she realized the chilling truth. It was empty.

She whirled around, wrenching the door open just as the zombie lunged in a grotesque charge. With a resonant thud, she slammed the door behind her. The growls from upstairs were more like gurgling symphonies of hunger. But her salvation lay below, in the armory's promise of a fighting chance.

What I need are guns and ammunition.

She plunged down the stairs, taking them three at a time in her descent. The echo of her footsteps acted as an alarm bell to the monstrosities above, and she heard their shambling feet scurrying in pursuit.

Several floors down, the door to salvation stood imposing before her. A lock could mean the difference between life and death in this moment. As her fingers grazed the cold metal handle, she offered a silent plea to any listening deity.

With delicate precision, she nudged the door open, her gaze sweeping the corridor for any hint of the undead. It was an eerie calm. As she stepped out, the door whispered shut behind her, a metallic sigh echoing her relief. She slunk toward the armory with stealthy determination.

A discordant symphony of screams and growls echoed through the corridors.

Reaching the armory, she was met with the frustrating sight of an RFID lock. Her gaze dropped to the hairclip in her hand. Picking this lock was out of the question. She scanned her surroundings, her mind whirling to solve the conundrum. How does one outsmart an RFID lock?

She noticed something lying on the floor, it was a baseball bat, its end streaked with crimson memories of previous encounters. She grasped it, weighing it in her hands as she stared down the imposing door. No, the door was too robust to yield under a bat's assault.

Her gaze drifted upwards. Hopes of a crawlspace in the ceiling came to her mind, a desperate architectural loophole. But a cursory glance dismissed that idea too. The ceiling was a solid canvas of lights and sprinklers, offering no easy escape. She was left standing there, a bloodstained bat in hand and an unyielding door mocking her.

More growls echoed down the corridor, dragging Samantha's attention from the mocking door to the ominous shadows approaching from around the corner. An unwelcome guest was making its approach. Samantha's pulse quickened as she considered retreating to the stairs, but a chorus of growls from behind the stairway door squashed that option. Cornered and armed only with a bat, she felt the vice of desperation tightening.

From the gloom emerged a small figure; a child, infected and turned, a stomach-turning monstrosity, snarling and growling a pathetic childlike rumble. It had been a boy, not even ten years old. A lump formed in her throat as she whispered, "Oh no..." Compassion surged, tearing at her heartstrings, but survival screamed louder. This was not a boy anymore, but a life-threatening predicament.

The zombie's head twitched and looked at her. The once angelic face twisted as a violent roar erupted from it. Black spittle spattered onto the floor and the boy charged, screaming a high-pitched growl.

"Oh no, oh no, oh no," she said. Hurting a child went against every instinct in her, but there was no time to think up an alternative. When the boy was close enough, she swung the bat at his head, and it splattered with a sickening crunch. "Oh God! What have I done? I am so sorry. Oh, little one, I am so sorry."

The deed was done. The boy was not a threat anymore.

More growls indicated she was running out of time as well as options. The lights flickered for a moment. *God, I hope the power doesn't go out. Imagine being in pitch black amid these things.* An idea occurred. *What happens to RFID locks when the power goes out... or when there is a fire? Safety protocol would require opening locks... though I don't think OSHA applies here.* She took off her shirt and tied it around the end of the bat. She took a lighter out of her pocket and started a small flame. Quickly she held the flame against the sprinkler. In a second, water spurted from the sprinkler head and she heard a click as the armory door opened.

She lunged for the door and entered the armory, pulling the door closed behind her, but it would not click shut. *With the doors unlocked those things will probably get in here in moments.*

The armory was a mess. Nearly all the guns were missing, and empty boxes of ammunition lay strewn over the floor. People had obviously come and loaded up in response to the internal outbreak. However, there were three identical shotguns in a corner on a shelf. *I guess people did not want to deafen themselves.* She had never seen a shotgun with a magazine feeder. It had the number 590 written on it. There was a vest with shells on it. She put the vest on and grabbed the shotgun. It had a black leather strap, so she slung the gun on her shoulder.

Guns are no use when you run out of shells or bullets. She looked around for more shells and saw a box labelled '10 cartridges'. She hoped a cartridge was the same as a shell, and grabbed it, putting it in her backpack. There were a couple of boxes labelled 'Magtech', she opened one and saw it matched the bullets for the gun.

She started loading the gun just as a woman burst in and put her back against the door. Samantha did not recognize the woman. She was about thirty, had black hair and wore a short skirt. Her legs were covered in dried blood. "They're here," said the woman.

No shit, thought Samantha as she loaded the seventeenth bullet into the gun's magazine. *There's no time to load the shotgun.*

The woman's slight frame was not enough to hold the door against the infected. She was pushed aside, fell to the ground, and a fat growling infected man burst in and fell over her and sunk her teeth into the woman's stomach. Three more infected were pushing there way into the room.

A strange calm descended on Samantha as she carefully took aim on the nearest target. *Bang!* A clean headshot from the gun. She took aim at the next target, a bald middle-aged, infected man who had locked rage filled white eyes on her. *Bang!* Her bullet went through his right eye. The woman on the floor had stopped screaming and the man on top of her lifted his gaze to Samantha.

Bang! The bullet clipped the back of his head, but he still got to his feet. *Bang! Bang!* She was aiming for his head, but the first shot hit his shoulder and the second hit his nose. He collapsed, but she put one more in the center of his head. *Bang!*

She had lost count of the bullets she fired. Two more people entered the room. She raised her gun to shoot and just as her trigger finger tensed, she realized they were not infected. It was a woman and a young girl. The woman was wearing a long white dress. The girl looked to be about eight years old, blonde haired, blue eyed, well brushed hair and had a blue jacket and black backpack.

"Jesus! I almost killed you," Samantha said.

The woman gave her a stern look. "Do not use the Lord's name in vain," she said.

Samantha raised an eyebrow. *You're thinking about that in this shit-storm*, she thought, but did not voice her opinion.

"Mommy they're coming," said the little girl.

"Get behind me, Leah," said the woman.

"And get out of my line of fire," added Samantha.

Two sprinting men arrived, one was uninfected, but covered in blood. The second man was infected and was inches from catching the first. They entered the armory. The first man did not notice the dead bodies on the floor and tripped over them, which cleared the line of sight for Samantha who fired two rapid shots. The first bullet grazed the infected man's head. The second one blew a third of the man's head off.

Samantha started reloading the gun's magazine.

Without hesitation the first man got to his feet and ran to the rear of the armory, grabbing a shotgun with a magazine. He checked the magazine and then pumped the shotgun once.

"How the fuck did this all happen," he said.

"Gerald!" admonished the woman, covering Leah's ears.

Gerald shook his head and strode out of the room. Seconds later there was an enormous bang from the shotgun.

"Shit! That's fucking loud!" shouted Gerald.

Samantha's ears were ringing. "That's going to bring every infected on the floor. Time to go!"

As Samantha began to leave, the woman pushed Leah into her path. "Take her," she said. "She's a good girl. She knows how to serve the Lord."

Samantha gave the woman an are-you-crazy look. The woman pointed to her hip. There was a blood stain there. *Bite marks.*

The woman closed her eyes for a moment, her grip tightening around Leah. When she opened them again, they were filled with a determined light. "Leah," she said softly, turning to her daughter. "I want you to listen to me, baby. You know I love you more than anything in this world, right?"

Leah nodded, silent tears streaming down her cheeks.

"I need you to be brave for mommy, okay?" she continued, her voice shaking. "I need you to go with um Samantha, isn't it? She's going to take care of you."

"But...but mommy..." Leah started, her voice barely a whisper.

"I know, baby," she interrupted gently. "I know it's scary. But I'm so, so proud of you. You're the bravest girl I know, and I need you to be brave now. Can you do that for me?"

Leah nodded, her small form shaking with sobs.

Samantha looked at the mother, her eyes welling up with tears. The mother looked back at her, her eyes pleading.

"Promise me," she whispered. "Promise me you'll take care of her."

Samantha's throat felt dry. She swallowed hard, then nodded. "I promise."

With that, the mother released her grip on Leah, reaching out a trembling hand to brush the hair out of her daughter's face. "Go with Samantha, sweet girl. Mommy loves you."

Leah let out a sob, but Samantha gently pulled her away, a fierce determination burning in her eyes.

It'll be hard enough getting myself out of this bunker without a kid to handle... She looked at the little girl and gave a big sigh as she realized she just could not leave her behind.

"Fine," she said in almost a whisper. "Stay right behind me."

"Yes ma'am," said Leah.

Despite it being the middle of an apocalypse, Samantha winced at being called "ma'am".

"We'll have to work our way up to the bunker doors and figure out how to get them open…" Samantha said.

"No," said the mother. "Those doors are the most secured in the facility and swarming with growlers. There is a passage that only a few know about. It is behind the Prophet's bed. You'll need a key that the Prophet always carries on him. If you ask him, he will let you and Leah through, because Leah is special to him. I was once honored enough to be bedded by him. That was a long time ago," she added wistfully and with a meaningful look at Leah.

Dirty old man, sowing his seed, thought Samantha. *I know where the Prophet's body is.*

"I'll ask him nicely," she said and grabbed Leah's arm.

They exited the armory. The ear shattering sound of the shotgun erupted from around the corner.

They could hear Gerald shouting. "Fuck, fuck, fuck."

He thought the shotgun would save him, but it's just bringing more of them down on him.

Samantha cautiously pushed open the stairwell door, her breath hitching as she caught sight of two infected creatures lurking quietly on the other side. Upon spotting her, their faces contorted into gruesome snarls, their eyes flashing menacingly. Without a moment's hesitation, Samantha aimed and shot the first creature squarely in the face.

The second creature, partially obscured by the collapsing body of the first, presented a moving, shadowy target. Samantha recoiled, bumping into Leah as she let loose a volley of shots into the creature's body. It kept moving until a final bullet found its mark in its head. Without wasting another moment, she quickly yanked Leah into the relative safety of the stairwell.

Goddamn, I've lost count of my bullets again.

The eerie chorus of growls and screams seemed to be closing in, echoing from all directions, although their immediate area was momentarily clear. Hastily, she ejected the gun's magazine and began to load it with bullets from her dwindling ammo box. In her haste, one bullet slipped from her fingers, clattering to the floor.

Leah, standing close by, quickly reached down and scooped up the dropped round. The small gesture, an act of assistance amidst their dire situation, wasn't lost on Samantha.

"Thank you, Leah," Samantha expressed her gratitude in a whisper, and once the weapon was loaded, she started ascending the stairs, with Leah sticking to her heels like a small, frightened shadow.

"How far..." Leah started, her voice a whisper-thin thread in the silence.

"Sshh!" Samantha cautioned, cutting her off gently. "Don't speak unless you have to. We can't afford to attract their attention."

Leah responded with a silent nod, her wide eyes brimming with understanding.

The growling from the infected below resonated through the stairs. Above them, the grating snarls of three more sent a cold shiver down Samantha's spine.

Should she risk taking out the immediate threat and potentially alert the infected below? But she had no other option, she needed to get to the Prophet's body upstairs before she could even think about facing whatever lurked below.

She steadied her breath, bracing herself for the inevitable. The next few moments were going to be a leap into the unknown, a dance with death she had no choice but to engage in.

Samantha edged her way up the stairs, each footfall a whispered plea to the unseen. The trio of infected above were oblivious to her approach. She settled her sights on the largest one, its distorted figure a grotesque sham of the man it once was. With a pull of the trigger, it crumpled to the floor, setting off a chain reaction.

The remaining two launched themselves at her, their roars echoing through the hollow space, inciting the infected below into a frenzy. A second gunshot echoed, bringing down the closest one. The final one hurled itself down the stairs towards her. Panic surged within her as she fired thrice, the first two shots just grazing it, the third hitting it in the creature's leg.

"Below, they're coming from below," Leah's voice trembled as she tugged on Samantha's elbow. The subsequent shot meant for the final infected ricocheted off the wall. Muttering a silent curse,

Samantha steadied her nerves. The rhythmic drumming of fast-approaching feet was amplifying in the stairwell, an impending storm.

With methodical precision, she took the headshot on the wounded creature before her, then spun around to face the new wave of threats emerging from below.

A curse slipped from her lips as she registered the horde. Seven distorted figures, eyes gleaming with an insatiable hunger. A mantra echoed in her mind, an anchor in the swirling chaos. *Don't panic, aim and shoot. Aim and shoot.*

The first of the sprinting infected burst into view, a disfigured shell of a human, its skin was a loathsome mix of hues—sickly greens and morbid browns. The once bright eyes were now an icy, milky white, devoid of anything human, focused solely on its prey with a chilling intensity. Its maw hung wide open, showcasing a macabre set of blackened teeth. From it, a dreadful growl issued, filling the air with the fetid stench of its own death and decay.

She waited for it to get closer. She breathed deeply, calmed herself and aimed. *Bang!* The first one fell. She instantly moved her aim to the second one. *Bang!* A burst of scarlet and black liquid erupted from its head, and it fell. The one behind staggered awkwardly over the bodies of the ones in front. This gave her time to carefully aim, and she blew a hole in the top of its head. This made an even bigger hurdle for the ones behind. She took her time with each shot and killed the remaining three effortlessly.

The trick is to stay calm, she told herself. She turned and grabbed Leah's hand and started running upstairs. It was not long before she got to the body of the Prophet.

Leah gasped. "It's the Prophet," she said.

"Yeah, he's dead. What a shame," Samantha said in a monotone.

She searched his trouser pockets, and then his jacket pockets but there was no key. She patted him down and there were no keys on him. "Damn he must have left his key somewhere."

What the hell am I supposed to do now, she thought. A door on the level above burst open and infected poured in.

She grabbed Leah to pull her downstairs, but Leah resisted. She was pointing at the Prophet's neck. Samantha looked closely, there was a necklace. She moved his collar and saw a key on it. With a quick tug she snapped the chain and got the key.

Samantha smiled. "Good girl, now let's run."

Samantha juggled the blueprints of the bunker in her mind. What floor was the Prophet's private quarters on? What odds would she face there in terms of infected numbers?

The sharp retort of gunfire echoed from below. There was a skirmish underway... that might mean an ally.

They descended multiple levels before she cautiously cracked the door open to scout the floor. It was swarming with infected, and her gut told her this wasn't the floor they were looking for. *One more level down*...if her memory served right. The infected on the stairs were a frantic mass, stumbling over each other in their frenzied attempt to catch them, oddly slowing their own advance.

Descending another flight, Samantha tried the next door, only to find it unyielding. One floor remained. If that was sealed, their fate would be sealed too. But was it the floor they needed? *There's only one way to find out.*

Samantha tugged Leah down the final flight of stairs, then flung the door open. The thunder of gunshots immediately filled her ears, echoing off the corridor's narrow walls. A makeshift barricade of a dozen survivors held the line against a seething mass of infected at the corridor's opposite end. Keeping a firm hold on Leah, Samantha wove them both behind the frantic line of defense, unnoticed by the survivors absorbed in their desperate fight for survival.

The Prophet's bedroom was close. She recognized it and snuck over, and tried the door handle; it was locked. *Hopefully this key works both locks,* she thought. She turned the key and with a muted click, the Prophet's sanctuary swung open. Out of the corner of her eye, she saw a surge of monstrous bodies flooding over the survivors, their screams and snarls muffled as the door to the bedroom closed behind her and Leah, sealing off the cacophony.

Leah was wide-eyed, her gaze bouncing around the room. "We're standing in the heart of the holy of holies," she said, her voice awestruck yet hushed, as if worried about disturbing the sanctity of the place.

Samantha closed the door behind her and locked it. She spared a moment to cast a wary glance around the room, the opulence doing little to impress her. "Let's not waste time standing in awe, we need to find that secret passage."

An expanse of unblemished white spread across the room; the carpet underfoot a soft, plush sea of ivory, the walls, a stark canvas devoid of decoration. Nestled in the center was a simple, single bed, its wooden frame painted an innocent white, dressed in matching sheets and covers.

Leah took in the simplicity with a kind of reverence. "Look at this, Samantha. The Prophet truly was a holy man, choosing to live so modestly," she said, her voice hushed, eyes gleaming with admiration.

He was a dirty old man… and this is not his vibe at all, Samantha thought.

Behind the crisp whiteness of the room, Samantha's gaze was drawn towards an inconspicuous sheet adorning the far wall. The only possible facade for a hidden passage, she mused. The escalating pounding on the door underscored the urgency of their predicament, the frenzied assault of the infected threatening to breach their sanctuary.

Without a second to waste, Samantha darted towards the wall, yanking down the sheet with a swift motion. As she suspected, the contours of a door appeared beneath. With an almost shaky haste, she turned the key in the lock, revealing the passage within. Hand firmly clasped in Leah's, they crossed the threshold together.

The sight awaiting them was beyond anything they could have prepared for. Samantha's mouth fell open in awe. She was about to curse but remembered innocent Leah beside her. "Oh...my...Gosh."

Leah's mouth dropped open in shock. "Shit!" she said. "I don't fucking believe it."

Samantha looked at Leah momentarily shocked. She returned her gaze to the new room they had discovered and she nodded. "Well…"

Chapter – Uncle Joe's Plan

AMANDA

Whitehouse Website Image

Joe's laptop screen flickered to life, cutting through the room's dim light. He logged in, his brows creasing in surprise. "Amanda, it seems you were right; we've got internet access."

A sense of relief washed over her as she slid into the chair beside him. "The internet was built by the Defense Department, it's backbone is a resilient creature bred to endure a nuclear attack, though I can't gauge for how long."

As Joe navigated to Google, a strange anomaly unfurled. "That's odd," he murmured. "This isn't Google." Despite typing the familiar web address, an image of the White House loomed on the screen. An unfamiliar string of text and a series of videos peppered the space below.

Joe's fingers moved cautiously, clicking on the first video in the queue. An unfolding scene painted the screen; a young woman stealthily breaking into what appeared to be a secured laboratory and snatching cylindrical tubes.

A voice, the unseen narrator, began to relay a tale. "The woman, an illegal, that you see in this footage, she's the seed of the chaos that now spreads out from Oakland, her actions sending ripples that are engulfing our nation and perhaps the world. Security footage caught her in a lab obtaining the pathogen that she later released in the water supply of Oakland and in a restaurant where the first case was reported."

They were all transfixed by the video, which showed a hand pouring the vial into a reservoir and then later pouring the remnant into a glass.

"Well how the hell did they get video of that?" said Amanda.

The footage transitioned, revealing the woman, now restrained and apparently under interrogation. Abruptly, the view switched to the familiar setting of the Oval Office, the figure of President Mitchel addressing the viewer. "We have apprehended the woman, known as Samantha Winters. Given the dire circumstances, and to answer the calls for justice, I've invoked emergency powers to command her execution."

"Kill her before she talks?" said Amanda.

The camera closed in on the President's face. "Now, let it be known that I am a President who doesn't falter in the face of adversity, but instead pursues justice with relentless determination. Under my leadership, our nation will reclaim its standing. This site will provide ongoing updates on the status of our recovery. Once this nation has fully recovered, we will return to elections. In the meantime, the military will relay the laws of martial law."

As the President's determined proclamation faded out, Joe shifted in his seat. "That was quite the theatrical display," he muttered, his tone laced with a biting sarcasm.

Amanda nodded. "It certainly raises more questions than it answers. Where was this lab she was breaking into? Why were they creating this pathogen? What was her motive? And you saw that fresh wound on her face after she was captured. That was hours after the first clip. It's such an obvious flaw in their narrative that I can't believe they didn't think about and remove it."

Bert smiled knowingly. "The truth is just the truth, but lies...lies can be tailor made to serve a purpose. People like to have sugar poured in their ears. The President knows that people will believe what they want to believe. They want someone to blame and who better than an immigrant. Facts be damned. It's going to feel real good to a lot of people to blame immigrants. Sugar in their ears."

Joe seemed to be very worked up. He was red faced and snorting. "I've been telling people for years, it's the government you have to look out for. The government is where the real danger always hides."

"Uncle Joe," said Billy. "You were always a bit too paranoid. Remember how you trapped those crows, thinking they were government drones?"

Joe nodded. "Sure, that was a mistake, but like the old saying goes; just because I am paranoid doesn't mean they're not out to get me."

Billy chimed in, "Maybe the other videos hold some answers."

Joe nodded, clicking on the next link. The screen showed marines disembarking a helicopter, their boots hitting the ground with military precision. The perspective shifted abruptly to a bird's-eye view, an unmanned drone capturing the squad's perilous advance into a city overrun with the infected. A caption read, "President Mitchel takes action to protect his citizens."

Joe raised a quizzical eyebrow. "What was even the point of that video?"

"Just to show the President's doing something, I guess," said Billy.

Amanda sighed. "I note he is not depicted collaborating with medical professionals or researchers. Instead, he's surrounded by military. He wants us to know he will enforce his rule on us. They're opting for a warlike narrative."

Joe's brows furrowed deeper. "This vilification of Samantha Winters…sounds like misdirection," he said, the distrust seeping into his voice. "If the people blame her, they won't look for who is really to blame."

Amanda curled her lip. "To execute someone quickly like that, it's like they're eager to quieten her. There's more to this. There must be clues somewhere on the internet. You know people must be trying to post stuff, but if all they get is this White House site then we are going to be left in the dark."

Joe responded by trying to get to other sites, a newfound resolve lining his features. Yet, every attempt to penetrate the vast information network of the internet redirected them back to the White House site, a digital maze with a single, unavoidable destination.

A momentary silence hung between them before Billy finally broke it, "I guess they've commandeered the DNS servers."

Amanda arched an eyebrow at him, "DNS?"

Billy jumped in with a helpful analogy, "Think of the DNS, the Domain Name System, like the internet's phonebook. You know, when you punch in a website name, it's the DNS that translates that into an actual numeric address, an IP, where the website lives."

Amanda did not understand. *This guy's a techie.*

Billy rubbed his hands together. "Right. But if we manage to circumvent the DNS and tap directly into the IP address..." He gestured to Joe so he could sit and take over typing.

His fingers danced across the keyboard, weaving a sequence of codes. "And if I manage to siphon off some info from the DNS cache and...replace it with our own local information...Voila! It should trust our DNS."

As the iconic Google search page flashed up on the screen, Billy exhaled a triumphant, "Yes!"

A cheer erupted around the table, their excitement reverberating in the small room. Billy pumped his fist in the air, while Amanda, more reserved, allowed herself a quiet smile.

"There are techies out there circumventing the DNS hijacking," said Billy. "The fact that search works is proof of that."

Scouring the recesses of the web, their search led them to a brand new site, hosted in South Africa. It had details on Samantha Winters. It depicted Samantha as an illegal immigrant, whose family were apprehended for being in the country illegally a year ago. She was entitled to stay in the country because she had been brought over as a child, but her mother and father were to be deported. She also had a little brother who was still a child and therefore would be deported with the parents.

Joe ran a hand through his hair, squinting at the screen. "It's a heartbreaking story, but you wouldn't think it would motivate her to start an apocalypse."

Amanda pointed to the screen. "It says she was a valedictorian, but never studied anything about biology, genetics, or biowarfare."

A chilling silence fell over the room as the weight of their discovery sank in. Each question that popped up in their pursuit of the truth seemed to beget more inconsistencies, more unknowns.

Amanda rose from her seat and paced the confines of the room, her footsteps echoing the rhythmic ticking of the clock on the wall. "We may have just witnessed the twilight of democracy," she said, her voice carrying a note of sorrow. "No elections and orders to come from the military."

Joe rubbed his chin. "I know a lot of folk in the military, they're not mindless you know. When they start doubting the President, there will be…resistance. We are going to need the military to get rid of these growlers."

Amanda nodded. "When our supplies dwindle to nothing, we'll be thrust into an alien world. When we emerge from the bunker we will be surrounded by growlers, and we barely survived our last encounter."

Billy swiveled his chair to face her, his eyes reflecting a mix of fear and uncertainty. "And us, the fortunate few with a bunker...How many survivors could there be out there, realistically? Not everyone had the resources or the foresight to invest in a bunker like Uncle Joe. And anyone who did not survive is going to be a growler. What is the world going to be like when we emerge from here?"

With a thoughtful expression, Joe rubbed the stubble on his chin. "The infected move with horrifying speed. But let's not forget, California is home to about twenty million firearms, and that's not even accounting the military."

Amanda shook her head, her eyes darkening with worry. "But guns can't protect against the pathogen. People are dying without a scratch on them."

Joe nodded. "And even for people who don't get infected by the pathogen, it is hard to shoot those damn growlers. They run fast and you got to hit them in the head. That's tough to do, as we discovered."

Billy heaved a sigh, his gaze growing distant. "Yeah...and I wonder if the rest of the world is going to be infected."

"When it's safe to emerge…" began Amanda.

"I think we'll be just trying to survive," said Bert. "Hiding from those growlers or killing them. Scavenging for food."

"While we are locked inside. We need to do something," Amanda said, her voice laced with determination. "First, we need to find out as much as we can. We must dissect every piece of information, every inconsistency. And we need to share what we learn."

Billy raised his eyebrows, "Share? With whom?"

"With the survivors. With the rest of the world. With any of them who will listen," Amanda replied. "We have the internet, for now at least. We can record videos, share our thoughts. Maybe someone else out there has other pieces of the puzzle."

"Make videos?" said Joe. "Okay, but don't put our faces in them."

Billy's eyes popped wide open, an edge of excitement creeping into his voice. "Check this out, guys. This guy, Carl, he has a site with info on the growlers from before the outbreak. He says he has videos made eighteen months ago by something called the Cult of the Phoenix."

Before the outbreak!

The trio huddled by Billy to see the computer screen where a young, bespectacled man dominated the frame. Billy cranked up the volume.

"...from our analysis, it appears these...creatures are actually semi-deceased, their brains manipulated by the virus to function as I've described. Our suspicions were aroused when we stumbled across these bizarre videos from the 'Phoenix Cult'."

A clip flickered onto the screen, showing an infected human, hair wild, sprinting relentlessly behind a pickup in a dust-choked desert. A calm, detached voice provided commentary. "The infected subject, number 7, has been clocked maintaining a pace of 27 mph over a distance of 5 miles."

As the scenery shifted to a man perched precariously atop a wall with a ladder propped against it, the zombies below pawed futilely at the air. "As demonstrated, although they have simple climbing skills, none of the subjects exhibit the capacity to ascend a ladder."

There were a series of clips showing the capabilities of growlers. The sight of one managing to manipulate a door handle prompted wide-eyed glances amongst the group. They all instinctively turned to gaze at their own secured bunker door. Joe dismissed their silent apprehension with a nonchalant shake of his head. "Relax, it's locked tight." A collective sigh of relief filled the room.

The video rolled on, now revealing an uninfected man dangling from a rope, while beneath him, several infected lunged upward, straining for the bait. "Take note, some of these infected are capable of propelling themselves up to fifteen feet high and covering a span of twenty feet. To create an effective barrier, one would need to stack shipping containers three high."

The bespectacled man returned; his earnest face filled the screen. "These troubling videos triggered our investigation. We've unearthed substantial evidence suggesting the President's involvement. I'll say it again, we believe the President is implicated in this outbreak. I'm Carl Rutger, and I'll continue to broadcast information as I uncover it. Stand strong, comrades, and long live the resistance."

The screen went blank.

"So this whole thing has been well planned. It's not some immigrant mad at being deported. It's an organization. We need to get that information out," said Billy.

Amanda raised a finger. "Talking of getting information out there; we know something that probably nobody else knows."

"Like what?" said Billy.

"Like the cure to the pathogen. Me and Joshua both took Zolga, and it worked. If we could go to the hospitals and get more of those pills…"

"Jesus, you're right," shouted Joe. "It will be more valuable than gold. If we keep that information to ourselves…"

Billy shook his head. "But, we can't wait to release that information. We have to start releasing it now, to save lives. A lot of people won't know how to bypass DNS and find their way to the information, but still we have to try. The hospitals will still probably have their supplies when we get out."

There was a pause.

Amanda considered Billy's words. Zolga was going to be worth a fortune. She really wanted to get all the supplies first, but she had to agree that they could not keep the information to themselves. She accepted that they should try to spread the news.

"Right," Amanda said, nodding. "But our first stop will be hospitals. Oakland's probably a no go, but Berkeley has a hospital, so does Walnut Creek. They might have a stock. If it's not completely overrun..."

Billy let out a sigh. "We can't stay in here forever. We're going to have to venture out at some point. Might as well be for a good cause."

"But," Joe added, sobering the atmosphere, "we need to remember there's still radiation out there from the fallout. We can't go until we know it's safe."

"How long could that be?" Billy asked, his forehead creased with worry.

Joe sighed. "It depends on a lot of variables. It could be weeks, maybe even longer."

"Then we'll prepare," Amanda decided, her tone filled with resolve. "We'll research everything we can about the local hospitals, their layouts, where they might store medications. We need to be ready to move the minute it's safe to do so."

"This Carl guy, that leaked this info…he is trying to get regular people like us to form some kind of…resistance?" Billy said. "It just seems far fetched that we could be of any use."

Joe snorted. "When the Nazis invaded France, people had a choice; to collaborate, to do nothing, or to resist. Whoever the fuck has done this…we need to resist their agenda, whatever it is."

"We may be just regular people, but resist is exactly what we should do," said Amanda.

Joe and Billy nodded, their determination reflecting Amanda's. They had a mission now, a purpose amidst the chaos and destruction. They were not just survivors huddled in a bunker anymore; they were a team. They had a plan, and they had hope.

Joe walked over to his weapons cabinets. "One thing is for sure. It's going to be a hell of a fight to get out of here."

Amanda took a deep breath. "And there's going to be whole new shit show of a world out there when we emerge," said Amanda. "And I'll be damned if I'm going to let the architects of this plague end up ruling us."

PROFESSOR MARK PRESTON

Depressing Place to be Executed

Carl drove Mark through a winding labyrinth of shadowy alleyways and hushed boulevards. The destination was an unassuming townhouse nestled amongst a row of similar structures, their uniformity a form of camouflage.

"We're here," Carl announced as he unlocked the front door. Mark followed Carl into the house, his mind struggling to reconcile the calm within these walls with the chaos he had left behind.

"This sanctuary is an FBI safehouse, fortified and insulated from the world outside," Carl narrated as they traversed the quiet corners of the townhouse. His hands swept over the thickened, unyielding steel frames of doors and windows, the tangible evidence of reinforcements. "And it's not just sturdy on the surface. It boasts its own autonomous power grid, and water supply; an island in itself." Mark, taking in Carl's words, could feel a semblance of security seeping into him as he scrutinized their new shelter.

The interior was spartan but functional; designed not for comfort but survival. It was a fortress, hidden in plain sight amidst the ordinary houses of the city.

"Get some sleep," Carl advised as he made his exit. "We have a lot of work ahead of us."

Mark nodded. "And the pathogen will reach us soon."

Carl stared at Mark for a moment. "We're going to have to ride it out here. Your bedroom's over there. There are clothes of various sizes in the closet. In the meantime, you might want to get some rest."

Mark took a deep breath and then entered the bedroom. In the quiet of his new refuge, he found himself alone with his thoughts. He collapsed on the bed, but sleep was elusive, his mind a whirlwind of concern and uncertainty. The reality of his situation was far beyond what he had ever imagined, a terrifying transformation from a scientist into a...what? An outlaw? A fugitive? A resistance figure?

He was no longer just a scientist, but a key player in a struggle he was still trying to comprehend. It was a daunting prospect, but he had no choice. He had seen the true face of the epidemic and the corruption that fueled it. It was his duty now to fight, to stand against the deceit, and bring the truth to light.

In the dim glow of the room, Mark allowed himself to sink into the uncomfortable reality of his new role. As the world outside spiraled into darkness, he resolved himself for the battle that lay ahead.

He stared out of the bedroom's window, which overlooked a quiet city street.

"The glass is bullet proof," said Carl.

"So I can watch the fall of civilization from safety and comfort," said Mark.

"And, hopefully ease that fall, and help civilization rise again," said Carl.

They both looked out as a dark cloud began to shroud the city.

Chapter - Clapp Spring Bunker – The Dungeon

SAMANTHA WINTERS

Nothing Creepy in Here

Stepping into the room, Samantha was met with a sight beyond her wildest imaginations, one that was shockingly unlike any she'd ever encountered. Dominating the center stood an odd-looking gynecological chair, stark and chilling in its implications.

The walls, bathed in a sinister shade of crimson, were adorned with a bewildering array of objects that demanded immediate attention from both Samantha and Leah. Among them, a shockingly large dildo mounted directly across from the entryway was impossible to ignore. Its size seemed implausible for any practical application, the attached straps adding to its intimidating presence.

A chilling gallery of implements filled the remainder of the wall space: whips and canes, their presence suggestive of pain and control, floggers with threatening tassels, and handcuffs and spreader bars promising restriction. Further adding to the discomforting ambiance were an assortment of gags, their purpose unnerving, and a collection of unidentifiable photographs, their subjects hidden from immediate view. Samantha took in the unnerving display, a wave of apprehension washing over her.

This is really odd. Sick.

Leah, her eyes saucer-wide, inched toward the wall. Her trembling finger pointed to a disturbing image: the Prophet, naked and restrained, with a young girl...donning the impossibly large dildo...

"Oh, you don't need to see that," said Samantha. *And neither do I.* Samantha instinctively shielded Leah's eyes from the distressing sight. Her heart pounded against her ribs, the image seared into her own eyes.

"What was that?" Leah murmured, her voice a small, shaken whisper in the shadow-laden room.

With a firm but gentle hand, Samantha guided Leah to face her. "Let's promise to leave what you just saw buried in this room, never to be spoken of again."

Leah bobbed her head in agreement, her voice barely a whisper. "I can do that. I can totally do that." She blinked as if the act deleted the memory. "Done."

A sense of urgency began to creep over Samantha. They needed to get out, to escape from the chilling scene they'd stumbled upon. Her eyes darted around the room, searching. But where was their exit? Where was their passage to safety from this nightmare?

Nestled inconspicuously in one wall was a diagonal cross. Upon closer inspection, she noticed a subtle separation, a hairline crack tracing an outline of a hidden door. She tried to pull at the cross, hoping to trigger a release, but it remained stubbornly immobile. Her eyes then landed on a small keyhole nestled in the intricate design of the cross. Sliding the key into the aged lock, she turned it.

A protesting groan of rusted metal hinges echoed in the room as the camouflaged door creaked open, unearthing a dauntingly steep staircase that disappeared into the shadowy heights above. A wave of colder air rolled over them, heavy with the pungent odor of stale water and the eerie scent of long-untouched decay. It was evident this area of the bunker saw little to no use.

Despite the foreboding ambience, Samantha knew. This was their path to freedom.

Leah looked at Samantha, her eyes wide with a blend of fear and hope. Samantha nodded at her, knowing words were unnecessary. They had to go on, and they had to do it now. She went first, clutching the cold railing, the stairs groaning beneath her weight.

Their journey upwards was a nerve-racking exercise. The gloom was thick, punctuated only by the sparse glow of the bulbs. They could hear their own breath, heavy and frantic, echoing around them. Occasionally, the silence was shattered by the far-off wails of the infected, the sounds warped and distorted by the labyrinthine passages of the bunker.

At the end of the stairs, they found a second door, this one bulkier and stronger-looking than the one downstairs. Samantha unlocked it, pushing with all her might to shift the weighty barrier.

With a final groan, the door yielded, swinging open to reveal a huge tunnel, eerily silent and seemingly stretching into infinity. It was an underground passage, seemingly forgotten and left to the ravages of time. The walls were damp with condensation, and the faintest hint of fresh air wafted through, the smell of freedom.

Samantha turned to Leah, "This is it. Let's get out of here."

Leah nodded, her face pale but resolute. They moved forward, leaving behind the monstrous nightmare of the bunker, and walked toward the uncertain, yet hopeful darkness that promised freedom.

I am in the middle of an island, with little food, little water, and the only company I have is the growlers behind me and a little girl. What the hell am I going to do?

The End

The Growler Chronicles Continues with …

Phase Two : Hide (Book 2 of The Growler Chronicles)

Phase Two: Hide
(Book 2 of The Growler Chronicles)
Chapter – Morning

MASON –
MARTINEZ, CALIFORNIA

In the soft hues of the early morning, a makeshift compound emerged from the dense fog, amidst the remnants of a once-thriving city, now ravaged by growlers and disease. The survivors erected a fortress of hope and resilience, a sanctuary they called home. Within its walls stood several sturdy barracks, crafted from the remnants of buildings long forgotten. Watchtowers rose like guardians on all four corners, where vigilant eyes scanned the horizon for any sign of danger. Its western side gently caressed by the calming waters where docks once welcomed ships from distant shores. As the first rays of sunlight kissed the horizon, a small boy ran from one of the buildings toward the southwest tower.

Mason climbed the wooden watchtower like he did most mornings. There had been a time when his father had told him not to, but Mason just wanted to be near his dad and help watch for growlers, so eventually his father had relented.

The compound was quiet at this time of the morning. A scavenging party would be going out later, but for now the only people around were patrolling guards, and the observers in the watchtowers.

His father always took morning shift and always used the southwest tower because it had a view of the bay as well as the clear southern approach. He'd been an avid sailor in the pre-world.

Mason pushed open the hatch with his head and shuffled into the observation deck. His father looked over momentarily, gave him a wink and then went back to scanning the southern approach.

Mason hugged his father at the waist and then walked to west end of the deck. He climbed up on the chair and brought the fixed binoculars up to his eyes. A blanket of thick fog sat on the water like wads of cotton wool.

"Ooh pretty!" he said.

"Yep," said his father. "Cover your ears," he added a few seconds later.

Mason did as he was told, and a shot rang out. He knew his dad had just taken out a wandering growler. They had been in the compound for months now. The military had set it up, then most of the army men had got sick and had to be... put down.

"Father?" said Mason turning his gaze from the sea. "If I got the black and died, would you put me down?"

"You've had the black, and you survived, so you have nothing to worry about."

Mason rolled his eyes. "But remember that lady that stole my chocolate? She got the black twice and the second time it killed her."

"Yes, but now we have the z-pills, that make you better."

Mason remembered the argument over the z-pills. Most of the compound did not think they were real, but they ended up trading for them just in case. Then the captain had got sick, and they gave him a z-pill and he got better… but no one was sure it was the z-pill that had saved him.

"But if I did die… would you put me down?"

"If you did die then your troubles are over, so why do you care?"

Mason thought about that. It was at least three minutes before he spoke again. "But I just want to know."

"Someone would put your body down," his father said with a sigh.

Mason returned to peering out at the fog.

"Are dragons real?" Mason asked.

"I don't think so," father responded.

"You don't think so?"

His father gave a very slight chuckle. "A few months ago, if you'd ask me if the dead could run around, I'd have said no with great certainty… so now, I don't rush to judgement."

"Father?"

His father did not respond for a moment.

"Father?"

"Yes," he said with a hint of exasperation in his tone.

"Why *did* the dead start running around?"

"Well… some people think it's all because of a lady called Samantha Winters."

Mason went back to looking through the viewers. "What do you think?"

"This Samantha Winters was a bit young to have engineered the outbreak."

"Father?"

"Just…" his father almost raised his voice. "Just watch in silence."

A few minutes later Mason saw a shape in the fog in the bay. A few seconds later the shape became a mast. A few more seconds later a small sailboat became visible. It was heading straight for the compound's docks. He could see only one person on the boat.

"Father…"

"Just be quiet," said his father.

"But there's a boat approaching."

His father swore quietly and moved over to the western view. "Let me take a look," he said and gently pushed Mason from the viewers. Mason watched his father peer through the viewers. His father pulled the alert rope that led into the barracks. A muffled bell rang, and people began pouring out of the buildings.

Mason watched as the boat brought in its sail, put out a dredging anchor. He admired the way the sailor feathered the approach. The boat kissed the pier. He lifted the door and slid down the ladder so he could meet the trader.

A group of heavily armed people were standing at the pier to greet the stranger. Mason had to push his way through the crowd to get to the front.

The stranger completed mooring the boat and then turned to face the welcoming committee. A mask and hood hid the trader's features, but when they spoke it was evidently a female.

"I am told you are honest people," said the stranger. "You welcome trade, and you are fair. Have I been misled?"

Meredith, the compound leader, stepped forward. "We treat honest traders fairly. What do you have to trade? Do you have food? Weapons? Ammunition?"

The trader shook her head. "I have two things to trade; a Spacelink endpoint, so you can access the internet, and a dozen Zolga pills, in case the Black shows up."

Meredith's mouth dropped open for a second. "And… what do you want in return?"

A couple of people pushed forward a little and the trader stepped back putting her hand on a sheathed knife. "I do not wish to be touched."

Meredith pushed her people back. "Give the lady space," she said and with a few grumbles they complied. She turned back to the trader. "Now what do you want in return?"

"I'll take a stack of the MREs I hear you have, and also a bag of dried fruit, and a box of 9mm ammunition."

There were some groans in the crowd and some chuckles.

"And my price is nonnegotiable," added the trader.

A silence followed. Mason could feel an unspoken tension in the crowd.

The trader sighed. "And if you decide that rather than pay me, it might be easier just to take my goods and kill me, you should know that I have friends who will only activate your Spacelink connections when I am clear of the harbor. I myself cannot do it."

Mason could feel the tension relax.

"We would never do such a thing," said Meredith. "We are honest and only kill in self-defense." She paused, looked at some of her people. Mason saw some nods. "We accept your price. May I ask where you got the Zolga pills. All the local hospitals have been stripped."

The trader was silent for a moment. "I will be back. Perhaps then I can tell you."

A shot rang out from the tower. Mason looked to see his father aiming to the south. A second shot rang out.

"Trouble?" shouted Meredith. "

A third and a fourth shot rang out. Some men ran to the western wall and a couple ran to the watchtower.

"We got a growler in body armor, including a helmet," said Mason's father.

"Just one?" asked Meredith.

Another shot rang out.

"Got it! Yeah, just one," said Mason's father.

The trader had backed up and had one foot on her boat. "I will stay on my boat until you have loaded my supplies. I will leave your goods on the pier."

"The growler made you nervous?" asked Meredith.

"I have seen men expend thousands of rounds of ammunition trying to deal with a herd of body armor wearing growlers. I don't think your compound could take a full assault. You need to build stone or concrete walls. Your fences won't work."

Meredith nodded. "We already have raided the local hardware stores for the supplies to build a better wall."

The trader looked toward the fence. "Well, I wouldn't wait long. There are groups of thousands of what used to be marines. All wearing body armor. And I tell you, you will not survive them."

Men arrived with the trader's goods. The exchange was made.

Mason pushed forward to get a closer look at the trader. He looked up at her face, but all he could see were eyes. They were deep dark brown. She looked to be in her twenties. From his low angle, he could see up into her hood. She had a small scar over her left eyebrow. She reached into her pocket and handed him something. He reached out, grabbed it and looked at what she had given him. It was a small candy bar. She winked at him as he put it in his pocket. He mouthed the words "Thank you," at her. She released her mooring, pushed her boat out and jumped aboard.

Meredith smiled at the trader. "You know how to make a kid smile."

The trader nodded. "I'll be back," she said as the boat moved out into the harbor. "I hope you guys make it. Especially you, little one." She looked at Mason.

At that moment a little blonde-haired girl walked onto the deck.

One of the men in the crowd turned to Meredith. "It's a tough world to drag a kid around in."

Meredith was silent.

"Oh, sorry. I … didn't mean…" the man stuttered.

"It's okay," said Meredith. "You're right. My Daryl is best off not having to face this new world. His death was, perhaps, a mercy."

Mason ran back to the compound's main meeting room. He jumped over the announcements table and looked at the posts board. There in the bottom right corner was a picture of a woman. "Wanted. Samantha Winters. The woman who released the outbreak." He looked closely at the picture. There above the woman's left eyebrow was that same scar he had seen on the trader.

He felt the candy bar in his pocket.

The bells started ringing. It was an alarm. An adult rushed in. It was one of the women who occasionally looked after him, but he could not remember her name. "There's a horde coming," she said. "Get to the barracks, just like in the drills."

Mason turned to her. "Are they wearing body armor?"

THE END (For Now)

Are you enjoying the Growler Chronicles? If so please help a starving author out by leaving a nice five star review.

The Growler Chronicles Books
- » Phase One: Run
- » Phase Two: Hide
- » Phase Three: Fight
- » Book Four: The Battle For Paradise
- » Book Five: Paradise Falls

Stand Alone Short Novellas set in the Growler Chronicles' World

- » Deacon
- » Jennifer
- » Gerald

Extra Content and News on J.C. Sampson at jcsampson.com

www.ingramcontent.com/pod-product-compliance
Lightning Source LLC
Chambersburg PA
CBHW051553250626
47157CB00001B/285